S0-BMG-423

OMNIVM
LVX
CIVIVM
MDCCCLII
MDCCC
LXXVIII

DARK LESSONS

Also in the MACMILLAN MIDNIGHT LIBRARY series

Child's Ploy

Witches' Brew

DARK LESSONS

Crime and Detection on Campus

EDITED BY

MARCIA MULLER

AND

BILL PRONZINI

MACMILLAN PUBLISHING COMPANY
New York

Macmillan Publishing Company
866 Third Avenue, New York, N.Y. 10022
Collier Macmillan Canada, Inc.

Library of Congress Cataloging in Publication Data
Main entry under title:
Dark lessons.
(Macmillan midnight library)
1. Detective and mystery stories, American.
2. Detective and mystery stories, English. 3. Crime
and criminals—Fiction. 4. Universities and colleges—
Fiction. I. Muller, Marcia. II. Pronzini, Bill.
III. Series.
PS648.D4D37 1984 813'.01'08 84-27325
ISBN 0-02-599220-1

10 9 8 7 6 5 4 3 2 1

Printed in the United States of America

Contents

Acknowledgments

"Murder at Pentecost," by Dorothy L. Sayers. From *Hangman's Holiday*. Copyright © 1933 by Dorothy L. Sayers. Reprinted by permission of Watkins/Loomis Agency, Inc.

"Murder at Mother's Knee," by Cornell Woolrich. Copyright © 1941 by Popular Publications, Inc.; © 1969 The Chase Manhattan Bank, N.A., Executors of the Estate of Cornell Woolrich. First published in *Dime Detective*. Reprinted by permission of Scott Meredith Literary Agency, Inc., 845 Third Avenue, New York, N.Y. 10022.

"The Lethal Logic," by Norbert Davis. From *Detective Fiction Weekly*, April 29, 1939, issue. Copyright © 1939 by The Red Star News Company. Copyright renewed © 1966 and Assigned to Popular Publications, Inc. Reprinted by special arrangement with Blazing Publications, Inc., proprietor and conservator of the respective copyrights and successor-in-interest to Popular Publications, Inc. All Rights Reserved.

"To Break the Wall," by Evan Hunter. Copyright © 1953 by Pocket Books, Inc.; © renewed 1981 by Evan Hunter. First published in *discovery no. 2*. Reprinted by permission of the author and his agents, John Farquharson Ltd.

"When Greek Meets Greek," by Graham Greene. From *Twenty-One Stories* by Graham Greene. Copyright © 1962 by Graham Greene. Reprinted by permission of Viking Penguin, Inc.

"Charles," by Shirley Jackson. From *The Lottery* by Shirley Jackson. Copyright © by 1948 by Shirley Jackson. Copyright © renewed 1976 by Laurence Hyman, Barry Hyman, Mrs. Sarah Webster and Mrs. Joanne Schnurer. Reprinted by permission of Farrar, Straus and Giroux, Inc.

"The Ten O'Clock Scholar," by Harry Kemelman. Copyright © 1952 by Mercury Publications, Inc. First published in *Ellery Queen's Mystery Magazine*. Reprinted by permission of Scott Meredith Literary Agency, Inc., 845 Third Avenue, New York, N.Y. 10022.

"The Problem of the Little Red Schoolhouse," by Edward D. Hoch. Copyright © 1976 by Edward D. Hoch. First published in *Ellery Queen's Mystery Magazine*. Reprinted by permission of the author.

Introduction

WHEN CHOOSING a setting for a story, suspense writers consider no institution too sacred. The halls of academe—from kindergarten to college—may seem an unlikely place for murder and mayhem, but in fiction they are often crowded with sinister characters bent on wicked undertakings. Professors regularly murder one another over intellectual disputes or matters of tenure; students kill for passion, ideals, or a good grade on a term paper; teachers are terrorized at all levels of the educational system; outsiders lurk near playgrounds, waiting to commit all sorts of terrible acts.

There is, in fact, such interest in what is now known as the academic mystery that many colleges and universities offer full courses in this type of crime fiction. Proving, perhaps, the theory that readers prefer situations and characters with which they can readily identify.

Academicians and general readers alike can find considerable variety within the academic mystery. Protagonists, for instance, may be teachers, students, or a variety of nonacademics ranging from parents to private detectives, from law enforcement officers to talented amateurs who have some connection with a case or with the characters involved. Many stories and novels rely on specialized knowledge of a subject taught at a particular school—be it English literature, Sanskrit, or fingerpainting. The best of these works give the reader a glimpse into the world of education, its secrets and attendant dangers.

One of the best-known university sleuths is Amanda Cross's intellectual feminist heroine, Kate Fansler. Fansler is a professor of English literature (a profession the author knows well, since in reality she is Carolyn Heilbrun, professor of English at Columbia University). She solves cases of a literary nature, such as *The James Joyce Murder* (1967), *Poetic Justice* (1970), and *The Theban Mysteries* (1971). Other excellent novels with professorial detectives include Dolores Hitchens's *Something about Midnight* (1949) and *Enrollment Cancelled* (1952), both featuring Mr. Pennyfeather; Robert Bernard's *Deadly Meeting* (1970), in which Bill Stratton wears the hero's mantle; and Will Harriss's *The Bay Psalm Book Murder* (1983), winner of the Mystery Writers of America Edgar as Best First Novel of its year and featuring Cliff Dunbar.

While many collegiate mysteries are set on fictional campuses, real institutions also attract their fair share of literary mayhem. Anthony Boucher's *The Case of the Seven of Calvary* (1937) takes place on the Berkeley campus of the University of California, as does Valerie Miner's *Murder in the English Department* (1983). In Kenneth Millar's *The Dark Tunnel* (1944), Professor Robert Branch investigates a colleague's death at a thinly disguised University of Michigan. No less hallowed an American institution than Harvard University is visited by violent death in Timothy Fuller's *Harvard Has a Homicide* (1936) and W. Bolingbroke Johnson's *The Widening Stain* (1942). And no less hallowed an English institution than Oxford is the scene of numerous fictional slaughters, among them Michael Innes's *Seven Suspects* (1936) and *The Long Farewell* (1958), and Edmund Crispin's *The Case of the Gilded Fly* (1945).

Matters are equally calamitous at the high school level. Evan Hunter's *The Blackboard Jungle* (1954) explores the theme of juvenile delinquency through the eyes of Richard Dadier, English teacher at a rough vocational high school in New York—a position Hunter himself once held. Jim Hollis visits murder and psychological terror on the staff and students of a Midwest school in *Teach You a Lesson* (1955). And back in New York City, teacher Ben Gordon solves four different and realistic academic mysteries in Ivan Ross's *Murder Out of School* (1960), *Requiem for a Schoolgirl* (1961), *Old Students Never Die* (1962), and *Teacher's Blood* (1964).

The educational community, of course, cannot always rely on amateur investigators from within its own ranks, and often professionals are called in to solve academic cases. Private detectives are featured prominently in several such mysteries, among them the team of Doan and Carstairs, who prowl and howl (Doan is a man, Carstairs is a Great Dane) their way to the solution of multiple murders on a Southern California college campus in Norbert Davis's amusing *Oh, Murderer Mine!* (1946); "Mac," who takes an undercover job as a high school physical education teacher in order to break up a juvenile gang of muggers, thieves, and dope dealers in Thomas B. Dewey's *The Mean Streets* (1955); and Lew Archer, who explores academic jealousies and passions at a California junior college in Ross Macdonald's *The Chill* (1964). Junior colleges also figure prominently in several of Archer's other cases: *The Wycherly Woman* (1961), *Black Money* (1966), and *The Blue Hammer* (1976). On the other side of the Atlantic, P. D. James's female private detective Cordelia Gray began her career with an investigation at Cambridge in *An Unsuitable Job for a Woman* (1972).

In some works, outside investigators become involved in an academic case for personal reasons. Mystery writer Harriet Vane returns to her college for a reunion in Dorothy L. Sayers's *Gaudy Night* (1935), only to be plunged into intrigue and murder. Miss Pym, of Josephine Tey's *Miss Pym Disposes* (1946), is a visitor at a school that trains physical education teachers, when circumstances lead her to solve the murder of a student. And in Dolores Hitchens's *The Abductors* (1962), a grade school teacher and one of her students are kidnapped from the schoolyard, forcing the teacher's alcoholic husband to determine their whereabouts and finally to bring about their rescue.

The stories in this anthology are as varied in format and content as the novels we have cited. They are set in large universities, small colleges, high schools, grade schools, a correspondence school, an old-fashioned one-room country schoolhouse, and even a kindergarten. Their protagonists are teachers, pupils, parents, professional investigators, amateur sleuths—and criminals of various types. And their authors are among the best of past and present masters of the art of literary suspense: Edgar Allan Poe, Graham Greene, Dorothy L. Sayers, Shirley Jackson, Evan Hunter, Stanley Ellin, Harry Kemelman, Nicolas Freeling, Edward D. Hoch, Barry N. Malzberg, George C. Chesbro, Talmage Powell, and Norbert Davis.

We think you'll recognize in these stories something of your own educational experience. And like us, you'll be thankful that *your* lessons were not nearly so dark. . . .

—Marcia Muller and Bill Pronzini

San Francisco, California
May 1984

William Wilson

EDGAR ALLAN POE

Edgar Allan Poe (1809–1849) was educated in the classical tradition in England, and doubtless was familiar with schoolboy rivalries. In "William Wilson" he adds a horrific element to what begins as simple competition between two young men who bear the same name, and takes it to its frightening and inevitable conclusion. Poe, the acknowledged creator of the detective story, was an editor, critic, and poet as well. His three stories featuring C. Auguste Dupin introduced the first important detective character, and other stories experiment with variations on the form. "The Gold Bug" (1843) is a cipher-solving story; "The Purloined Letter" (1844) is a secret-agent adventure; "The Mystery of Marie Roget" (1842) is a fictionalized account of a true crime; and "The Murders in the Rue Morgue" (1841) is a locked-room thriller.

What say of it? what say [of] CONSCIENCE grim,
That spectre in my path?
—*Chamberlayne's Pharronida.*

LET ME CALL MYSELF, for the present, William Wilson. The fair page now lying before me need not be sullied with my real appellation. This has been already too much an object for the scorn—for the horror—for the detestation of my race. To the uttermost regions of the globe have not the indignant winds bruited its unparalleled infamy? Oh, outcast of all outcasts most abandoned!—to the earth art thou not forever dead? to its honors, to its flowers, to its golden aspirations?—and a cloud, dense, dismal, and limitless, does it not hang eternally between thy hopes and heaven?

I would not, if I could, here or to-day, embody a record of my later years of unspeakable misery, and unpardonable crime. This epoch—these later years—took unto themselves a sudden elevation in turpitude, whose origin alone it is my present purpose to assign. Men usually grow base by degrees. From me, in an instant, all virtue dropped bodily as a mantle. From comparatively trivial wickedness I passed, with the stride of a giant, into more than the enormities of an Elah-Gabalus. What chance—what one event brought this evil thing to pass, bear with me while I relate. Death approaches; and the shadow which foreruns him has thrown a softening influence over my spirit. I long, in passing through the dim valley, for the sympathy—I had nearly said for the pity—of my fellow men. I would fain have them believe that I have been, in some measure, the slave of circumstances beyond human control. I would wish them to seek out for me, in the details I am about to give, some little oasis of *fatality* amid a wilderness of error. I would have them allow—what they cannot refrain from allowing—that, although temptation may have ere-while existed as great, man was never *thus*, at least, tempted before—certainly, never *thus* fell. And is it therefore that he has never thus suffered? Have I not indeed been living in a dream? And am I not now dying a victim to the horror and the mystery of the wildest of all sublunary visions?

I am the descendant of a race whose imaginative and easily excitable temperament has at all times rendered them remark-able; and, in my earliest infancy, I gave evidence of having fully inherited the family character. As I advanced in years it was more strongly developed; becoming, for many reasons, a cause of serious disquietude to my friends, and of positive injury to myself. I grew self-willed, addicted to the wildest caprices, and a prey to the most ungovernable passions. Weak-minded, and beset with constitutional infirmities akin to my own, my parents could do but little to check the evil propensities which distin-guished me. Some feeble and ill-directed efforts resulted in com-plete failure on their part, and, of course, in total triumph on mine. Thenceforward my voice was a household law; and at an age when few children have abandoned their leading-strings, I was left to the guidance of my own will, and became, in all but name, the master of my own actions.

My earliest recollections of a school-life, are connected with a large, rambling, Elizabethan house, in a misty-looking village of England, where were a vast number of gigantic and gnarled trees, and where all the houses were excessively ancient. In truth, it was a dream-like and spirit-soothing place, that venera-ble old town. At this moment, in fancy, I feel the refreshing chilliness of its deeply-shadowed avenues, inhale the fragrance of its thousand shrubberies, and thrill anew with undefinable delight, at the deep hollow note of the churchbell, breaking, each hour, with sullen and sudden roar, upon the stillness of the dusky atmosphere in which the fretted Gothic steeple lay imbed-ded and asleep.

It gives me, perhaps, as much of pleasure as I can now in any manner experience, to dwell upon minute recollections of the school and its concerns. Steeped in misery as I am—misery, alas! only too real—I shall be pardoned for seeking relief, however slight and temporary, in the weakness of a few rambling details. These, moreover, utterly trivial, and even ridiculous in themselves, assume, to my fancy, adventitious importance, as connected with a period and a locality when and where I recognize the first ambiguous monitions of the destiny which afterwards so fully overshadowed me. Let me then remember.

The house, I have said, was old and irregular. The grounds were extensive, and a high and solid brick wall, topped with a bed of mortar and broken glass, encompassed the whole. This prison-like rampart formed the limit of our domain; beyond it we saw but thrice a week—once every Saturday afternoon, when, attended by two ushers, we were permitted to take brief walks in a body through some of the neighbouring fields—and twice during Sunday, when we were paraded in the same formal manner to the morning and evening service in the one church of the village. Of this church the principal of our school was pastor. With how deep a spirit of wonder and perplexity was I wont to regard him from our remote pew in the gallery, as, with step solemn and slow, he ascended the pulpit! This reverend man, with countenance so demurely benign, with robes so glossy and so clerically flowing, with wig so minutely powdered, so rigid and so vast,—could this be he who, of late, with sour visage, and in snuffy habiliments, administered, ferule in hand, the Draconian laws of the academy? Oh, gigantic paradox, too utterly monstrous for solution!

At an angle of the ponderous wall frowned a more ponderous gate. It was riveted and studded with iron bolts, and surmounted with jagged iron spikes. What impressions of deep awe did it inspire! It was never opened save for the three periodical egressions and ingressions already mentioned; then, in every creak of its mighty hinges, we found a plenitude of mystery—a world of matter for solemn remark, or for more solemn meditation.

The extensive enclosure was irregular in form, having many capacious recesses. Of these, three or four of the largest constituted the play-ground. It was level, and covered with fine hard gravel. I well remember it had no trees, nor benches, nor anything similar within it. Of course it was in the rear of the house. In front lay a small parterre, planted with box and other shrubs; but through this sacred division we passed only upon rare occasions indeed—such as a first advent to school or final departure thence, or perhaps, when a parent or friend having called for us, we joyfully took our way home for the Christmas or Midsummer holydays.

But the house!—how quaint an old building was this!—to me how veritably a palace of enchantment! There was really no end to its windings—to its incomprehensible subdivisions. It was difficult, at any given time, to say with certainty upon which of its two stories one happened to be. From each room to every other there were sure to be found three or four steps either in ascent or descent. Then the lateral branches were innumerable—inconceivable—and so returning in upon themselves, that our most exact ideas in regard to the whole mansion were not very far different from those with which we pondered upon infinity. During the five years of my residence here, I was never able to ascertain with precision, in what remote locality lay the little sleeping apartment assigned to myself and some eighteen or twenty other scholars.

The school-room was the largest in the house—I could not help thinking, in the world. It was very long, narrow, and dismally low, with pointed Gothic windows and a ceiling of oak. In a remote and terror-inspiring angle was a square enclosure of eight or ten feet, comprising the *sanctum*, "during hours," of our principal, the Reverend Dr. Bransby. It was a solid structure, with massy door, sooner than open which in the absence of the "Dominie," we would all have willingly perished by the *peine forte et dure*. In other angles were two other similar boxes, far less reverenced, indeed, but still greatly matters of awe. One of these was the pulpit of the "classical" usher, one of the "English and mathematical." Interspersed about the room, crossing and recrossing in endless irregularity, were innumerable benches and desks, black, ancient, and timeworn, piled desperately with much-bethumbed books, and so beseamed with initial letters, names at full length, grotesque figures, and other multiplied efforts of the knife, as to have entirely lost what little of original form might have been their portion in days long departed. A huge bucket with water stood at one extremity of the room, and a clock of stupendous dimensions at the other.

Encompassed by the massy walls of this venerable academy, I passed, yet not in tedium or disgust, the years of the third lustrum of my life. The teeming brain of childhood requires no external world of incident to occupy or amuse it; and the apparently dismal monotony of a school was replete with more intense excitement than my riper youth has derived from luxury, or my full manhood from crime. Yet I must believe that my first mental development had in it much of the uncommon—even much of the *outré*. Upon mankind at large the events of very early existence rarely leave in mature age any definite impression. All is gray shadow—a weak and irregular remembrance—an indistinct regathering of feeble pleasures and phantasmagoric pains. With me this is not so. In childhood I must have felt with the energy of a man what I now find stamped upon memory in lines as vivid, as deep, and as durable as the *exergues* of the Carthaginian medals.

Yet in fact—in the fact of the world's view—how little was there to remember! The morning's awakening, the nightly summons to bed; the connings, the recitations; the periodical half-holidays, and perambulations; the play-ground, with its broils, its pastimes, its intrigues;—these, by a mental sorcery long forgotten, were made to involve a wilderness of sensation, a world of rich incident, an universe of varied emotion, of excitement the most passionate and spirit-stirring. *"Oh, le bon temps, que ce siècle de fer!"*

In truth, the ardor, the enthusiasm, and the imperiousness of my disposition, soon rendered me a marked character among my schoolmates, and by slow, but natural gradations, gave me an ascendancy over all not greatly older than myself;—over all with a single exception. This exception was found in the person of a scholar, who, although no relation, bore the same christian and surname as myself;—a circumstance, in fact, little remarkable; for, notwithstanding a noble descent, mine was one of those everyday appellations which seem, by prescriptive right, to have been, time out of mind, the common property of the mob. In this narrative, I have therefore designated myself as William Wilson,—a fictitious title not very dissimilar to the real. My namesake alone, of those who in school phraseology constituted "our set," presumed to compete with me in the studies of the class—in the sports and broils of the play-ground—to refuse implicit belief in my assertions, and submission to my will—indeed, to interfere with my arbitrary dictation in any respect whatsoever. If there is on earth a supreme and unqualified despotism, it is the despotism of a master mind in boyhood over the less energetic spirits of its companions.

Wilson's rebellion was to me a source of the greatest embarrassment;—the more so as, in spite of the bravado with which in public I made a point of treating him and his pretensions, I secretly felt that I feared him, and could not help thinking the equality which he maintained so easily with myself, a proof of his true superiority; since not to be overcome cost me a perpetual struggle. Yet this superiority—even this equality—was in truth acknowledged by no one but myself; our associates, by some unaccountable blindness, seemed not even to suspect it. Indeed, his competition, his resistance, and especially his impertinent and dogged interference with my purposes, were not more pointed than private. He appeared to be destitute alike of the ambition which urged, and of the passionate energy of mind which enabled me to excel. In his rivalry he might have been supposed actuated solely by a whimsical desire to thwart, astonish, or mortify myself; although there were times when I could not help observing, with a feeling made up of wonder, abasement, and pique, that he mingled with his injuries, his insults, or his contradictions, a certain most inappropriate, and assuredly most unwelcome *affectionateness* of manner. I could only conceive this singular behavior to arise from a consummate self-conceit assuming the vulgar airs of patronage and protection.

Perhaps it was this latter trait in Wilson's conduct, conjoined with our identity of name, and the mere accident of our having entered the school upon the same day, which set afloat the notion that we were brothers, among the senior classes in the academy. These do not usually inquire with much strictness into the affairs of their juniors. I have before said, or should have said, that Wilson was not, in the most remote degree, connected with my family. But assuredly if we *had* been brothers we must have been twins; for, after leaving Dr. Bransby's, I casually learned that my namesake was born on the nineteenth of January, 1813—and this is a somewhat remarkable coincidence; for the day is precisely that of my own nativity.

It may seem strange that in spite of the continual anxiety occasioned me by the rivalry of Wilson, and his intolerable spirit of contradiction, I could not bring myself to hate him altogether. We had, to be sure, nearly every day a quarrel in which, yielding me publicly the palm of victory, he, in some manner, contrived to make me feel that it was he who had deserved it; yet a sense of pride on my part, and a veritable dignity on his own, kept us always upon what are called "speaking terms," while there were many points of strong congeniality in our tempers, operating to awake in me a sentiment which our position alone, perhaps, prevented from ripening into friendship. It is difficult, indeed, to define, or even to describe, my real feelings towards him. They formed a motley and heterogeneous admixture;—some petulant animosity, which was not yet hatred, some esteem, more respect, much fear, with a world of uneasy curiosity. To the moralist it will be unnecessary to say, in addition, that Wilson and myself were the most inseparable of companions.

It was no doubt the anomalous state of affairs existing between us, which turned all my attacks upon him (and they were many, either open or covert) into the channel of banter or practical joke (giving pain while assuming the aspect of mere fun) rather than into a more serious and determined hostility. But my endeavours on this head were by no means uniformly successful, even when my plans were the most wittily concocted; for my namesake had much about him, in character, of that unassuming and quiet austerity which, while enjoying the poignancy of its own jokes, has no heel of Achilles in itself, and absolutely refuses to be laughed at. I could find, indeed, but one vulnerable point, and that, lying in a personal peculiarity, arising, perhaps, from constitutional disease, would have been spared by any antagonist less at his wit's end than myself;—my rival had a weakness in the faucial or guttural organs, which precluded him from raising his voice at any time *above a very low whisper.* Of this defect I did not fail to take what poor advantage lay in my power.

Wilson's retaliations in kind were many; and there was one form of his practical wit that disturbed me beyond measure. How his sagacity first discovered at all that so petty a thing would vex me, is a question I never could solve; but, having discovered, he habitually practised the annoyance. I had always felt aversion to my uncourtly patronymic, and its very common, if not plebeian praenomen. The words were venom in my ears; and when, upon the day of my arrival, a second William Wilson came also to the academy, I felt angry with him for bearing the name, and doubly disgusted with the name because a stranger bore it, who would be the cause of its twofold repetition, who would be constantly in my presence, and whose concerns, in the ordinary routine of the school business, must inevitably, on account of the detestable coincidence, be often confounded with my own.

The feeling of vexation thus engendered grew stronger with every circumstance tending to show resemblance, moral or physical, between my rival and myself. I had not then discovered the remarkable fact that we were of the same age; but I saw that we were of the same height, and I perceived that we were even singularly alike in general contour of person and outline of feature. I was galled, too, by the rumor touching a relationship, which had grown current in the upper forms. In a word, nothing could more seriously disturb me, (although I scrupulously concealed such disturbance,) than any allusion to a similarity of mind, person, or condition existing between us. But, in truth, I had no reason to believe that (with the exception of the matter of relationship, and in the case of Wilson himself,) this similarity had ever been made a subject of comment, or even observed at all by our schoolfellows. That *he* observed it in all its bearings, and as fixedly as I, was apparent; but that he could discover in such circumstances so fruitful a field of annoyance, can only be attributed, as I said before, to his more than ordinary penetration.

His cue, which was to perfect an imitation of myself, lay both in words and in actions; and most admirably did he play his part. My dress it was an easy matter to copy; my gait and general manner were, without difficulty, appropriated; in spite of his constitutional defect, even my voice did not escape him. My louder tones were, of course, unattempted, but then the key, it was identical; *and his singular whisper, it grew the very echo of my own.*

How greatly this most exquisite portraiture harassed me, (for it could not justly be termed a caricature,) I will not now venture to describe. I had but one consolation—in the fact that the imitation, apparently, was noticed by myself alone, and that I had to endure only the knowing and strangely sarcastic smiles of my namesake himself. Satisfied with having produced in my bosom the intended effect, he seemed to chuckle in secret over the sting he had inflicted, and was characteristically disregardful of the public applause which the success of his witty endeavours might have so easily elicited. That the school, indeed, did not feel his design, perceive its accomplishment, and participate in his sneer, was, for many anxious months, a riddle I could not resolve. Perhaps the *gradation* of his copy rendered it not so readily perceptible; or, more possibly, I owed my security to the masterly air of the copyist, who, disdaining the letter, (which in a painting is all the obtuse can see,) gave but the full spirit of his original for my individual contemplation and chagrin.

I have already more than once spoken of the disgusting air of patronage which he assumed toward me, and of his frequent officious interference with my will. This interference often took the ungracious character of advice; advice not openly given, but hinted or insinuated. I received it with a repugnance which gained strength as I grew in years. Yet, at this distant day, let me do him the simple justice to acknowledge that I can recall no occasion when the suggestions of my rival were on the side of those errors or follies so usual to his immature age and seeming inexperience; that his moral sense, at least, if not his general talents and worldly wisdom, was far keener than my own; and that I might, to-day, have been a better, and thus a happier man, had I less frequently rejected the counsels embodied in those meaning whispers which I then but too cordially hated and too bitterly despised.

As it was, I at length grew restive in the extreme under his distasteful supervision, and daily resented more and more openly what I considered his intolerable arrogance. I have said that, in the first years of our connexion as schoolmates, my feelings in regard to him might have been easily ripened into friendship; but, in the latter months of my residence at the academy, although the intrusion of his ordinary manner had, beyond doubt, in some measure, abated, my sentiments, in nearly similar proportion, partook very much of positive hatred. Upon one occasion he saw this, I think, and afterwards avoided, or made a show of avoiding me.

It was about the same period, if I remember aright, that, in an altercation of violence with him, in which he was more than usually thrown off his guard, and spoke and acted with an openness of demeanor rather foreign to his nature, I discovered, or fancied I discovered, in his accent, his air, and general appearance, a something which first startled, and then deeply interested me, by bringing to mind dim visions of my earliest infancy—wild, confused and thronging memories of a time when memory herself was yet unborn. I cannot better describe the sensation which oppressed me than by saying that I could with difficulty shake off the belief of my having been acquainted with the being who stood before me, at some epoch very long ago—some point of the past even infinitely remote. The delusion, however, faded rapidly as it came; and I mention it at all but to define the day of the last conversation I there held with my singular namesake.

The huge old house, with its countless subdivisions, had several large chambers communicating with each other, where slept the greater number of the students. There were, however, (as must necessarily happen in a building so awkwardly planned,) many little nooks or recesses, the odds and ends of the structure; and these the economic ingenuity of Dr. Bransby had also fitted up as dormitories; although, being the merest closets, they were capable of accommodating but a single individual. One of these small apartments was occupied by Wilson.

One night, about the close of my fifth year at the school, and immediately after the altercation just mentioned, finding every one wrapped in sleep, I arose from bed, and, lamp in hand, stole through a wilderness of narrow passages from my own bedroom to that of my rival. I had long been plotting one of those ill-natured pieces of practical wit at his expense in which I had hitherto been so uniformly unsuccessful. It was my intention, now, to put my scheme in operation, and I resolved to make him feel the whole extent of the malice with which I was imbued. Having reached his closet, I noiselessly entered, leaving the lamp, with a shade over it, on the outside. I advanced a step, and listened to the sound of his tranquil breathing. Assured of his being asleep, I returned, took the light, and with it again approached the bed. Close curtains were around it, which, in the prosecution of my plan, I slowly and quietly withdrew, when the bright rays fell vividly upon the sleeper, and my eyes, at the same moment, upon his countenance. I looked;—and a numbness, an iciness of feeling instantly pervaded my frame. My breast heaved, my knees tottered, my whole spirit became possessed with an objectless yet intolerable horror. Gasping for breath, I lowered the lamp in still nearer proximity to the face. Were these—*these* the lineaments of William Wilson? I saw, indeed, that they were his, but I shook as if with a fit of the ague in fancying they were not. What *was* there about them to confound me in this manner? I gazed;—while my brain reeled with a multitude of incoherent thoughts. Not thus he appeared—assuredly not *thus*—in the vivacity of his waking hours. The same name! the same contour of person! the same day of arrival at the academy! And then his dogged and meaningless imitation of my gait, my voice, my habits, and my manner! Was it, in truth, within the bounds of human possibility, that *what I now saw* was the result, merely, of the habitual practice of this sarcastic imitation? Awe-stricken, and with a creeping shudder, I extinguished the lamp, passed silently from the chamber, and left, at once, the halls of that old academy, never to enter them again.

After a lapse of some months, spent at home in mere idleness, I found myself a student at Eton. The brief interval had been sufficient to enfeeble my remembrance of the events at Dr. Bransby's, or at least to effect a material change in the nature of the feelings with which I remembered them. The truth—the tragedy—of the drama was no more. I could now find room to doubt the evidence of my senses; and seldom called up the subject at all but with wonder at the extent of human credulity, and a smile at the vivid force of the imagination which I hereditarily possessed. Neither was this species of scepticism likely to be diminished by the character of the life I led at Eton. The vortex of thoughtless folly into which I there so immediately and recklessly plunged, washed away all but the froth of my past hours, engulfed at once every solid or serious impression, and left to memory only the veriest levities of a former existence.

I do not wish, however, to trace the course of my miserable profligacy here—a profligacy which set at defiance the laws, while it eluded the vigilance of the institution. Three years of folly, passed without profit, had but given me rooted habits of vice, and added, in a somewhat unusual degree, to my bodily stature, when, after a week of soulless dissipation, I invited a small party of the most dissolute students to a secret carousal in my chambers. We met at a late hour of the night; for our debaucheries were to be faithfully protracted until morning. The wine flowed freely, and there were not wanting other and perhaps more dangerous seductions; so that the grey dawn had already faintly appeared in the east, while our delirious extravagance was at its height. Madly flushed with cards and intoxication, I was in the act of insisting upon a toast of more than wonted profanity, when my attention was suddenly diverted by the violent, although partial unclosing of the door of the apartment, and by the eager voice of a servant from without. He said that some person, apparently in great haste, demanded to speak with me in the hall.

Wildly excited with wine, the unexpected interruption rather delighted than surprised me. I staggered forward at once, and a few steps brought me to the vestibule of the building. In this low and small room there hung no lamp; and now no light at all was admitted, save that of the exceedingly feeble dawn which made its way through the semi-circular window. As I put my foot over the threshold, I became aware of the figure of a youth about my own height, and habited in a white kerseymere morning frock, cut in the novel fashion of the one I myself wore at the moment. This the faint light enabled me to perceive; but the features of his face I could not distinguish. Upon my entering he strode hurriedly up to me, and seizing me by the arm with a gesture of petulant impatience, whispered the words "William Wilson!" in my ear.

I grew perfectly sober in an instant.

There was that in the manner of the stranger, and in the tremulous shake of his uplifted finger, as he held it between my eyes and the light, which filled me with unqualified amazement; but it was not this which had so violently moved me. It was the pregnancy of solemn admonition in the singular low, hissing utterance; and, above all, it was the character, the tone, *the key*, of those few, simple, and familiar, yet *whispered* syllables, which came with a thousand thronging memories of by-gone days, and struck upon my soul with the shock of a galvanic battery. Ere I could recover the use of my senses he was gone.

Although this event failed not of a vivid effect upon my disordered imagination, yet was it evanescent as vivid. For some weeks, indeed, I busied myself in earnest inquiry, or was wrapped in a cloud of morbid speculation. I did not pretend to disguise from my perception the identity of the singular individual who thus perseveringly interfered with my affairs, and harassed me with his insinuated counsel. But who and what was this Wilson?—and whence came he?—and what were his purposes? Upon neither of these points could I be satisfied; merely ascertaining, in regard to him, that a sudden accident in his family had caused his removal from Dr. Bransby's academy on the afternoon of the day in which I myself had eloped. But in a brief period I ceased to think upon the subject; my attention being all absorbed in a contemplated departure for Oxford. Thither I soon went; the uncalculating vanity of my parents furnishing me with an outfit and annual establishment, which would enable me to indulge at will in the luxury already so dear to my heart,—to vie in profuseness of expenditure with the haughtiest heirs of the wealthiest earldoms in Great Britain.

Excited by such appliances to vice, my constitutional temperament broke forth with redoubled ardor, and I spurned even the common restraints of decency in the mad infatuation of my revels. But it were absurd to pause in the detail of my extravagance. Let it suffice, that among spendthrifts I out-Heroded Herod, and that, giving name to a multitude of novel follies, I added no brief appendix to the long catalogue of vices then usual in the most dissolute university of Europe.

It could hardly be credited, however, that I had, even here, so utterly fallen from the gentlemanly estate, as to seek acquaintance with the vilest arts of the gambler by profession, and, having become an adept in his despicable science, to practise it habitually as a means of increasing my already enormous income at the expense of the weak-minded among my fellow-collegians. Such, nevertheless, was the fact. And the very enormity of this offence against all manly and honourable sentiment proved, beyond doubt, the main if not the sole reason of the impunity with which it was committed. Who, indeed, among my most abandoned associates, would not rather have disputed the clearest evidence of his senses, than have suspected of such courses, the gay, the frank, the generous William Wilson—the noblest and most liberal commoner at Oxford—him whose follies (said his parasites) were but the follies of youth and unbridled fancy—whose errors but inimitable whim—whose darkest vice but a careless and dashing extravagance?

I had been now two years successfully busied in this way, when there came to the university a young *parvenu* nobleman, Glendinning—rich, said report, as Herodes Atticus—his riches, too, as easily acquired. I soon found him of weak intellect, and, of course, marked him as a fitting subject for my skill. I frequently engaged him in play, and contrived, with the gambler's usual art, to let him win considerable sums, the more effectually to entangle him in my snares. At length, my schemes being ripe, I met him (with the full intention that this meeting should be final and decisive) at the chambers of a fellow-commoner, (Mr. Preston,) equally intimate with both, but who, to do him justice, entertained not even a remote suspicion of my design. To give to this a better colouring, I had contrived to have assembled a party of some eight or ten, and was solicitously careful that the introduction of cards should appear accidental, and originate in the proposal of my contemplated dupe himself. To be brief upon a vile topic, none of the low finesse was omitted, so customary upon similar occasions that it is a just matter for wonder how any are still found so besotted as to fall its victims.

We had protracted our sitting far into the night, and I had at length effected the manoeuvre of getting Glendinning as my sole antagonist. The game, too, was my favorite *écarté*. The rest of the company, interested in the extent of our play, had abandoned their own cards, and were standing around us as spectators. The *parvenu*, who had been induced by my artifices in the early part of the evening, to drink deeply, now shuffled, dealt, or played, with a wild nervousness of manner for which his intoxication, I thought, might partially, but could not altogether account. In a very short period he had become my debtor to a large amount, when, having taken a long draught of port, he did precisely what I had been coolly anticipating—he proposed to double our already extravagant stakes. With a well-feigned show of reluctance, and not until after my repeated refusal had seduced him into some angry words which gave a color of *pique* to my compliance, did I finally comply. The result, of course, did but prove how entirely the prey was in my toils; in less than an hour he had quadrupled his debt. For some time his countenance had been losing the florid tinge lent it by the wine; but now, to my astonishment, I perceived that it had grown to a pallor truly fearful. I say to my astonishment. Glendinning had been represented to my eager inquiries as immeasurably wealthy; and the sums which he had as yet lost, although in themselves vast, could not, I supposed, very seriously annoy, much less so violently affect him. That he was overcome by the wine just swallowed, was the idea which most readily presented itself; and, rather with a view to the preservation of my own character in the eyes of my associates, than from any less interested motive, I was about to insist, peremptorily, upon a discontinuance of the play, when some expressions at my elbow from among the company, and an ejaculation evincing utter despair on the part of Glendinning, gave me to understand that I had effected his total ruin under circumstances which, rendering him an object for the pity of all, should have protected him from the ill offices even of a fiend.

What now might have been my conduct it is difficult to say. The pitiable condition of my dupe had thrown an air of embarrassed gloom over all; and, for some moments, a profound silence was maintained, during which I could not help feeling my cheeks tingle with the many burning glances of scorn or reproach cast upon me by the less abandoned of the party. I will even own that an intolerable weight of anxiety was for a brief instant lifted from my bosom by the sudden and extraordinary interruption which ensued. The wide, heavy folding doors of the apartment were all at once thrown open, to their full extent, with a vigorous and rushing impetuosity that extinguished, as if by magic, every candle in the room. Their light, in dying, enabled us just to perceive that a stranger had entered, about my own height, and closely muffled in a cloak. The darkness, however, was now total; and we could only *feel* that he was standing in our midst. Before any one of us could recover from the extreme astonishment into which this rudeness had thrown all, we heard the voice of the intruder.

"Gentlemen," he said, in a low, distinct, and never-to-be-forgotten *whisper* which thrilled to the very marrow of my bones, "Gentlemen, I make no apology for this behaviour, because in thus behaving, I am but fulfilling a duty. You are, beyond doubt, uninformed of the true character of the person who has to-night won at *écarté* a large sum of money from Lord Glendinning. I will therefore put you upon an expeditious and decisive plan of obtaining this very necessary information. Please to examine, at your leisure, the inner linings of the cuff of his left sleeve, and the several little packages which may be found in the somewhat capacious pockets of his embroidered morning wrapper."

While he spoke, so profound was the stillness that one might have heard a pin drop upon the floor. In ceasing, he departed at once, and as abruptly as he had entered. Can I—shall I describe my sensations?—must I say that I felt all the horrors of the damned? Most assuredly I had little time given for reflection. Many hands roughly seized me upon the spot, and lights were immediately reprocured. A search ensued. In the lining of my sleeve were found all the court cards essential in *écarté,* and, in the pockets of my wrapper, a number of packs, fac-similes of those used at our sittings, with the single exception that mine were of the species called, technically, *arrondées;* the honours being slightly convex at the ends, the lower cards slightly convex at the sides. In this disposition, the dupe who cuts, as customary, at the length of the pack, will invariably find that he cuts his antagonist an honour; while the gambler, cutting at the breadth, will, as certainly cut nothing for his victim which may count in the records of the game.

Any burst of indignation upon this discovery would have affected me less than the silent contempt, or the sarcastic composure, with which it was received.

"Mr. Wilson," said our host, stooping to remove from beneath his feet an exceedingly luxurious cloak of rare furs, "Mr. Wilson, this is your property." (The weather was cold; and, upon quitting my own room, I had thrown a cloak over my dressing wrapper, putting it off upon reaching the scene of play.) "I presume it is supererogatory to seek here (eyeing the folds of the garment with a bitter smile) for any farther evidence of your skill. Indeed, we have had enough. You will see the necessity, I hope, of quitting Oxford—at all events, of quitting instantly my chambers."

Abased, humbled to the dust as I then was, it is probable that I should have resented this galling language by immediate personal violence, had not my whole attention been at the moment arrested by a fact of the most startling character. The cloak which I had worn was of a rare description of fur; how rare, how extravagantly costly, I shall not venture to say. Its fashion, too, was of my own fantastic invention; for I was fastidious to an absurd degree of coxcombry, in matters of this frivolous nature. When, therefore, Mr. Preston reached me that which he had picked up upon the floor, and near the folding doors of the apartment, it was with an astonishment nearly bordering upon terror, that I perceived my own already hanging on my arm, (where I had no doubt unwittingly placed it,) and that the one presented me was but its exact counterpart in every, in even the minutest possible particular. The singular being who had so disastrously exposed me, had been muffled, I remembered, in a cloak; and none had been worn at all by any of the members of our party with the exception of myself. Retaining some presence of mind, I took the one offered me by Preston; placed it, unnoticed, over my own; left the apartment with a resolute scowl of defiance; and, next morning ere dawn of day, commenced a hurried journey from Oxford to the continent, in a perfect agony of horror and of shame.

I fled in vain. My evil destiny pursued me as if in exultation, and proved, indeed, that the exercise of its mysterious dominion had as yet only begun. Scarcely had I set foot in Paris ere I had fresh evidence of the detestable interest taken by this Wilson in my concerns. Years flew, while I experienced no relief. Villain!—at Rome, with how untimely, yet with how spectral an officiousness, stepped he in between me and my ambition! At Vienna, too—at Berlin—and at Moscow! Where, in truth, had I *not* bitter cause to curse him within my heart? From his inscrutable tyranny did I at length flee, panic-stricken, as from a pestilence; and to the very ends of the earth *I fled in vain.*

And again, and again, in secret communion with my own spirit, would I demand the questions "Who is he?—whence came he?—and what are his objects?" But no answer was there found. And then I scrutinized, with a minute scrutiny, the forms, and the methods, and the leading traits of his impertinent supervision. But even here there was very little upon which to base a conjecture. It was noticeable, indeed, that, in no one of the multiplied instances in which he had of late crossed my path, had he so crossed it except to frustrate those schemes, or to disturb those actions, which, if fully carried out, might have resulted in bitter mischief. Poor justification this, in truth, for an authority so imperiously assumed! Poor indemnity for natural rights of self-agency so pertinaciously, so insultingly denied!

I had also been forced to notice that my tormentor, for a very long period of time, (while scrupulously and with miraculous dexterity maintaining his whim of an identity of apparel with myself,) had so contrived it, in the execution of his varied interference with my will, that I saw not, at any moment, the features of his face. Be Wilson what he might, *this,* at least, was but the veriest of affectation, or of folly. Could he, for an instant, have supposed that, in my admonisher at Eton—in the destroyer of my honor at Oxford,—in him who thwarted my ambition at Rome, my revenge at Paris, my passionate love at Naples, or what he falsely termed my avarice in Egypt,—that in this, my arch-enemy and evil genius, I could fail to recognise the William Wilson of my school boy days,—the namesake, the companion, the rival,—the hated and dreaded rival at Dr. Bransby's? Impossible!—But let me hasten to the last eventful scene of the drama.

Thus far I had succumbed supinely to this imperious domination. The sentiment of deep awe with which I habitually regarded the elevated character, the majestic wisdom, the apparent omnipresence and omnipotence of Wilson, added to a feeling of even terror, with which certain other traits in his nature and assumptions inspired me, had operated, hitherto, to impress me with an idea of my own utter weakness and helplessness, and to suggest an implicit, although bitterly reluctant submission to his arbitrary will. But, of late days, I had given myself up entirely to wine; and its maddening influence upon my hereditary temper rendered me more and more impatient of control. I began to murmur,—to hesitate,—to resist. And was it only fancy which induced me to believe that, with the increase of my own firmness, that of my tormentor underwent a proportional diminution? Be this as it may, I now began to feel the inspiration of a burning hope, and at length nurtured in my secret thoughts a stern and desperate resolution that I would submit no longer to be enslaved.

It was at Rome, during the Carnival of 18—, that I attended a masquerade in the palazzo of the Neapolitan Duke Di Broglio. I had indulged more freely than usual in the excesses of the wine-table; and now the suffocating atmosphere of the crowded rooms irritated me beyond endurance. The difficulty, too, of forcing my way through the mazes of the company contributed not a little to the ruffling of my temper; for I was anxiously seeking, (let me not say with what unworthy motive) the young, the gay, the beautiful wife of the aged and doting Di Broglio. With a too unscrupulous confidence she had previously communicated to me the secret of the costume in which she would be habited, and now, having caught a glimpse of her person, I was hurrying to make my way into her presence.—At this moment I felt a light hand placed upon my shoulder, and that ever-remembered, low, damnable *whisper* within my ear.

In an absolute phrenzy of wrath, I turned at once upon him who had thus interrupted me, and seized him violently by the collar. He was attired, as I had expected, in a costume altogether similar to my own; wearing a Spanish cloak of blue velvet, begirt about the waist with a crimson belt sustaining a rapier. A mask of black silk entirely covered his face.

"Scoundrel!" I said, in a voice husky with rage, while every syllable I uttered seemed as new fuel to my fury, "scoundrel! impostor! accursed villain! you shall not—you *shall not* dog me unto death! Follow me, or I stab you where you stand"—and I broke my way from the ball-room into a small antechamber adjoining—dragging him unresistingly with me as I went.

Upon entering, I thrust him furiously from me. He staggered against the wall, while I closed the door with an oath, and commanded him to draw. He hesitated but for an instant; then, with a slight sigh, drew in silence, and put himself upon his defence.

The contest was brief indeed. I was frantic with every species of wild excitement, and felt within my single arm the energy and power of a multitude. In a few seconds I forced him by sheer strength against the wain-scoting, and thus, getting him at mercy, plunged my sword, with brute ferocity, repeatedly through and through his bosom.

At that instant some person tried the latch of the door. I hastened to prevent an intrusion, and then immediately returned to my dying antagonist. But what human language can adequately portray *that* astonishment, *that* horror which possessed me at the spectacle then presented to view? The brief moment in which I averted my eyes had been sufficient to produce, apparently, a material change in the arrangements at the upper or farther end of the room. A large mirror,—so at first it seemed to me in my confusion—now stood where none had been perceptible before; and, as I stepped up to it in extremity of terror, mine own image, but with features all pale and dabbled in blood, advanced to meet me with feeble and tottering gait.

Thus it appeared, I say, but was not. It was my antagonist—it was Wilson, who then stood before me in the agonies of his dissolution. His mask and cloak lay, where he had thrown them, upon the floor. Not a thread in all his raiment—not a line in all the marked and singular lineaments of his face which was not, even in the most absolute identity, *mine own!*

It was Wilson; but he spoke no longer in a whisper, and I could have fancied that I myself was speaking while he said:

"*You have conquered, and I yield. Yet, henceforward art thou also dead—dead to the World, to Heaven and to Hope! In me didst thou exist—and, in my death, see by this image, which is thine own, how utterly thou has murdered thyself.*"

Murder at Pentecost

DOROTHY L. SAYERS

The academic world was no mystery to Dorothy L. Sayers (1893–1957). The daughter of the headmaster of Christchurch Cathedral Choir School, Oxford, she herself became a scholar at Somerville College, Oxford, receiving top honors in medieval literature, and in 1915 becoming one of the first women to obtain her degree. Although she is best known for her detective novels featuring the inquisitive nobleman Lord Peter Wimsey, many of Ms. Sayers's works are scholarly, and she wrote and lectured on religion, philosophy, and medieval literature during the last decade of her life. Influences of her academic background are reflected in her popular literature; most notably in Gaudy Night, *when Peter Wimsey's fiancée, mystery writer Harriet Vane, returns to her alma mater—which closely resembles Somerville—and becomes caught up in a murder investigation. In* "Murder at Pentecost," *Ms. Sayers's other well-known series character, wine salesman Montague Egg, makes full use of his deductive powers in solving the murder of a college master.*

"BUZZ OFF, Flathers," said the young man in flannels. "We're thrilled by your news, but we don't want your religious opinions. And, for the Lord's sake, stop talking about 'undergrads,' like a ruddy commercial traveller. Hop it!"

The person addressed, a pimply youth in a commoner's gown, bleated a little, but withdrew from the table, intimidated.

"Appalling little tick," commented the young man in flannels to his companion. "He's on my staircase, too. Thank Heaven, I move out next term. I suppose it's true about the Master? Poor old blighter—I'm quite sorry I cut his lecture. Have some more coffee?"

"No, thanks, Radcott. I must be pushing off in a minute. It's getting too near lunch-time."

Mr. Montague Egg, seated at the next small table, had pricked up his ears. He now turned, with an apologetic cough, to the young man called Radcott.

"Excuse me, sir," he said, with some diffidence. "I didn't intend to overhear what you gentlemen were saying, but might I ask a question?" Emboldened by Radcott's expression, which, though surprised, was frank and friendly, he went on: "I happen to be a commercial traveller—Egg is my name, Montague Egg, representing Plummet & Rose, wines and spirits, Piccadilly. Might I ask what is wrong with saying 'undergrads'? Is the expression offensive in any way?"

Mr. Radcott blushed a fiery red to the roots of his flaxen hair.

"I'm frightfully sorry," he said ingenuously, and suddenly looking extremely young. "Damn stupid thing of me to say. Beastly brick."

"Don't mention it, I'm sure," said Monty.

"Didn't mean anything personal. Only, that chap Flathers gets my goat. He ought to know that nobody says 'undergrads' except townees and journalists and people outside the university."

"What ought we to say? 'Undergraduates'?"

" 'Undergraduates' is correct."

"I'm very much obliged," said Monty. "Always willing to learn. It's easy to make a mistake in a thing like that, and, of course, it prejudices the customer against one. The *Salesman's Handbook* doesn't give any guidance about it; I shall have to make a memo for myself. Let me see. How would this do? 'To call an Oxford gent an—' "

"I think I should say 'Oxford man'—it's the more technical form of expression."

"Oh, yes. 'To call an Oxford man an undergrad proclaims you an outsider and a cad.' That's very easy to remember."

"You seem to have a turn for this kind of thing," said Radcott, amused.

"Well, I think perhaps I have," admitted Monty, with a touch of pride. "Would the same thing apply at Cambridge?"

"Certainly," replied Radcott's companion. "And you might add that 'To call the university the 'varsity is out of date, if not precisely narsity.' I apologise for the rhyme. 'Varsity has somehow a flavour of the 'nineties."

"So has the port I'm recommending," said Mr. Egg brightly. "Still, one's sales-talk must be up to date, naturally; and smart, though not vulgar. In the wine and spirit trade we make refinement our aim. I am really much obliged to you, gentlemen, for your help. This is my first visit to Oxford. Could you tell me where to find Pentecost College? I have a letter of introduction to a gentleman there."

"Pentecost?" said Radcott. "I don't think I'd start there, if I were you."

"No?" said Mr. Egg, suspecting some obscure point of university etiquette. "Why not?"

"Because," replied Radcott surprisingly, "I understand from the regrettable Flathers that some public benefactor has just murdered the Master, and in the circumstances I doubt whether the Bursar will be able to give proper attention to the merits of rival vintages."

"Murdered the Master?" echoed Mr. Egg.

"Socked him one—literally, I am told, with a brickbat enclosed in a Woolworth sock—as he was returning to his house from delivering his too-well-known lecture on Plato's use of the Enclitics. The whole school of *Literae Humaniores* will naturally be under suspicion, but, personally, I believe Flathers did it himself. You may have heard him informing us that judgment overtakes the evil-doer, and inviting us to a meeting for prayer and repentance in the South Lecture-Room. Such men are dangerous."

"Was the Master of Pentecost an evil-doer?"

"He has written several learned works disproving the existence of Providence, and I must say that I, in common with the whole Pentecostal community, have always looked on him as one of Nature's worst mistakes. Still, to slay him more or less on his own doorstep seems to me to be in poor taste. It will upset the examination candidates, who face their ordeal next week. And it will mean cancelling the Commem. Ball. Besides, the police have been called in, and are certain to annoy the Senior Common Room by walking on the grass in the quad. However, what's done can't be undone. Let us pass to a pleasanter subject. I understand that you have some port to dispose of. I, on the other hand, have recently suffered bereavement at the hands of a bunch of rowing hearties, who invaded my rooms the other night and poured my last dozen of Cockburn '04 down their leathery and undiscriminating throttles. If you care to stroll around with me to Pentecost, Mr. Egg, bringing your literature with you, we might be able to do business."

Mr. Egg expressed himself as delighted to accept Radcott's invitation, and was soon trotting along the Cornmarket at his conductor's athletic heels. At the corner of Broad Street the second undergraduate left them, while they turned on, past Balliol and Trinity, asleep in the June sunshine, and presently reached the main entrance of Pentecost.

Just as they did so, a small elderly man, wearing a light overcoat and carrying an M.A. gown over his arm, came ambling short-sightedly across the street from the direction of the Bodleian Library. A passing car just missed whirling him into eternity, as Radcott stretched out a long arm and raked him into safety on the pavement.

"Look out, Mr. Temple," said Radcott. "We shall be having *you* murdered next."

"Murdered?" queried Mr. Temple, blinking. "Oh, you refer to the motor-car. But I saw it coming. I saw it quite distinctly. Yes, yes. But why 'next'? Has anybody else been murdered?"

"Only the Master of Pentecost," said Radcott, pinching Mr. Egg's arm.

"The Master? Dr. Greeby? You don't say so! Murdered? Dear me! Poor Greeby! This will upset my whole day's work." His pale-blue eyes shifted, and a curious, wavering look came into them. "Justice is slow but sure. Yes, yes. The sword of the Lord and of Gideon. But the blood—that is always so disconcerting, is it not? And yet, I washed my hands, you know." He stretched out both hands and looked at them in a puzzled way. "Ah, yes—poor Greeby has paid the price of his sins. Excuse my running away from you—I have urgent business at the police-station."

"If," said Mr. Radcott, again pinching Monty's arm, "you want to give yourself up for the murder, Mr. Temple, you had better come along with us. The police are bound to be about the place somewhere."

"Oh, yes, of course, so they are. Yes. Very thoughtful of you. That will save me a great deal of time, and I have an important chapter to finish. A beautiful day, is it not, Mr.—I fear I do not know your name. Or do I? I am growing sadly forgetful."

Radcott mentioned his name, and the oddly assorted trio turned together towards the main entrance to the college. The great gate was shut; at the postern stood the porter, and at his side a massive figure in blue, who demanded their names.

Radcott, having been duly identified by the porter, produced Monty and his credentials.

"And this," he went on, "is, of course, Mr. Temple. You know him. He is looking for your Superintendent."

"Right you are, sir," replied the policeman. "You'll find him in the cloisters. . . . At his old game, I suppose?" he added, as the small figure of Mr. Temple shuffled away across the sun-baked expanse of the quad.

"Oh, yes," said Radcott. "He was on to it like a shot. Must be quite exciting for the old bird to have a murder so near home. Where was his last?"

"Lincoln, sir; last Tuesday. Young fellow shot his young woman in the Cathedral. Mr. Temple was down at the station the next day, just before lunch, explaining that he'd done it because the poor girl was the Scarlet Woman."

"Mr. Temple," said Radcott, "has a mission in life. He is the sword of the Lord and of Gideon. Every time a murder is committed in this country, Mr. Temple lays claim to it. It is true that his body can always be shown to have been quietly in bed or at the Bodleian while the dirty work was afoot, but to an idealistic philosopher that need present no difficulty. But what *is* all this about the Master, actually?"

"Well, sir, you know that little entry between the cloisters and the Master's residence? At twenty minutes past ten this morning, Dr. Greeby was found lying dead there, with his lecture-notes scattered all round him and a brickbat in a woollen sock lying beside his head. He'd been lecturing in a room in the Main Quadrangle at 9 o'clock, and was, as far as we can tell, the last to leave the lecture-room. A party of American ladies and gentlemen passed through the cloisters a little after 10 o'clock, and they have been found, and say there was nobody about there then, so far as they could see—but, of course, sir, the murderer might have been hanging about the entry, because, naturally, they wouldn't go that way but through Boniface Passage to the Inner Quad and the chapel. One of the young gentlemen says he saw the Master cross the Main Quad on his way to the cloisters at 10.5, so he'd reach the entry in about two minutes after that. The Regius Professor of Morphology came along at 10.20, and found the body, and when the doctor arrived, five minutes later, he said Dr. Greeby must have been dead about a quarter of an hour.

So that puts it somewhere round about 10.10, you see, sir."

"When did these Americans leave the chapel?"

"Ah, there you are, sir!" replied the constable. He seemed very ready to talk, thought Mr. Egg, and deduced, rightly, that Mr. Radcott was well and favourably known to the Oxford branch of the Force. "If that there party had come back through the cloisters, they might have been able to tell us something. But they didn't. They went on through the Inner Quad into the garden, and the verger didn't leave the chapel, on account of a lady who had just arrived and wanted to look at the carving on the reredos."

"And did the lady also come through the cloisters?"

"She did, sir, and she's the person we want to find, because it seems as though she must have passed through the cloisters very close to the time of the murder. She came into the chapel just on 10.15, because the verger recollected of the clock chiming a few minutes after she came in and her mentioning how sweet the notes was. You see the lady come in, didn't you, Mr. Dabbs?"

"I saw *a* lady," replied the porter, "but then I see a lot of ladies one way and another. This one came across from the Bodleian round about 10 o'clock. Elderly lady, she was, dressed kind of old-fashioned, with her skirts round her heels and one of them hats like a rook's nest and a bit of elastic round the back. Looked like she might be a female don—leastways, the way female dons used to look. And she had the twitches—you know—jerked her head a bit. You get hundreds like 'em. They goes to sit in the cloisters and listen to the fountain and the little birds. But as to noticing a corpse or a murderer, it's my belief they wouldn't know such a thing if they saw it. I didn't see the lady again, so she must have gone out through the garden."

"Very likely," said Radcott. "May Mr. Egg and I go in through the cloisters, officer? Because it's the only way to my rooms, unless we go round by St. Scholastica's Gate."

"All the other gates are locked, sir. You go on and speak to the Super; he'll let you through. You'll find him in the cloisters with Professor Staines and Dr. Moyle."

"Bodley's Librarian? What's he got to do with it?"

"They think he may know the lady, sir, if she's a Bodley reader."

"Oh, I see. Come along, Mr. Egg."

Radcott led the way across the Main Quadrangle and through a dark little passage at one corner, into the cool shade of the cloisters. Framed by the arcades of ancient stone, the green lawn drowsed tranquilly in the noonday heat. There was no sound but the echo of their own footsteps, the plash and tinkle of the little fountain and the subdued chirping of chaffinches, as they paced the alternate sunshine and shadow of the pavement. About mid-way along the north side of the cloisters they came upon another dim little covered passageway, at the entrance to which a police-sergeant was kneeling, examining the ground with the aid of an electric torch.

"Hullo, sergeant!" said Radcott. "Doing the Sherlock Holmes, stunt? Show us the bloodstained footprints."

"No blood, sir, unfortunately. Might make our job easier if there were. And no footprints neither. The poor gentleman was sandbagged, and we think the murderer must have climbed up here to do it, for the deceased was a tall gentleman and he was hit right on the top of the head, sir." The sergeant indicated a little niche, like a blocked-up window, about four feet from the ground. "Looks as if he'd waited up here, sir, for Dr. Greeby to go by."

"He must have been well acquainted with his victim's habits," suggested Mr. Egg.

"Not a bit of it," retorted Radcott. "He'd only to look at the lecture-list to know the time and place. This passage leads to the Master's House and the Fellows' Garden and nowhere else, and it's the way Dr. Greeby would naturally go after his lecture, unless he was lecturing elsewhere, which he wasn't. Fairly able-bodied, your murderer, sergeant, to get up here. At least—I don't know."

Before the policeman could stop him, he had placed one hand on the side of the niche and a foot on a projecting band of masonry below it, and swung himself up.

"Hi, sir! Come down, please. The Super won't like that."

"Why? Oh, gosh! Fingerprints, I suppose. I forgot. Never mind; you can take mine if you want them, for comparison. Give you practice. Anyhow, a baby in arms could get up here. Come on, Mr. Egg; we'd better beat it before I'm arrested for obstruction."

But at this moment Radcott was hailed by a worried-looking don, who came through the passage from the far side, accompanied by three or four other people.

"Oh, Mr. Radcott! One moment, Superintendent, this gentleman will be able to tell you what you want to know; he was at Dr. Greeby's lecture. That is so, is it not, Mr. Radcott?"

"Well, no, not exactly, sir," replied Radcott, with some embarrassment. "I should have been, but, by a regrettable accident, I cut—that is to say, I was on the river, sir, and didn't get back in time."

"Very vexatious," said Professor Staines, while the Superintendent merely observed:

"Any witness to your being on the river, sir?"

"None," replied Radcott. "I was alone in a canoe, up a backwater—earnestly studying Aristotle. But I really didn't murder the Master. His lectures were—if I may say so—dull, but not to that point exasperating."

"That is a very impudent observation, Mr. Radcott," said the Professor severely, "and in execrable taste."

The Superintendent, murmuring something about routine, took down in a note-book the alleged times of Mr. Radcott's departure and return, and then said:

"I don't think I need detain any of you gentlemen further. If we want to see you again, Mr. Temple, we will let you know."

"Certainly, certainly. I shall just have a sandwich at the café and return to the Bodleian. As for the lady, I can only repeat that she sat at my table from about half-past nine till just before ten, and returned again at ten-thirty. Very restless and disturbing. I do wish, Dr. Moyle, that some arrangement could be made to give me that table to myself, or that I could be given a place apart in the library. Ladies are always restless and disturbing. She was still there when I left, but I very much hope she has now gone for good. You are sure you don't want to lock me up now? I am quite at your service.''

''Not just yet, sir. You will hear from us presently.''

''Thank you, thank you. I should like to finish my chapter. For the present, then, I will wish you good-day.''

The little bent figure wandered away, and the Superintendent touched his head significantly.

''Poor gentleman! Quite harmless, of course. I needn't ask you, Dr. Moyle, where *he* was at the time?''

''Oh, he was in his usual corner of Duke Humphrey's Library. He admits it, you see, when he is asked. In any case, I know definitely that he was there this morning, because he took out a Phi book, and of course had to apply personally to me for it. He asked for it at 9.30 and returned it at 12.15. As regards the lady, I think I have seen her before. One of the older school of learned ladies, I fancy. If she is an outside reader, I must have her name and address somewhere, but she may, of course, be a member of the University. I fear I could not undertake to know them all by sight. But I will inquire. It is, in fact, quite possible that she is still in the library, and, if not, Franklin may know when she went and who she is. I will look into the matter immediately. I need not say, professor, how deeply I deplore this lamentable affair. Poor dear Greeby! Such a loss to classical scholarship!''

At this point, Radcott gently drew Mr. Egg away. A few yards farther down the cloisters, they turned into another and rather wider passage, which brought them out into the Inner Quadrangle, one side of which was occupied by the chapel. Mounting three dark flights of stone steps on the opposite side, they reached Radcott's rooms, where the undergraduate thrust his new acquaintance into an armchair, and, producing some bottles of beer from beneath the window-seat, besought him to make himself at home.

''Well,'' he observed presently, ''you've had a fairly lively introduction to Oxford life—one murder and one madman. Poor old Temple. Quite one of our prize exhibits. Used to be a Fellow here, donkey's years ago. There was some fuss, and he disappeared for a time. Then he turned up again, ten years since, perfectly potty; took lodgings in Holywell, and has haunted the Bodder and the police-station alternately ever since. Fine Greek scholar he is, too. Quite reasonable, except on the one point. I hope old Moyle finds his mysterious lady, though it's nonsense to pretend that they keep tabs on all the people who use the library. You've only got to walk in firmly, as if the place belonged to you, and, if you're challenged, say in a loud, injured tone that you've been a reader for years. If you borrow a gown, they won't even challenge you."

"Is that so, really?" said Mr. Egg.

"Prove it, if you like. Take my gown, toddle across to the Bodder, march straight in past the showcases and through the little wicket marked 'Readers Only,' into Duke Humphrey's Library; do what you like, short of stealing the books or setting fire to the place—and if anybody says anything to you, I'll order six dozen of anything you like. That's fair, isn't it?"

Mr. Egg accepted this offer with alacrity, and in a few moments, arrayed in a scholar's gown, was climbing the stair that leads to England's most famous library. With a slight tremor, he pushed open the swinging glass door and plunged into the hallowed atmosphere of mouldering leather that distinguishes such temples of learning.

Just inside, he came upon Dr. Moyle in conversation with the door-keeper. Mr. Egg, bending nonchalantly to examine an illegible manuscript in a showcase, had little difficulty in hearing what they said, since, like all official attendants upon reading-rooms, they took no trouble to lower their voices.

"I know the lady, Dr. Moyle. That is to say, she has been here several times lately. She usually wears an M.A. gown. I saw her here this morning, but I didn't notice when she left. I don't think I ever heard her name, but seeing that she was a senior member of the University—"

Mr. Egg waited to hear no more. An idea was burgeoning on his mind. He walked away, courageously pushed open the Readers' Wicket, and stalked down the solemn mediaeval length of Duke Humphrey's Library. In the remotest and darkest bay, he observed Mr. Temple, who, having apparently had his sandwich and forgotten about the murder, sat alone, writing busily, amid a pile of repellent volumes, with a large attaché-case full of papers open before him.

Leaning over the table, Mr. Egg addressed him in an urgent whisper:

"Excuse me, sir. The police Superintendent asked me to say that they think they have found the lady, and would be glad if you would kindly step down at once and identify her."

"The lady?" Mr. Temple looked up vaguely. "Oh, yes—the lady. To be sure. Immediately? That is not very convenient. Is it so very urgent?"

"They said particularly to lose no time, sir," said Mr. Egg.

Mr. Temple muttered something, rose, seemed to hesitate whether to clear up his papers or not, and finally shovelled them all into the bulging attaché-case, which he locked upon them.

"Let me carry this for you, sir," said Monty, seizing it promptly and shepherding Mr. Temple briskly out. "They're still in the cloisters, I think, but the Super said, would you kindly wait a few moments for him in the porter's lodge. Here we are."

He handed Mr. Temple and his attaché-case over to the care of the porter, who looked a little surprised at seeing Mr. Egg in academic dress, but, on hearing the Superintendent's name, said nothing. Mr. Egg hastened through quad and cloisters and mounted Mr. Radcott's staircase at a run.

"Excuse me, sir," he demanded breathlessly of that young gentleman, "but what is a Phi book?"

"A Phi book," replied Radcott, in some surprise, "is a book deemed by Bodley's Librarian to be of an indelicate nature, and catalogued accordingly, by some dead-and-gone humorist, under the Greek letter *phi*. Why the question?"

"Well," said Mr. Egg, "it just occurred to me how simple it would be for anybody to walk into the Bodleian, disguise himself in a retired corner—say in Duke Humphrey's Library—walk out, commit a murder, return, change back to his own clothes and walk out. Nobody would stop a person from coming in again, if he—or she—had previously been seen to go out—especially if the disguise had been used in the library before. Just a change of clothes and an M.A. gown would be enough."

"What in the world are you getting at?"

"This lady, who was in the cloisters at the time of the murder. Mr. Temple says she was sitting at his table. But isn't it funny that Mr. Temple should have drawn special attention to himself by asking for a Phi book, to-day of all days? If he was once a Fellow of this college, he'd know which way Dr. Greeby would go after his lecture; and he may have had a grudge against him on account of that old trouble, whatever it was. He'd know about the niche in the wall, too. And he's got an attaché-case with him that might easily hold a lady's hat and a skirt long enough to hide his trousers. And why is he wearing a topcoat on such a hot day, if not to conceal the upper portion of his garments? Not that it's any business of mine—but—well, I just took the liberty of asking myself. And I've got him out there, with his case, and the porter keeping an eye on him."

Thus Mr. Egg, rather breathlessly. Radcott gaped at him.

"Temple? My dear man, you're as potty as he is. Why, he's always confessing—he confessed to this—you can't possibly suppose—"

"I daresay I'm wrong," said Mr. Egg. "But isn't there a fable about the man who cried 'Wolf!' so often that nobody would believe him when the wolf really came? There's a motto in the *Salesman's Handbook* that I always admire very much. It says: 'Discretion plays a major part in making up the salesman's art, for truths that no one can believe are calculated to deceive.' I think that's rather subtle, don't you?"

Murder at Mother's Knee

CORNELL WOOLRICH

The spinster schoolteacher has been a stock character of crime fiction for many years; but in the hands of Cornell Woolrich, such a character takes on a subtly different dimension, as you'll discover when you meet Miss Prince in "Murder at Mother's Knee." This story, like all of Woolrich's fiction, is filled with the twin ingredients of terror and pulse-pounding suspense. Woolrich (1903-1968) was a tragic figure who suffered a lifelong sense of unfulfillment and doom, which perhaps explains his ability to so vividly express palpable dread in his short fiction and in such classic novels as The Bride Wore Black *(1940),* Black Alibi *(1942), and* Phantom Lady *(1942, as William Irish).*

MISS PRINCE KNEW all the signs that meant homework hadn't been done. The hangdog look, the guiltily lowered head. She stood there by the Gaines boy's desk, one hand extended. "Well, I'm waiting, Johnny."

The culprit squirmed uncomfortably to his feet. "I—I couldn't do it, teacher."

"Why not?"

"I—I didn't know what to write about."

"That's no excuse," Miss Prince said firmly. "I gave the class the simplest kind of theme this time. I said to write about something you know, something that really happened, either at home or elsewhere. If the others were able to, why weren't you?"

"I couldn't think of anything that happened."

Miss Prince turned away. "Well, you'll stay in and sit there until you do. When I give out homework I expect it to be done!" She returned to her desk, stacked the collected creative efforts to one side, and took up the day's lesson.

Three o'clock struck and the seats before her emptied like magic in one headlong, scampering rush for the door. All but the second one back on the outside aisle.

"You can begin now, Johnny," said Miss Prince relentlessly. "Take a clean sheet of paper and quit staring out the window."

Although the boy probably wouldn't have believed it, she didn't enjoy this any more than he did. He was keeping her in just as much as she was keeping him in. But discipline had to be maintained.

The would-be-author seemed to be suffering from an acute lack of inspiration. He chewed the rubber of his pencil, fidgeted, stared at the blackboard, and nothing happened.

"You're not trying, Johnny!" she said severely, at last.

"I can't think of anything," he lamented.

"Yes, you can. Stop saying that. Write about your dog or cat, if you can't think of anything else."

"I haven't any."

She went back to her papers. He raised his hand finally, to gain her attention. "Is it all right to write about a dream?"

"I suppose so, if that's the best you can do," she acquiesced. It seemed to be the only way out of the predicament. "But I wanted you to write something that really happened. This was to test your powers of observation and description."

"This was part-true and only part a dream," he assured her.

He bent diligently to the desk, to make up for time lost. At the end of fifteen minutes he stood before her with the effort completed. "All right, you can go home now," she consented wearily. "And the next time you come to school without your homework—" But the door had already closed behind him.

She smiled slightly to herself, with a sympathetic understanding he wouldn't have given her credit for, and placed the latest masterpiece on top of the others, to take home with her. As she did so, her eye, glancing idly along the opening sentences, was caught by something. She lingered on, reading, forgetting her original intention of rising from her desk and going out to the cloakroom to get her hat.

The epistle before her, in laborious straight up-and-down, childish handwriting, read:

Johnny Gaines
English Comp. 2

Something that happened in our house

One night I wasn't sleeping so good on account of something I eat, and I dreamed I was out in a boat and the water was rough and rocking me up and down a lot. So then I woke up and the floor in my room was shaking kind of and so was my bed and everything. And I even heard a table and chair fall down, downstairs. So I got kind of scared and I sneaked downstairs to see what was the matter. But by that time it stopped again and everything was quiet.

My mother was in the kitchen straitening things up again, and she didn't want me to come near there when she first saw me. But I looked in anyway. Then she closed the outside door and she told me some kind of a varmint got in the house from outside, and my pa had a hard time getting it and killing it, and that was why everything fell over. It sure must have been a bad kind of one, because it scared her a lot, she was still shaking all the time. She was standing still, but she was all out of breath. I asked her where it was and she said he carried it outside with him to get rid of it far away from the house.

Then I saw where his hat got to when he was having all that trouble catching it, and he never even missed it. It fell through the stove onto the ashes. So she picked it up out of there when I showed her, and the ashes made it look even cleaner than before when he had it on. Almost like new.

Then she got some water and a brush and started to scrub the kitchen floor where she said the varmint got it dirtied up. But I couldn't see where it was because she got in the way. And she wouldn't let me stay and watch, she made me go upstairs again.

So that was all that happened.

When she had finished, Miss Prince turned her head abruptly toward the door as if to recall the author of the composition.

She sat on there for a while, tapping her pencil thoughtfully against the edge of her teeth.

Miss Prince settled herself uneasily on one of the straight-backed chairs against the wall that the desk-sergeant had indicated to her, and waited, fiddling with her handbag.

She felt out of place in a police station anteroom, and wondered what had made her come like this.

A pair of thick-soled brogues came walloping out, stopped short before her, and she looked up. She'd never been face to face with a professional detective before. This one didn't look like one at all. He looked more like a businessman who had dropped into the police station to report his car stolen, or something.

"Anything I can do for you?" he asked.

"It's—it's just something that I felt I ought to bring to your attention," she faltered. "I'm Emily Prince of the English Department at the Benjamin Harrison Public School." She fumbled for the composition, extended it toward him. "One of my pupils handed this to me yesterday afternoon."

He read it over, handed it back to her. "I don't get it," he grinned. "You want me to pinch the kid that wrote this for murdering the King's English?"

She flashed him an impatient look. "I think it's obvious that this child witnessed an act of violence, a crime of some sort, without realizing its full implication," she said coldly. "You can read between the lines. I believe that a murder has taken place in that house, and gone undiscovered. I think the matter should be investigated."

She stopped short. He had begun to act in a most unaccountable manner. The lower part of his face began to twitch, and a dull-red flush overspread it. "Excuse me a minute," he said in a choked voice, stood up abruptly, and walked away from her. She noticed him holding his hand against the side of his face, as if to shield it from view. He stopped a minute at the other end of the room, stood there with his shoulders shaking, then turned and came back. He coughed a couple of times on the way over.

"If there's anything funny about this, I fail to see it!"

"I'm sorry," he said, sitting down again. "It hit me so sudden, I couldn't help it. A kid writes a composition, the first thing that comes into his head, just so he can get it over with and go out and play, and you come here and ask us to investigate. Aw, now listen, lady—"

She surveyed him with eyes that were not exactly lanterns of esteem. "I cross-questioned the youngster. Today, after class. Before coming here. He insists it was *not* made up—that it's true."

"Naturally he would. The detail—I mean the assignment, was for them to write about something true, wasn't it? He was afraid he'd have to do it over if he admitted it was imaginary."

"Just a minute, Mr.—"

"Kendall," he supplied.

"May I ask what your duties are?"

"I'm a detective attached to the Homicide Squad. That's what you asked for."

It was now her turn to get in a dirty lick. "I just wanted to make sure," she said dryly. "There's been no way of telling since I've been talking to you."

"Ouch!" he murmured.

"There are certain details given here," she went on, flourishing the composition at him, "that are not within the scope of a child's imagination. Here's one: his mother was standing still, but she was all out of breath. Here's another: a hat lying in just such and such a place. Here's the most pertinent of the lot: her scrubbing of the kitchen floor at that hour of the night. It's full of little touches like that. It wouldn't occur to a child to make up things like that. They're *too* realistic. A child's flights of fancy would incline toward more fantastic things. Shadows and spooks and faces at the window. I *deal* in children—I know how their minds work."

"Well," he let her know stubbornly, "I deal in murders. And I don't run out making a fool of myself on the strength of a composition written by a kid in school!"

She stood up so suddenly her chair skittered back into the wall. "Sorry if I've wasted your time. I'll know better in the future!"

"It's not mine you've wasted," he countered. "It's your own, I'm afraid."

A few minutes after her class had been dismissed the next day, a "monitor," one of the older children used to carry messages about the building, knocked on her door. "There's a man outside would like to talk to you, Miss Prince."

She stepped out into the hall. The man, Detective Kendall of the Homicide Squad, was tossing a piece of chalk up and down in the hollow of his hand.

"Thought you might like to know," he said, "that I stopped that Gaines youngster on his way to school this morning and asked him a few questions. It's just like I told you yesterday. The first words out of his mouth were that he made the whole thing up. He couldn't think of anything, and it was nearly 4 o'clock, so he scribbled down the first thing that came into his head."

If he thought this would force her to capitulate, he was sadly mistaken. "Of course he'd deny it—to *you*. That's about as valid as a confession extracted from an adult by third-degree methods. The mere fact that you stopped to question him about it frightened him into thinking he'd done something wrong. He wasn't sure just what, but he'd played safe by saying he'd made it up."

He thrust his jaw forward. "You know what I think is the matter with you?" he told her bluntly. "I think you're *looking* for trouble!"

"Thank you for your cooperation, it's been overwhelming!" she said, snatching something from him as she turned away. "And will you kindly refrain from marking the walls with that piece of chalk! Pupils are punished when they do it!"

She returned stormily to the classroom. The Gaines boy sat hunched forlornly, looking very small in the sea of empty seats. "I've found out it wasn't your fault for being late, Johnny," she relented. "You can go now, and I'll make it up to you by letting you out earlier tomorrow."

He scuttled for the door.

"Johnny, just a minute. I'd like to ask you something."

His face clouded as he came back slowly.

"Was that composition of yours true or made up?"

"Made up, Miss Prince," he mumbled, scuffling his feet.

Which only proved to her that he was more afraid of the anonymous man with a badge than of his own teacher.

"Johnny, do you live in a large house?"

"Yes'm, pretty big," he admitted.

"Well, er—do you think your mother would care to rent out a room to me? I have to leave where I am living now, and I'm trying to find another place."

He swallowed. "You mean move into our house and *live* with us?" Obviously his child's mind didn't regard having a teacher at such close quarters as a blessing.

She smiled reassuringly. "I won't interfere with you in your spare time, Johnny. I think I'll walk home with you now—I'd like to know as soon as possible."

"We'll have to take the bus, Miss Prince, it's pretty far out," he told her.

It was even farther than she had expected it to be, a weather-beaten, rather depressing-looking farm-type of building, well beyond the last straggling suburbs, in full open country. It was set back from the road, and the whole area around it had an air of desolation and neglect. Its unpainted shutters hung askew, and the porch roof was warped and threatened to topple over at one end.

Something *could* have happened out here quite easily, she thought, judging by the looks of the place alone.

A toilworn, timid-looking woman came forward to meet them as they neared the door, wiping her hands on an apron. "Mom, this is my teacher, Miss Prince," Johnny introduced.

At once the woman's expression became even more harassed and intimidated. "You been doing something you shouldn't again? Johnny, why can't you be a good boy?"

"No, this has nothing to do with Johnny's conduct," Emily Prince hastened to explain. She repeated the request for lodging she had already made to the boy.

It was obvious, at a glance, that the suggestion frightened the woman. "I dunno," she kept saying. "I dunno what Mr. Mason will say about it. He ain't in right now."

Johnny was registered at school under the name of Gaines. Mr. Mason must be the boy's stepfather then. It was easy to see that the poor woman before her was completely dominated by him, whoever he was. That, in itself, from Miss Prince's angle, was a very suggestive factor. She made up her mind to get inside this house if she had to coax, bribe, or browbeat her way in.

She opened her purse, took out a large-size bill, and allowed it to be seen in her hand, in readiness to seal the bargain.

The boy's mother was obviously swayed by the sight of it but was still being held back by fear of something. "We could use the money, of course," she wavered. "But—but wouldn't it be too far out for you, here?"

Miss Prince faked a slight cough. "Not at all. The country air would be good for me. Couldn't I at least see one of the rooms?" she coaxed. "There wouldn't be any harm in that, would there?"

"N-no, I suppose not," Mrs. Mason faltered.

She led the way up a badly creaking inner staircase. "There's really only one room fit for anybody," she apologized.

"I'd only want it temporarily," Miss Prince assured her. "Maybe a week or two at the most."

She looked around. It really wasn't as bad as she had been led to expect by the appearance of the house from the outside. In other words, it was the masculine share of the work, the painting and external repairing, that was remiss. The feminine share, the interior cleaning, was being kept up to the best of Mrs. Mason's ability. There was another little suggestive sidelight in that, thought Miss Prince.

She struck while the iron was hot. "I'll take it," she said firmly, and thrust the money she had been holding into the other's undecided hand before she had time to put forward any further objections.

That did the trick.

"I—I guess it's all right," Mrs. Mason breathed, guiltily wringing her hands in the apron. "I'll tell Mr. Mason it's just for the time being." She tried to smile to make amends for her own trepidation. "He's not partial to having strangers in with us—"

"Why?" Miss Prince asked in her own mind, with a flinty question mark.

"But you being Johnny's teacher—when will you be wanting to move in with us?"

Miss Prince had no intention of relinquishing her tactical advantage. "I may as well stay, now that I'm out here," she said. "I can have my things sent out."

She closed the door of her new quarters and sat down to think.

The sun was already starting to go down when she heard an approaching tread coming up the neglected dirt track that led to the door. She edged over to the window and peered cautiously down. Mason, if that was he, was singularly unprepossessing, even villainous-looking at first glance, much more so than she had expected him to be. He was thick-set, strong as a steer in body, with bushy black brows and small, alert eyes. He had removed a disreputable, shapeless hat just as he passed below her window, and was wiping his completely bald head with a soiled bandanna. The skin of his scalp was sunburned, and ridged like dried leather.

She left the window and hastened across the room to gain the doorway and overhear his first reaction to the news of her being there. She strained her ears. This first moment or two was going to offer an insight that was never likely to repeat itself, no matter how long she stayed in this house.

"Where's Ed?" she heard him grunt unsociably. This was the first inkling she had had that there was still another member of the household.

"Still over in town, I guess," she heard Mrs. Mason answer. She was obviously in mortal terror as she nerved herself to make the unwelcome announcement—the listener above could tell by the very ring of her voice. "Johnny's teacher come to stay with us—a little while."

There was suppressed savagery in his rejoinder. "What'd you do that for?" And then a sound followed that Emily Prince couldn't identify for a second. A sort of quick, staggering footfall. A moment later she realized what it must have been. He had given the woman a violent push to express his disapproval.

She heard her whimper: "She's up there right now, Dirk."

"Get rid of her!" was the snarling answer.

"I can't, Dirk, she already give me the money, and—and she

ain't going to be here but a short spell anyway."

She heard him come out stealthily below her, trying to listen up just as she was trying to listen down. An unnatural silence fell, then prolonged itself unnaturally. It was like a grotesque cat-and-mouse play, one of them directly above the other, both reconnoitering at once.

He turned and went back again at last, when she was about ready to keel over from the long strain of holding herself motionless. She crept back inside her room and drew a long breath.

If that hadn't been a guilty reaction, what was? But still it wasn't evidence by any means.

The porch floor throbbed again, and someone else had come in. This must be the Ed she had heard them talk about. She didn't try to listen this time. There would never be a second opportunity quite like that first. Whatever was said to him would be in a careful undertone. Mrs. Mason came out shortly after, called up: "Miss Prince, like to come down to supper?"

The teacher steeled herself, opened the door and stepped out. This was going to be a battle of wits. On their side they had an animal-like craftiness. On hers she had intellect, a trained mind, and self-control.

She felt she was really better equipped than they for warfare of this sort. She went down to enter the first skirmish.

They were at the table already eating—such a thing as waiting for her had never entered their heads. They ate crouched over, and that gave them the opportunity of watching her surreptitiously. Mrs. Mason said: "You can sit here next to Johnny. This is my husband. And this is my stepson, Ed."

The brutality on Ed's face was less deeply ingrained than on Mason's. It was only a matter of degree, however. Like father, like son.

"Evenin'," Mason grunted.

The son only nodded, peering upward at her in a half-baleful, half-suspicious way, taking her measure.

They ate in silence for a while, though she could tell that all their minds were busy on the same thing: her presence here, trying to decide what it might mean.

Finally Mason spoke. "Reckon you'll be staying some time?"

"No," she said quietly, "just a short while."

The son spoke next, after a considerable lapse of time. She could tell he'd premeditated the question for a full ten minutes. "How'd you happen to pick our place?"

"I knew Johnny, from my class. And it's quieter out here."

She caught the flicker of a look passing among them. She couldn't read its exact meaning, whether acceptance of her explanation or skepticism.

They shoved back their chairs, one after the other, got up and turned away, without a word of apology. Mason sauntered out into the dark beyond the porch. Ed Mason stopped to strike a match to a cigarette he had just rolled. Even in the act of doing that, however, she caught his head turned slightly toward her, watching her when he thought she wasn't looking.

The older man's voice sounded from outside: "Ed, come out here a minute, I want to talk to you."

She knew what about—they were going to compare impressions, possibly plot a course of action.

The first battle was a draw.

She got up and went after Mrs. Mason. "I'll help you with the dishes." She wanted to get into that kitchen.

She couldn't see it at first. She kept using her eyes, scanning the floor surreptitiously while she wiped Mrs. Mason's thick, chipped crockery. Finally she thought she detected something. A shadowy bald patch, so to speak. It was both cleaner than the surrounding area, as though it had been scrubbed vigorously, and at the same time it was overcast. There were the outlines of a stain still faintly discernible. But it wasn't very conspicuous, just the shadow of a shadow.

She said to herself: "*She'll* tell me. I'll find out what I want to know."

She moved aimlessly around, pretending to dry off something, until she was standing right over it. Then she pretended to fumble her cloth, let it drop. She bent down, and planted the flat of her hand squarely on the shadowy place, as if trying to retain her balance. She let it stay that way for a moment.

She didn't have to look at the other woman. A heavy mug slipped through her hands and shattered resoundingly at her feet. Emily Prince straightened up, and only then glanced at her. Mrs. Mason's face had whitened a little. She averted her eyes.

"She's told me," Miss Prince said to herself with inward satisfaction.

There hadn't been a word exchanged between the two of them.

She went upstairs to her room a short while after. If somebody had been murdered in the kitchen, what disposal had been made of the body? Something must have been done with it—a thing like that just doesn't disappear.

She sat on the edge of the cot, wondering: "Am I going to have nerve enough to sleep here tonight, under the same roof with a couple of murderers?" She drew the necessary courage, finally, from an unexpected quarter. The image of Detective Kendall flashed before her mind, laughing uproariously at her. "I certainly am! I'll show him whether I'm right or not!" And she proceeded to blow out the lamp and lie down.

In the morning sunlight the atmosphere of the house was less macabre. She rode to school with Johnny on the bus, and for the next six hours put all thoughts of the grisly matter she was engaged upon out of her mind, while she devoted herself to parsing, syntax, and participles.

After she had dismissed class that afternoon she went to her former quarters to pick up a few belongings. This was simply to allay suspicion on the part of the Masons. She left the greater part of her things undisturbed, to be held for her.

She was waiting for the bus, her parcels beside her, when Kendall came into sight on the opposite side of the street. He was the last person she wanted to meet under the circumstances. She pretended not to recognize him, but it didn't work. He crossed over to her, stopped, touched his hat-brim, and grinned. "You seem to be moving. Give you a hand with those?"

"I can manage," she said distantly.

He eyed the bus route speculatively, then followed it with his gaze out toward her eventual destination. "It wouldn't be out to the Mason place?" Which was a smarter piece of deduction than she had thought him capable of.

"It happens to be."

To her surprise his face sobered. "I wouldn't fool around with people of that type," he said earnestly. "It's not the safest thing, you know."

Instantly she whirled on him, to take advantage of the flaws she thought she detected in his line of reasoning. "You're being inconsistent, aren't you? If something happened out there which they want to keep hidden, I agree it's not safe. But *you* say nothing happened out there. Then why shouldn't it be safe?"

"Look," he said patiently, "you're going at this from the wrong angle. There's a logical sequence to things like this." He told off his fingers at her, as though she were one of her own pupils. "First, somebody has to be missing or unaccounted for. Second, the body itself, or evidence sufficiently strong to take the place of an actual body, has to be brought to light. The two of them are interchangeable, but one or the other of them always has to precede an assumption of murder. That's the way we work. *Your* first step is a composition written by an eight-year-old child. Even in the composition itself, which is your whole groundwork, there's no direct evidence of any kind. No assault was seen by the kid, no body of any victim was seen either before or after death. In other words, you're reading an imaginary crime between the lines of an account that's already imaginary in itself. You can't get any further away from facts than that."

She loosed a blast of sarcasm at him sufficient to have withered the entire first three rows of any of her classes. "You're wasting your breath, my textbook expert. The trouble with hard-and-fast rules is that they always let a big chunky exception slip by."

He shoved a helpless palm at her. "But there's nobody missing, man, woman, or child, within our entire jurisdiction, and that goes out well beyond the Mason place. Word would have come in to us by now if there were! How're you going to get around that?"

"Then why don't you go out after it?" she flared. "Why don't you take this main road, this interstate highway that runs through here, and zone it off, and then work your way back along it, zone by zone, and find out if anyone's missing from other jurisdictions? Believe me," she added crushingly, "the only reason I suggest *you* do it is that you have the facilities and I haven't!"

He nodded with tempered consideration. "That could be done," he admitted. "I'll send out inquiries to the main townships along the line. I'd hate to have to give my reasons for checking up, though, in case I was ever pinned down to it: 'A kid in school here wrote a composition in which he mentioned he saw his mother scrubbing the kitchen floor at two in the morning.' " He grinned ruefully. "Now why don't you just let it go at that and leave it in our hands? In case I get a bite on any of my inquiries, I could drop out there myself and look things over—"

She answered this with such vehemence that he actually retreated a step. "I'll do my own looking over, thank you! I mayn't know all the rules in the textbook, but at least I'm able to think for myself. My mind isn't in handcuffs! Here comes my bus. Good day, Mr. Kendall!"

He thrust his hat back and scratched under it. "Whew!" she heard him whistle softly to himself, as she clambered aboard with her baggage.

It was still too early in the day for the two men to be on hand when she reached the Mason place. She found Mrs. Mason alone in the kitchen. A stolen glance at the sector of flooring that had been the focus of her attention the previous night revealed a flagrant change. Something had been done to it since then, and whatever it was, the substance used must have been powerfully corrosive. The whole surface of the wood was now bleached and shredded, as though it had been eaten away by something. Its changed aspect was far more incriminating now than if it had been allowed to remain as it was. They had simply succeeded in proving that the stain was *not* innocent, by taking such pains to efface it. However, it was no longer evidence now, even if it had been to start with. It was only a place where evidence had been.

She opened the back door and looked out at the peaceful sunlit fields that surrounded the place, with a wall of woodland in the distance. In one direction, up from the house, they had corn growing. The stalks were head-high, could have concealed anything. A number of black specks—birds—were hovering above one particular spot, darting busily in and out. They'd rise above it and circle and then go down again; but they didn't stray very far from it. Only that one place seemed to hold any attention for them.

Down the other way, again far off—so far off as to be almost indistinguishable—she could make out a low quadrangular object that seemed to be composed of cobblestones or large rocks. It had a dilapidated shed over it on four uprights. A faint, wavering footpath led to it. "What's that?" she asked.

Mrs. Mason didn't answer for a moment. Then she said, somewhat unwillingly: "Used to be our well. Can't use it now, needs shoring up. Water's all sediment."

"Then where do you get water from?" Miss Prince asked.

"We've been going down the road and borrowing it from the people at the next place down, carrying it back in a bucket. It's a long ways to go, and they don't like it much neither."

Miss Prince waited a moment, to keep the question from sounding too leading. Then she asked casually: "Has your well been unfit to use for very long?"

She didn't really need the answer. New grass was sprouting up everywhere, but it had barely begun to overgrow the footpath. She thought the woman's eyes avoided her, but that might have been simply her chronic hangdog look. " 'Bout two or three weeks," she mumbled reluctantly.

Birds agitated in a cornfield. A well suddenly unfit for use for the last two or three weeks. And then, in a third direction, straight over and across, the woods, secretive and brooding. Three possibilities.

She said to herself: "She told me something I wanted to know once before. Maybe I can get her to tell me what I want to know now." Those who live in the shadow of fear have poor defenses. The teacher said briskly: "I think I'll go for a nice long stroll in the open."

She put her to a test, probably one of the most peculiar ever devised. Instead of turning and striking out at once, as a man would have in parting from someone, she began to retreat slowly, half-turned backwards toward her as she drew away, chattering as she went, as though unable to tear herself away.

She retreated first in the general direction of the cornfield, as though intending to ramble among the stalks. The woman just stood there immobile in the doorway, looking after her.

The teacher closed in again, as though inadvertently, under necessity of something she had just remembered. "Oh, by the way, could you spare me an extra chair for my room I—"

Then when she again started to part company with her, it was in a diametrically opposite direction, along the footpath that led to the well. "Any kind of a chair will do," she called back talkatively. "Just so long as it has a seat and four—"

The woman just stood there, eyeing her without a flicker.

She changed her mind, came back again the few yards she had already traveled. "The sun's still hot, even this late," she prattled. She pretended to touch the top of her head. "I don't think I care to walk in the open. I think I'll go over that way instead—those woods look nice and cool from here. I always did like to roam around in woods—"

The woman's eyes seemed to be a little larger now, and she swallowed hard. Miss Prince could distinctly see the lump go down the scrawny lines of her throat. She started to say something, then she didn't after all. It was obvious, the way her whole body had seemed to lean forward for a moment, then subside against the door-frame. Her hands, inert until now, had begun to mangle her apron.

But not a sound came from her. Yet, though the test seemed to have failed, it had succeeded.

"I know the right direction now," Miss Prince was saying to herself grimly, as she trudged along. "It's in the woods. It's somewhere in the woods."

She went slowly. Idly. Putting little detours and curleycues into her line of progress, to seem aimless, haphazard. She knew, without turning, long after the house was a tiny thing behind her, that the woman was still there in the doorway, straining her eyes after her, watching her all the way to the edge of the woods. She knew too, that that had been a give-and-take back there. The woman had told her what she wanted to know, but she had told the woman something too. If nothing else, that she wasn't quite as scatterbrained, as frivolous, as she had seemed to be about which direction to take for her stroll. Nothing definite maybe, but just a suspicion that she wasn't out here just for her health.

She'd have to watch her step with them, as much as they'd have to watch theirs with her. A good deal depended on whether the woman was an active ally of the two men, or just a passive thrall involved against her will.

She was up to the outermost trees now, and soon they had closed around her. The house and its watcher was gone from sight, and a pall of cool blue twilight had dimmed everything. She made her way slowly forward. The trees were not set thickly together but they covered a lot of ground.

She had not expected anything so miraculous as to stumble on something the moment she stepped in here. It was quite likely that she would leave none the wiser this time. But she intended returning here again and again if necessary, until—

She was getting tired now, and she was none too sure of her whereabouts. She spotted a half-submerged stump protruding from the damp, moldy turf and sat down on it, fighting down a suspicion that was trying to form in the back of her mind that she was lost. A thing like that, if it ever got to that Kendall's ears, would be all that was needed to complete his hilarity at her expense. The stump was green all over with some sort of fungus, but she was too tired to care. The ground in here remained in a continual state of moldy dampness, she noticed. The sun never had a chance to reach through the leafy ceiling of the trees and dry it out.

She had been sitting there perhaps two minutes at the most, when a faint scream of acute fright reached her from a distance. It was thin and piping, and must have been thin even at its source. She jarred to her feet. It had sounded like the voice of a child, not a grown-up. It repeated itself, and two others joined in with it, as frightened as the first, if less shrilly acute. She started to run, as fast as the trackless ground would allow, toward the direction from which she believed the commotion was coming.

She could hear waters splashing, and then without any warning she came crashing out into the margin of a sizable and completely screened-off woodland pool. It was shaped like a figure 8.

At the waist, where it narrowed, there was an irregular bridge of flat stones, although the distances between them were unmanageable except by sprinting. There was a considerable difference in height between the two sections, and the water coursed into the lower one in a placid, silken waterfall stretching the entire width of the basin. This lower oval was one of the most remarkable sights she had ever seen. It was shallow, the water was only about knee-high in it, and under the water was dazzling creamy-white sand. There was something clean and delightful looking about it.

Two small boys in swimming trunks, one of them Johnny Gaines, were arched over two of the stepping-stones, frantically tugging at a third boy who hung suspended between them, legs scissoring wildly over the water and the sleek sand below. "Keep moving them!" she heard Johnny shriek just as she got there. "Don't let 'em stay still!"

She couldn't understand the reason for their terror. The water below certainly wasn't deep enough to drown anybody—

"Help us, lady!" the other youngster screamed. "Help us get him back up over the edge here!"

She kicked off her high-heeled shoes, picked her way out to them along the stones, displaced the nearest one's grip with her own on the floundering object of rescue. He wouldn't come up for a minute, even under the added pull of her adult strength, and she couldn't make out what was holding him. There was nothing visible but a broil of sand-smoking water around his legs. She hauled backwards from him with every ounce of strength in her body, and suddenly he came free.

The three of them immediately retreated to the safety of the bank, and she followed. "Why were you so frightened?" she asked.

"Don't you know what that is?" Johnny said, still whimpering. "Quicksand! Once that gets you—"

There could be no mistaking the genuineness of their fright. Johnny's two companions had scuttled off for home without further ado, finishing their dressing as they went.

"Look, I'll show you." He picked up a fist-sized rock and threw it in. What happened sent a chill down her spine. The stone lay there for a moment, motionless and perfectly visible through the crystalline water. Then there was a slight concentric swirl of the sand immediately around it, a dimple appeared on its surface, evened out again, and suddenly the stone wasn't there any more. The sand lay as smooth and satiny as ever. The delayed timing was what was so horrible to watch.

"We'd better go," she said, taking a step backward from it.

"The upper pool's all right, it's only got gravel at the bottom," Johnny was explaining, wiping his hair with a handful of leaves.

She didn't hear him. She was examining the branch of a bush growing beside the bank that had swung back into place in her wake. It formed an acute angle such as is never found in nature. It was badly fractured halfway along its length. She reached for a second branch, a third, and fingered them. Their spines were all broken the same way.

Her face paled a little. She moved around the entire perimeter of the bush, handling its shoots. Then she examined the neighboring bushes. The fractures were all on the landward side, away from the pool. The tendrils that overhung the water itself—that anyone in difficulties in the sand could have been expected to grasp—were all undamaged, arching gracefully the way they had grown.

She came away with a puzzled look on her face. But only that, no increased pallor.

At the edge of the woods, just before they came out into the open again, the youngster beside her coaxed plaintively: "Miss Prince, don't gimme 'way about going swimming in there, will you?"

"Won't they notice your hair's damp?"

"Sure, but I can say I went swimming in the mill-pond, down by the O'Brien place. I'm allowed to go there."

"Oh, it's just that—that place we just came from they don't want you to go near?"

He nodded.

That could have been because of the quicksand. Then again it could have been for other reasons. "Have they always told you to keep away from there?" she hazarded.

It paid off. "No'm, only lately," he answered.

Only lately. She decided she was going to pay another visit to that cannibal sandbed. With a long pole, perhaps.

The evening meal began in deceptive calmness. Although the two Masons continued to watch her in sullen silence, there seemed to be less of overt suspicion and more of just casual curiosity in their underbrow glances. But a remark from Johnny suddenly brought on a crisis when she was least expecting it. The youngster didn't realize the dynamite in his question. "Did I pass, in that composition I handed in?" he asked all at once. And then, before she could stop him in time, he blurted out: "You know, the one about the dream I had, where I came down and—"

Without raising eyes from the table she could sense the tightening of the tension around her. It was as noticeable as though an electric current were streaking around the room. Ed Mason forgot to go ahead eating, he just sat looking down at his plate. Then his father stopped too, and looked at his plate. There was a soft slur of shoe-leather inching along the floor from somewhere under the table.

Mrs. Mason said in a stifled voice, "Sh-h, Johnny."

There was only one answer she could make. "I haven't got around to reading it yet." Something made her add: "It's up there on the table in my room right now."

Mason resumed eating. Then Ed followed suit.

She had given them all the rope they needed: Let them go ahead and hang themselves now. If the composition disappeared, as she was almost certain it was going to, that would be as good as an admission that—

She purposely lingered below, helping Mrs. Mason as she had the night before. When she came out of the kitchen and made ready to go up to her room, they were both sprawled out in the adjoining room. Whether one of them had made a quick trip up the stairs and down again, she had no way of knowing—until she got up there herself.

Mason's eyes followed her in a strangely steadfast way as she started up the stairs. Just what the look signified she couldn't quite make out. It made her uneasy, although it wasn't threatening in itself. It had some other quality that she couldn't figure out, a sort of shrewd complacency. Just before she reached the turn and passed from sight he called out: "Have a good night's sleep, Miss." She saw a mocking flicker of the eyes pass between him and Ed.

She didn't answer. The hand with which she was steadying the lamp she was taking up with her shook a little as she let herself into her room and closed the door. She moved a chair in front of it as a sort of barricade. Then she hurried to the table and sifted through the homework papers stacked on it.

It was still there. It hadn't been touched. It was out of the alphabetical order she always kept her papers in, but it had been left there for her to read at will.

That puzzled, almost crestfallen look that she'd had at the

pool came back to her face again. She'd been positive she would find it missing.

How long she'd been asleep she could not tell, but it must have been well after midnight when something roused her. She didn't know exactly what it was at first; then as she sat up and put her feet to the floor, she identified it as a strong vibration coming from some place below. As though two heavy bodies were threshing about in a struggle down there.

She quickly put something on and went out to listen in the hall. A chair went over with a vicious crack. A table jarred. She could hear an accompaniment of hard breathing, an occasional wordless grunt. But she was already on her way down by that time, all further thought of concealment thrown to the winds.

Mason and his son were locked in a grim, heaving struggle that floundered from one end of the kitchen to the other, dislodging everything in its path. Mrs. Mason was a helpless onlooker, holding a lighted lamp back beyond danger of upsetting, and ineffectually whimpering: "Don't! Dirk! Ed! Let each other be now!"

"Hold the door open, quick, Ma! I've got him!" Mason gasped just as Miss Prince arrived on the scene.

The woman edged over sidewise along the wall and flung the door back. Mason catapulted his adversary out into the night. Then he snatched up a chicken lying in a pool of blood over in a corner, sent that after him, streaking a line of red drops across the floor. "Thievin' drunkard!" he shouted, shaking a fist at the sprawling figure outside. "Now you come back when you sober up, and I'll let you in!" He slammed the door, shot the bolt home. "Clean up that mess, Ma," he ordered gruffly. "That's one thing I won't 'low, is no chicken-stealing drunkards in my house!" He strode past the open-mouthed teacher without seeming to see her, and stamped up the stairs.

"He's very strict about that," Mrs. Mason whispered confidentially. "Ed don't mean no harm, but he helps himself to things that don't belong to him when he gets likkered up." She sloshed water into a bucket, reached for a scrubbing brush, sank wearily to her knees, and began to scour ruddy circles of chicken blood on the floor. "I just got through doin' this floor with lye after the last time," she murmured.

Miss Prince found her voice at last. It was still a very small, shaky one. "Has—has this happened before?"

"Every so often," she admitted. "Last time he run off with the O'Brien's Ford, drove it all the way out here just like it belonged to him. Mr. Mason had to sneak it back where he took it from, at that hour of the night."

An odor of singeing felt suddenly assailed the teacher's nostrils. She looked, discovered a felt hat, evidently the unmanageable Ed's, fallen through the open scuttle-hold of the wood-burning stove onto the still-warm ashes below. She drew it up and beat it against the back of a chair.

There was a slight rustle from the doorway and Johnny was standing there in his night-shirt, sleepily rubbing one eye. "I had another of those dreams, Ma," he complained. "I dreamed the whole house was shaking and—"

"You go back to bed, hear?" his mother said sharply. "And don't go writin' no more compositions about it in school, neither!" She fanned out her skirt, trying to screen the crimson vestiges on the floor from him. "Another of them wood-varmints got into the house, and your Pa and your Uncle Ed had to kill it, that's all!"

Miss Prince turned and slunk up the stairs, with a peculiar look on her face—the look of someone who has made a complete fool of herself. She slammed the door of her room behind her with—for her—unusual asperity. She went over to the window and stood looking out. Far down the highway she could make out the dwindling figure of Ed Mason in the moonlight, steering a lurching, drunken course back toward town and singing, or rather hooting, at the top of his voice as he went.

"Appearances!" she said bitterly. "Appearances!"

She always seemed to meet Kendall just when she didn't want to. He appeared at her elbow next morning just as she alighted from the bus in town. "How're things going? Get onto anything yet?"

She made a move to brush by him without answering.

"I haven't received anything definite yet on any of those inquiries I sent out," he went on.

She turned and faced him. "You won't, either. You can forget the whole thing! All right, laugh, you're entitled to it! You were right and I was wrong."

"You mean you don't think—"

"I mean I practically saw the same thing the boy did, with my own eyes, last night and it was just a family row! I've made a fool out of myself and gone to a lot of trouble, for nothing."

"What're you going to do?"

"I'm going to pack my things and leave."

"Don't take it too hard—" he tried to console her.

She stalked off. At least, she had to admit to herself, he'd been decent enough not to say, "I told you so," and laugh right in her face. Oh, well, he was probably saving it up to enjoy it more fully back at the station house with his cronies.

Mrs. Mason was alone in the kitchen again when she returned that afternoon to get her things together. There hadn't been time before school in the morning. The woman looked at her questioningly, but the teacher didn't say anything about her imminent departure. Time enough to announce it when she came down again.

In her room she picked up the dress she'd had on the afternoon before and started to fold it over. Something caught her eye. There was a stain, a blotch, that she hadn't noticed until now. She looked at it more closely, as though unable to account for it. Then she remembered sitting down on a half-submerged stump for a moment, just before hearing the boys' cries of distress. "No more appearances!" she warned herself, and tossed the dress into the open bag.

She picked up the batch of school papers lying on the table to follow suit with them. There was that composition of Johnny's that had started all the trouble. She started to reread it. She was standing up at first. Before she had finished she was seated once more. She turned and looked over at the dress she had just put away. Then she got up and took it out again.

There was a timid knock on the door and Mrs. Mason looked in at her. "I thought maybe you'd like me to help you get your things together," she faltered.

Miss Prince eyed her coolly. "I didn't say anything about leaving. What gave you that idea? I'm staying—at least, for a little while longer."

The woman's hands started out toward her, in a palsied gesture of warning. She seemed about to say something. Then she quickly closed the door.

Her main worry was to get down the venerable stairs without causing them to creak and betray her. The house lay steeped in midnight silence. She knew that Mason and his son were inveterate snorers when asleep—she had heard them at other times, even downstairs when they dozed after meals. Tonight she could not hear them.

She didn't use the flashlight she had brought with her, for fear of attracting attention while still within the house. The real need for that would be later, out in the woods. The stairs accomplished without mishap, it was an easy matter to slip the bolt on the back door and leave without much noise. There was a full moon out, but whether it would be much help where she was going, she doubted.

She stole around to the back of the rickety tool-house and retrieved the long-poled pitchfork she had concealed there earlier in the evening. Its tines were bent, and with a little manipulation, it might serve as a sort of grappling hook if—if there was anything for it to hook onto. A button was all she needed, a rotting piece of suiting. Evidence. Until she had that, she couldn't go to Kendall, she had to keep on working alone. Not after what she had admitted to him that morning.

She struck out across the silver-dappled fields. The trees

closed around her finally, a maw of impenetrable blackness after the moonlight, and she brought her flashlight into play, following its wan direction-finder in and out among the looming, ghostly trunks.

The bed of quicksand loomed whitely even in the dark. There was something sinister about it, like a vast evil eye lying there in wait. The coating of water refracted the shine of her light to a big phosphorescent balloon when she cast the beam downward. She discovered her teeth chattering and clamped them shut. She looked around for something to balance her light, finally nested it in a bush so that the interlaced twigs supported it. She shifted a little farther along the bank and posed the pitchfork like someone about to spear fish.

She lunged out and downward with it. The soft feel of the treacherous sand as the tines dove in was transferred repugnantly along the pole to her hands. That was all she had time to notice. She didn't even see it sink in.

A leathery hand was pressed to the lower half of her face, a thick anaconda-like arm twined about her waist from behind, and the light winked out. Her wrists were caught together as they flew up from the pitchfork-pole, and held helpless.

"Got her, Ed?" a quiet voice said.

"Got her," a second voice answered.

There hadn't been any warning sound. They must have been lurking there ahead of her, to be able to spring the trap so unexpectedly.

Her pinioned hands were swung around behind her, brought together again. The hand had left her mouth. "You int'rested in what's down there?" the man behind her asked threateningly.

"I don't know what you mean. Take your hands off me!"

"You know what we mean. And we know what you mean. Don't you suppose we're onto why you're hanging around our place? Now you'll get what you were lookin' for." He addressed his father. "Take off her shoes and stockings and lie 'em on the bank. Careful, don't tear 'em now."

"What's that for?"

"She came out here alone, see, early tomorrow morning, and it looked so pretty she went wading without knowing what it was, and it got her."

She kicked frantically, trying to stop them. She was helpless in their hands. Her ankles were caught, one at a time, and stripped.

"They'll dredge for her, won't they?" Dirk Mason mentioned with sinister meaning.

"She'll be on top, won't she?" was the grisly reassurance. "Once they get her out, they'll be no call for them to go ahead dredging any further down."

She ripped out a scream of harrowing intensity. If it had been twice as shrill, it couldn't have reached past the confines of these woods. And who was there in the woods to hear her? "Think we ought to stuff something in her mouth?" the older man asked.

"No, because we gotta figure on her being found later. Don't worry, no one'll hear her."

She was fighting now the way an animal fights for its life. But she was no match for the two of them. Not even a man would have been.

They were ready for the incredible thing they were about to do. "Grab her legs and swing her, so she goes out far enough." There was a moment of sickening indecision, while she swung suspended between them, clear of the ground. Then her spinning body shot away from them.

Water sprayed over her as she struck. The fall was nothing. It was like landing on a satin quilt, the sand was so soft. She rolled over, tore her arms free, and threshed to a kneeling position. There was that awful preliminary moment in which nothing happened, as with that stone she had seen Johnny throw in yesterday. Then a sudden pull, a *drawing,* started in—weak at first, barely noticeable, giving the impression of being easy to counteract. And each move she made wound the sand tighter around her bared feet, ankles, calves.

Meanwhile, something was happening on the bank, or at least, farther back in the woods; but she was only dimly aware of it, too taken up in her own floundering struggles. It reached her vaguely, like something through a heavy mist. An intermittent winking as of fireflies here and there, each one followed by a loud crack like the breaking of a heavy bough. Then heavy forms were crashing through the thickets in several directions at once, two of them fleeing along the edge of the pool, others fanning out farther back, as if to intercept them. There was one final crack, a fall, and then a breathless voice nearby said: "Don't shoot—I give up!"

A light, stronger than the one she had brought, suddenly flashed out, caught her, steadied, lighting up the whole pool. Her screams had dwindled to weak wails now, simply because she hadn't enough breath left. She was writhing there, still upright, but her legs already gone past the knees.

"Hurry up, and help me with this girl!" a voice shouted somewhere behind the blinding light. "Don't you see what they've done to her?" The pole of the same pitchfork she had used was thrust out toward her. "Hang onto this!" She clutched it with both hands. A moment later a noosed rope had splashed into the water around her. "Pass your arms through that and tighten it around you. Grab hold now and kick out behind you!"

For minutes nothing happened; she didn't seem to move at all, though there must have been at least three of them pulling on the rope. "Are we hurting you?" Then suddenly there was a crumbling feeling of the sand around her trapped legs and she came free.

Kendall was one of them, of course, and even the brief glimpse she had of his face by torchlight made her wonder how she could have ever felt averse to running into him at any time. She certainly didn't feel that way now.

They carried her out of the woods in a "chair" made of their hands and put her into a police car waiting at the edge of the fields.

"You'd better get back there and go to work," she said. "Even before you got the rope around me, the downward pull had stopped, I noticed. I seemed to be standing on something . . . How did you get out here on time?"

"One of those inquiries I sent out finally paid off. A commercial traveler named Kenneth Johnson was reported missing, from way over in Jordanstown. He was supposed to show up at Indian River, out beyond here in the other direction, and he never got there—dropped from sight somewhere along the way, car and all. He was carrying quite a gob of money with him. He left three weeks ago, but it wasn't reported until now, because he was only expected back around this time. I only got word a half hour ago. I thought of the Masons right away, thanks to you. I started right out here with a couple of my partners to look around, never dreaming that you were still here yourself. Then a little past the next house down, the O'Brien place, we met the kid, Johnny, running along the road lickety-split, on his way to phone in to us and get help. His mother had finally got pangs of conscience and thrown off her fear of her husband and stepson long enough to try to save you from what she guessed was going to happen."

She went out there again first thing the next morning. Kendall came forward to meet her as she neared the pool. He told her they'd finally got the car out a little after daybreak, with the help of a farm-tractor run in under the trees, plenty of stout ropes, and some grappling hooks. She could see the weird-looking sand-encrusted shape standing there on the bank, scarcely recognizable for what it was.

"Kenneth Johnson, all right," Kendall said quietly, "and still inside it when we got it out. But murdered before he was ever swallowed up in the sand. I have a confession from the two Masons. He gave Ed a hitch back along the road that night. Mason got him to step in for a minute on some excuse or other, when they'd reached his place, so he'd have a chance to rifle his wallet. Johnson caught him in the act, and Mason and his father murdered him with a flatiron. Then they put him back in the car, drove him over here, and pushed it in. No need to go any closer, it's not a very pretty sight."

On the way back he asked: "But what made you change your mind so suddenly? Only yesterday morning when I met you you were ready to—"

"I sat down on a stump not far from the pool, and afterwards I discovered axle-grease on my dress. It was so damp and moldy in there that the clot that had fallen from the car hadn't dried out yet. Why should a car be driven in there where there was no road?

"But the main thing was still that composition of Johnny's. Remember where Johnny said the hat had fallen? Through the stove onto the ashes. But in the reenactment they staged for me, Ed Mason's hat also fell through the open scuttlehold in the stove onto the ashes below. Is it probable that a hat, flung off somebody's head in the course of a struggle, would land in the identical place *twice*? Hardly. Things like that just don't happen. The second hat had been deliberately placed there for me to see, to point up the similarity to what had happened before."

That night, safely back in her old quarters in town, she was going over back-schoolwork when her landlady knocked on the door. "There's a gentleman downstairs to see you. He says it's not business, but social."

Miss Prince smiled a little. "I think I know who it is. Tell him I'll be right down as soon as I've finished grading this composition."

She picked up the one Johnny Gaines had written. She marked it A-plus, the highest possible mark she could give, without bothering for once about grammar, punctuation, or spelling. Then she put on her hat, turned down the light, and went out to meet Kendall.

The Lethal Logic

NORBERT DAVIS

Norbert Davis (1909–1949) was among the best of the writers whose work appeared regularly in Black Mask, Dime Detective, *and other pulp magazines in the thirties and early forties. Davis also wrote for such slicks as* Collier's, American Magazine, *and* The Saturday Evening Post; *and published three excellent mystery novels about the team of Doan and Carstairs (one of them—*Oh, Murderer Mine!*—has a collegiate setting). His fiction is fast-paced, occasionally lyrical in a hard-boiled way, and often quite funny. "The Lethal Logic," which first appeared in* Detective Fiction Weekly *in 1939, is somewhat more restrained and straightforward than his usual pulp efforts; but it is nonetheless tightly plotted and effective. It also provides a vivid capsule portrait of life at a small California college in the late 1930s.*

LANGDON CAUGHT Carlson on the path that ran from the parking lot in back of the Library across in front of the Education building. He stopped Carlson with a quickly nervous flutter of his hands and a nervous, ducking bow.

"Professor Carlson. Just—one moment . . ."

Carlson said: "Yes?" impatiently.

Langdon was a nondescript clerical-looking little man with fine white hair that the wind ruffled. His smile was vague and ready-to-please. He wore a black suit—not a dark one, but black. It was too big for him, and the pockets of the coat were bulging now with pamphlets that had rough edged pages.

"I've been looking for Dean Michels, Professor. Do you know where . . ."

"He had a luncheon engagement," Carlson said.

"Oh, yes. Of course. If you should see him, will you tell him the copies of his new text have come in? I thought he'd be anxious to know . . ."

"I'll tell him."

"Thank you, Professor."

Carlson walked on across to the Law steps. He walked fast, not because he was in a hurry, but because of the surging impatience that was with him always and that he never could control. He was tall and thin and stooped, and his face had a dark, fine-edged eagerness that had bitten deep lines around his mouth and eyes. He scowled a little as a habit.

There were law students gathered on the steps, waiting for their one o'clocks. Carlson stopped to take a last puff of his cigarette, dropped it, ground it under his heel. He started up the steps and saw Vaster standing at the top. He drew in his breath in a noiseless, swearing whisper and looked down at his climbing feet, hoping for the best, but he knew it would be quite useless, and it was.

"Professor Carlson," said Vaster. "Please—if you could give

me a second. You know in the lecture this morning . . . that about intent. About subjective and objective intent. Now you said if there was a man walking in the woods at night following another man and intending to kill him, and he saw a stump and thought it was the other man and shot the stump and the other man wasn't anywhere near the stump . . . You said whether or not that was an attempt to commit murder depended on—on . . . I didn't get that part, Professor Carlson."

Carlson sighed deeply. He went through it carefully and slowly, emphasizing and repeating each point. Vaster had round dull blue eyes, and they blinked mechanically at the end of each of Carlson's sentences, and every time they blinked, Vaster nodded. Vaster had a thick neck and wide sloping shoulders and a thickly lumpy body. He had a flattened, shapeless nose and big lips.

Carlson, watching him as he talked, thought he could see the small, dull brain behind the slope of Vaster's skull, see it actually groping around in the mist, blindly and stubbornly trying to find and follow Carlson's logical path.

Carlson wondered why there had to be minds like that—and why, if they were really necessary, their owners picked out a place like the Law School to foregather. They never seemed to choose any of the several other departments where stupidity was at a premium. The students on the steps had stopped talking among themselves and gathered in a tight, concentrated knot around Carlson and Vaster. Their heads, like Vaster's, all nodded in unison every time Carlson made a point, and he felt like a yogi demonstrating mass hypnotism.

He broke it off abruptly, telling Vaster to see him in his office if he wanted further explanations. As the group split to let him through, he saw that there had been one student who hadn't gathered with them, and he knew at once that it would be Dieckmann. Dieckmann had a mind as sharp as a razor. He was sitting on the top of the steps, absently smoking a pipe. He was short and stocky and hard-looking with a square, tanned face and very bright blue eyes. He nodded at Carlson and winked.

Carlson almost winked back, but caught himself. He walked on under the cool, shadowed archway of gray granite, thinking that it was a shame Dieckmann couldn't parcel out the unneeded bits of his brilliance here and there. He decided, on second thought, that it was probably a good thing he couldn't. As an older and more famous professor had said: Some lawyers are smart and some are elected judges.

Going past the library door, Carlson went in through the faculty entrance, along the narrow, dark corridor that always smelled damply of the last rain and into the rear end of the library. He turned to the left and went past the stacks of state reports.

Janice Lee, Michels' secretary, came around the corridor at the end of the last stack. She was a small girl with smooth, blue-black hair. Her face was very white and smooth, and her soft, small lips framed a whispered answer to Carlson's greeting. She went on by him with a quick thud-thud of rubber heels.

Carlson turned the corner she had come around and saw Reeve sitting in a reading chair that had been moved in close against the last stack. He had a big, loose-leaf volume of Advance Reports open on his lap. He wore a green eye shade. His head was bent and one hand trailed down over the arm of the chair and touched the floor.

Reeve was a student, and he often slept in the library, apparently under the theory that he might absorb some of the knowledge packed around him through his subconscious mind. Carlson had never seen him in this part before, but he thought nothing of it until he had gone three steps on beyond him.

He stopped, then. It was cool and quiet and shadowed here. Carlson stood still, staring straight ahead of him and frowning, for as long as it would take to count ten slowly. Then he turned around and looked back at Reeve. Reeve hadn't moved, and he didn't.

Carlson went back the three steps and touched him on the shoulder. Reeve was slumped down in the chair. He bent forward slowly from the waist until his face bumped against the book he had on his lap.

Carlson moistened his lips and swallowed. He looked quickly both ways along the corridor, and then he took hold of Reeve's shoulder and carefully straightened him back into his first position. He stood there, motionless and uncertain for a long minute. Then he turned and walked quickly around the jog in the corridor and into Dean Michels' reception office.

It was empty. Janice Lee's desk was at the side, and there was a letter half-written in her typewriter. The door of the inner office was ajar.

Carlson tapped on it and said: "Michels."

Michels' pleasing, smooth voice answered: "Yes?"

Carlson went inside the office and stood in front of Michels' big desk. He was frowning and pulling at his lower lip.

"What is it?" Michels asked.

"His name," Carlson said absently. "What the devil was that name?" He looked at Michels. "Reeve is sitting outside in a chair. He's dead."

"What—" Michels began, and then his big, loose face seemed to stretch grotesquely. "Dead! You said—"

Carlson nodded. "Dead. Murdered. Stabbed in the back. What was that fool's name? Ah! Harms!" He picked up the telephone on Michels' desk, and when the University operator answered, said: "Get me the city police department."

Michels sat as though he were afraid to move, staring.

While he waited, Carlson said: "Harms is a lieutenant—a detective—on the police force. I met him once at a banquet. He's very stupid."

A voice in the receiver said: "Police department."

"I'd like to speak to Lieutenant Harms," Carlson said.

Lieutenant Harms had a rumbling, aimless voice. "Harms speaking."

"This is Carlson—at the University."

Harms remembered him. "Oh. Hello, Professor."

"We've got some business for you out here. A student by the name of Reeve has been murdered in the Law library."

"I'll be right out!"

"Don't hurry," Carlson advised. "He'll stay here." He hung up the receiver.

Michels spoke in a mumbling whisper. "Terrible . . . terrible . . ."

Carlson shrugged. "I don't know why. He was rather a nasty little rat. I never did like him."

Carlson lived in a bachelor apartment on the west side of the campus. He had just come in from dinner and arranged things to his satisfaction. He had the radio tuned carefully between two stations so that the resulting sound was a pleasant blur. He was looking at a Chinese newspaper. He took several of them. He couldn't read Chinese, but he always went through each one carefully from the front page to the last, comforting himself with the thought that if there was any bad news current in the world, he wouldn't find it out.

The doorbell rang, and he folded up his paper and went to answer it. It was Harms.

"Hello, Professor," said Harms. "Say, I didn't get much of a chance to talk to you this afternoon, so I thought I'd drop around."

Harms went with his voice. He was big and fat and flat-footed. He had yellow teeth and a cigar in the corner of his mouth, and he smiled all the time with a sort of jovial ferocity, as though his feet hurt.

There was another man with him, and the other man walked in the door so close behind Harms that the two of them gave the effect of a couple of prisoners doing the lock-step.

"Who's this?" Carlson asked, pointing at the other man.

"Him?" said Harms, apparently surprised that anyone would notice his companion. "Oh, that's Dogan. He's my partner."

"I got a headache," said Dogan.

He was a small man, hunch-shouldered and white-faced. He looked like the movie version of a gangster's bodyguard except for the fact that he was cross-eyed and wore thick glasses.

"You got any aspirin?" he asked.

"In the bathroom," Carlson said. "I'll get—"

"I'll find it," said Dogan. He went into the bathroom and came out with a bottle of aspirin tablets. He rolled four out on his palm. "You got any whiskey?"

Carlson took a bottle out of the cabinet and gave him a glass. Dogan poured the glass half-full, popped the aspirin tablets in his mouth, and swallowed them and the whiskey with one gulp.

"I got a hell of a headache," he said dully. He went and sat down in a straight chair in the corner.

"Now, about this fellow, Reeve," said Harms. "The doc says he was stuck with an ice pick."

"Yes?" said Carlson politely.

"Uh-huh. And not very long before you found him. Say about a half-hour or less."

"Is that so?"

"Yeah. You know who did it?"

"No."

"Could you find out?"

"Certainly."

"Oh," said Harms. "Certainly, huh? How?"

"By assembling the requisite factual data and reasoning from that to an inevitable logical conclusion."

"Oh," said Harms gloomily. "I don't think I could do that."

"You're right."

Harms squinted at him. "Why do you think I couldn't?"

"I don't think, I know. You haven't the mental ability to reason in a logical sequence. Like all policemen, all you're capable of a pseudo logic. You go from conclusion to premise. In other words, you pick out a suspect and try to prove he committed the crime."

"Is that what I've been doing all these years?" Harms wondered. "It works pretty good most of the time."

Carlson shrugged. "Doubtless. So why don't you go and use it on this case? Or, are you? Do you think I committed the crime?"

"I dunno. Did you?"

"As a matter of fact—no. But if I had, you'd never be able to convict me for it."

"Why not?"

"Because I know about ten times as much about criminal law as any judge you've got on this circuit and at least fifty times as much as your district attorney."

"Is that a fact?" Harms asked.

"Yes. If you don't believe me, try me out."

"I guess I kind of believe you," said Harms, more gloomily. "It don't seem like there's any respect for law in this country. I tried to take some fingerprints and ask some questions this afternoon, and all I got was a lot of horse laughs from them law students. They told me to go look at the Constitution. I couldn't get nowhere."

Carlson nodded sympathetically. "Most of them are just learning that the law is a pretty silly business, and they haven't gotten over the shock yet."

"Yeah," said Harms indefinitely. "Well, look. On this case, I got to pinch somebody right away quick."

"Why?"

"Because of that damned college newspaper. It's run by students, and no student likes cops. If I don't pinch somebody, them guys are gonna start writin' funny articles about me, and the articles will be picked up and re-printed in the city papers, and then I'll be out on my ear. How's for you findin' out who did it with your logical premises and such?"

"No."

"Why not?"

"Because I don't care who did it."

"Maybe he'll murder somebody else."

"Let him."

"It's your fault," said Harms accusingly. "All your fault."

"My fault."

"Sure. You got me into this. You called me."

Carlson grinned. "So sorry."

"All right, then," said Harms grimly. "I'm gonna pinch that girl."

"What girl?"

"The dean's secretary. Janice Lee."

Carlson stared incredulously. "Why?"

Harms moved his big shoulders. "She's a girl, and she's right pretty, and she was near it when it happened."

Carlson exploded, "My God! You don't mean to tell me that any modern police officer follows that antiquated bit of flubdub. *Cherchez la femme!* Faugh! It makes me sick!"

"Well," said Harms. "She coulda been carryin' on with the dean, and this Reeve coulda spotted it . . ."

Carlson said clearly and slowly: "She had nothing whatever to do with it. Neither did Dean Michels. If you arrest either one of them on any such insane theory, it will ruin her life and his career."

"I got to arrest somebody—quick."

Carlson drew a deep breath. "All right. Look at it realistically. Reeve was stabbed in the Law library with an ice pick. That gives you three factual bases on which to reason. Stabbed, ice pick, Law library. There are no ice picks around the Law library ordinarily, and the ordinary person doesn't carry one habitually, and, if he did, wouldn't go around stabbing people indiscriminately with it. Following me?"

"Yeah," Harms admitted.

"From this, we can permissably reason that some person brought an ice pick into the Law library with a purpose in mind. Without trying to reduce any of the logical by-roads to absurdities, I think we can safely reason that the purpose was to stab Reeve."

"Sure," Harms agreed. "That's what he did."

"Don't start that false logic again. I've just given you one clue to his identity."

"What?"

"The murder was premeditated. The murderer had a grudge against Reeve—that is, a reason, real or fancied, for killing him."

Carlson thought a moment, then:

"I'll give you another clue. He was familiar with the Law library—very familiar. The premise for that is because he could go in and find Reeve and get out without being seen, or he was so usual and expected a sight that no one would bother about it if they did see him. Now go find him."

"Huh!" Harms said sourly. "I'll stick to the girl. Come on, Dogan."

Carlson let them get as far as the door, and then he sighed wearily and said: "All right. You win. I'll find out who did it for you."

Harms reassumed his ferocious grin. "Good! When?"

Carlson sighed again. "It won't take me more than a couple of hours. It's a stupidly simple problem."

At night the campus always assumed a different aspect in Carlson's eyes. The buildings loomed tall and shadowy with lights pin-pricking out of the scattered windows. There was something majestically mysterious about it, as there was supposed to be something majestically mysterious about knowledge. But then—again like knowledge—when you saw it in the clear light of day the mystery went away, and it was only a group of things conceived by man and built by man—impermanent and weather-beaten and faintly shoddy as are all things conceived and built by man.

There was no one on the Law steps, and Carlson's heels clicked briskly going up them. There was a light above, in the center of the archway, and it threw spidery shadows that wiggled on the worn brick of the walk. Watching the shadows, Carlson unaccountably shivered.

He stopped short, amazed at himself. He had felt like shivering. He still did. Little cold prickles seemed to raise the hair at the back of his neck. Carlson snorted. Now that was nothing but damned foolishness. Only the ignorant are afraid. But nevertheless, he turned and looked behind him.

Of course there was nothing in sight. But he had a vague, sneaking premonition—he hated premonitions—that if he had turned just a little sooner, there would have been something.

He snorted again and turned and marched steadily along the corridor to the Law library, and the little chill of fear followed him right along, touching the back of his neck with its gentle, icy fingers. Carlson opened the door of the main entrance and shut it behind him and leaned against it.

He was perspiring, and he swore at himself for doing it with a practiced, fluent bitterness. Straightening up, he walked on into the library. It was only a little after nine o'clock, and there were several students studying.

Carlson stood in the doorway for a second and then walked down the length of the room to one of the tables at the back. Dieckmann was sitting alone at the table. He was hunched forward, and the book he was reading was spread out flat under the green-shaded bulb of the reading light.

Carlson sat down opposite him. "Dieckmann."

Dieckmann raised his eyes. They were bright and shrewd and quickly alert, and he smiled at Carlson, showing the glisten of his white teeth.

Carlson said: "I'm investigating Reeve's murder."

"Yes?" said Dieckmann.

There was no one sitting near them, and Carlson talked in a low voice, almost a whisper: "Reeve was a certain recognizable type of person. When he was small, he was the kind of little boy who write dirty words on sidewalks and fences. He never outgrew it. His hobby here was looking up cases that dealt with salacious crimes."

"Yes," said Dieckmann.

"There is a case like that in 151 Northern. Quite a famous one. In it the judge—the case was on appeal of course—reprinted quite a lot of testimony of the lower court, either because he was the same type as Reeve or because he was too damned lazy to write enough of his own for an adequate opinion. I read the case when the volume came out about five years ago. I didn't pay any particular attention to it—except as an added example of judicial stupidity—but I never forget anything I read. The complaining witness in that case was a young girl, and her name was Dieckmann."

Dieckmann nodded. "My sister."

"Oh," said Carlson slowly. "I'm sorry. I saw Reeve reading the case the other day. Did he know the girl was your sister?"

"No. He noticed the name, though. He was trying to find out."

Carlson said, "Did you kill him, Dieckmann?"

Dieckmann's smile broadened. "Why do you ask?"

"Because you're worth a hundred of Reeve, so I would figure you had about ninety-nine more murders to go before I should start interfering."

Dieckmann shook his head. "It won't be necessary to wait. I didn't kill Reeve. He was annoying me to some extent, but if I had really wanted to get rid of him, I'd have thought up something less messy and more effective than murder."

Carlson nodded. "Thanks." He got up and started away from the table.

"Professor," said Dieckmann.

Carlson stopped. "Yes?"

"I'd be a little careful if I were you."

Carlson stared sharply. "Why do you say that?"

"Just casual advice," Dieckmann said indifferently. He began to read his book again.

Carlson went back to the front of the library. There was an attendant—a student—on duty at the desk, and Carlson asked him: "Where did Reeve keep his books?"

The attendant's eyes were curious and a little shocked. "At—at the end of that first shelf—on top. Right next to *Corpus Juris.*"

Carlson found the spot. Reeve, like many other students, did a lot of his studying in the library because it was handy for reference work, and he made a habit—as did the others—of keeping his books in the library to save carrying them back and forth from his room.

The shelf contained two casebooks and several regulation stiff-backed notebooks. Carlson thumbed through three of the notebooks and found nothing but inadequate notes and briefed cases in Reeve's spattering, spidery scrawl. There was something in the pocket at the back of the fourth. Carlson pulled it out far enough to see that it was a particularly vicious French postcard.

He made a wry face and shoved it back out of sight. He replaced the notebook on the shelf, noticing that the binding at the back was stretched. He took the notebook out once more, opened and shut it thoughtfully several times while he examined the binding, then put it on the shelf again.

He walked back and addressed the attendant: "Did you clean up around here tonight?"

"Yes, sir."

"You know where Reeve usually—ah—studied, don't you? Not in the main room here, but between the third and fourth stacks at that little table?"

"Yes, sir."

"Find any books on that table?"

The attendant nodded doubtfully. "Well . . . yes, sir."

"Reports?"

"Yes, sir."

"Same kind Reeve usually read?"

The attendant flushed. "Yes, sir."

Carlson nodded and said: "Thanks," absently. He walked diagonally across the library and into the passageway that led through the middle of the stacks of books. He turned off between the third and fourth stacks, walked clear to the end and looked down at the little table there in a thoughtfully absent way.

The third and fourth stacks extended clear to the wall. There was no way to get around behind them, which was why Reeve had picked the particular spot to pursue his research work. It gave him complete privacy.

Carlson went back to the middle aisle, turned down between the fourth and fifth stacks. The fifth stack didn't go clear to the wall. There was a passageway. Carlson walked through it, past the sixth, seventh, and eighth stacks, and came out at a spot about ten feet from where Reeve's body had been when he had first seen it.

He went to the spot and stopped, looking down at the chair in which Reeve had been sitting. Finally he took the copy of Advance Reports that Reeve had been holding on his lap from the shelf and looked at the case index in it. He shook his head and replaced the book, looking around.

Twenty feet further along the corridor was the door to Lapham's office. Lapham taught the history of Law, and he was at present in Mississippi doing some research work. His office was not in use. Carlson tried the door. It should have been locked, but it wasn't.

Carlson turned on the light in the office. There was a fine layer of dust over all the furniture, and nothing had been disturbed that he could see.

"That's it," he said to himself in a satisfied mutter.

He went back and lifted the chair Reeve had been sitting in. It was a heavy one. It weighed about fifteen pounds, he judged. In his mind, he conjured up an image of Reeve. Reeve had been soft and fat and pudgy. He had weighed about a hundred and seventy, if not more. Carlson did some mental addition and nodded again, pleased with himself.

Carlson went out the faculty entrance, and it was as though that little instinctive prickle of fear had been waiting patiently in the darkness outside the door for him. It stayed with him as he hurried diagonally across the campus, and he had to use the whole force of his will to keep himself from running. The familiar shrubs assumed weird and menacing shapes, and in the pockets of shadow under the archways strangely shaped things waited and watched him go past.

He came out of the quadrangle, crossed the road to the student's coöperative store. It was a long, low building. The store was closed now, but Carlson peered through the blinds that covered the front door and found a light somewhere at the back. He pounded repeatedly and noisily on the door.

Another light came on, brighter and closer, and a voice said cautiously through the door: "Who is it?"

"Carlson."

"Oh. Professor Carlson." The lock clicked, and one of the doors squeaked open.

Carlson slid through it and closed it behind him and looked down at Langdon. Langdon's fine white hair was rumpled slightly, and the fingers of his right hand were stained with ink. He was smiling his shy, gentle smile, a little bewildered now, but still anxious to please.

"Good evening, Professor. I was working on our books. It's the end of the month, you know, and we close our accounts . . ."

Carlson nodded impatiently, "Langdon, I'm investigating Reeve's murder."

"Oh," said Langdon.

Carlson watched him. "Langdon, you've been selling and renting erotica to the students, haven't you?"

Langdon's smile went away. "I—I—"

"Don't bother to lie. I know you have. Reeve was one of your customers. You went over to the library this noon either to get some books he was through with, or give him some new ones, or both. Isn't that true?"

Langdon moistened his lips, silently.

Carlson said: "And you found him dead, didn't you?"

Langdon's head moved in a stiff nod. "I didn't—didn't know he had been—killed. Thought he—a stroke—"

"He kept his pamphlets in one of his notebooks he wasn't using. You knew that. You went to the shelf where he kept his notebooks and took the pamphlets out, didn't you?"

"I—I thought they shouldn't—be found . . ."

Carlson nodded. "I saw them in your pocket when you met me. You gave me that story about wanting to see Dean Michels because you wanted an alibi in case anyone had seen you around the library."

Langdon opened his mouth and hunted for words. "Professor Carlson—not—not what you think. . . . Just rare unexpurgated editions—classics . . ."

"You lie. But that doesn't matter. Where was Reeve when you saw him?

Langdon stared. "Where he always was."

"You mean at that little table between the third and fourth stacks?"

"Yes. I saw his face—his eyes . . . I knew—something . . ."

"How close did you come to him?"

"About—about three steps."

Carlson smiled grimly. "You missed being murdered by just those three steps. The murderer was hiding behind Reeve and the chair, watching you. If you had come close enough to saw him?"

Langdon's breath made a whistling sound in his throat.

Carlson pointed his finger. "Get out of here, Langdon. I'll give you until tomorrow morning. Be gone by then. Don't ever come back. Do you understand?"

"Yes, sir," said Langdon.

Carlson went outside. He drew a deep breath, and the air felt clear and fresh and pure in his throat. He moved his shoulders in an annoyed shrug.

He crossed the street and headed back toward the quadrangle. He was walking with his head bent a little, staring at the side-walk in front of him. He went through an archway and ten steps on into the darkness of the campus, and then there were two shadows on the ground in front of him. His own and a heavier, thicker one.

Carlson whirled on his heel. Vaster was standing within arm's reach of him. His dull, round eyes were opened very wide now, and his big lips looked moistly loose.

"Vaster," Carlson said, and his voice scratched in his throat.

"Hello, Professor Carlson."

Carlson swallowed and swallowed again. "You killed Reeve, Vaster."

Vaster had his right hand behind his back. "Yes. You knew it all the time, didn't you?"

Carlson had an aching pulse in his throat. "I knew it—all the time?"

"Yes. Reeve told you."

Carlson couldn't think of any words but those he had just heard, and he repeated them blankly: "Reeve—told me?"

"Yes."

Carlson shook his head, trying to clear it. "I don't understand. You mean that Reeve told me you killed him?"

"No. He told you I cheated."

"Cheated?" Carlson said incredulously.

"Yes. On that last Crime examination. I had all the cases and points written out on tissue paper. He was sitting near me, and he saw me looking at them."

Carlson's mind wavered dizzily. "But you didn't pass the last Crime examination!"

Vaster's head nodded. "Sure. Because he told you I cheated. So you flunked me."

Carlson stared unbelievingly. The whole thing was a fantastic nightmare. Reeve hadn't said anything about Vaster cheating, and Carlson hadn't flunked Vaster because he cheated. He had flunked him because Vaster's examination paper had been childishly inadequate. If Vaster had cheated, he certainly hadn't done a very good job.

Carlson said: "You *killed* Reeve for that?"

"He laughed at me," said Vaster. "Every time he saw me, he'd laugh and nod his head."

"You fool!" said Carlson breathlessly.

He backed up one step, and Vaster came after him that step, silently. Vaster brought his right hand from behind his back, and he was holding an ice pick. It made a thin, needle-like glimmer in the darkness.

"Vaster!" said Carlson, and the word rattled in the dryness of his throat.

He took another step back, and Vaster came another step after him.

Harms' rumbling voice said: "Hey, there." He was a vaguely big shadow in the darkness ten feet away.

In one motion, Vaster whirled and threw the ice pick at him. It went in a whirling, glittering arc. Harms dropped down on one knee and let it go over his head.

Vaster knocked Carlson aside with a stiff-armed blow in the face and ran. He ran twenty feet and then Dogan's scrawny shape bobbed up from somewhere and ran beside him step for step. Dogan's thin, small legs suddenly tangled with Vaster's heavy ones, and the two of them went down in a long, sliding sprawl on the brick walk. Vaster lay there motionless, and Dogan got up and sat down on top of him.

"You hurt him?" Harms asked.

"Not very much," Dogan said wearily. "My head aches again. It aches terrible. I wish I could go home."

Carlson's cheek hurt where Vaster had hit him. He put his hand up to it, while the darkness wavered around him.

"You did it, all right," said Harms, a sneaking admiration in his tone. "Damned if you didn't. How'd you know it was him?"

Carlson sighed. "When I found Reeve, he was sitting in a place in the library he had never sat before. There were three possibilities. First, the fact that he was sitting there when he was murdered was pure coincidence. Second, that he was murdered because he was sitting there. Third, that he was sitting there because he was murdered. The third was the most likely, I thought, and it proved to be the correct one.

"When he was murdered, Reeve was sitting where he usually sat, at a little table between the third and fourth stacks. The murderer picked him up, chair and all, and carried him around in back of the stacks, intending to put him in Lapham's empty office until he had more time to dispose of the body. He didn't quite get there. Someone or something interrupted him. So he sat Reeve down where he was, put a book in his lap, with the hope that everyone would think he had just dozed off while studying and not investigate until the murderer had time to come back again and get him."

"Yeah," said Harms. "So how does that lead to Vaster?"

"As shown from what he did, the murderer had two characteristics. He was stupid. If he hadn't been, instead of stabbing Reeve and carrying him to Lapham's office, he would have gotten Reeve to go inside the office under his own power and then stabbed him. It would have been much easier and much less risky. The murderer was also enormously strong. He picked up Reeve and the chair he was sitting in and carried them about fifty feet. The two of them must have weighed close to two hundred pounds, and they were very awkward to carry."

"Well, I'll be damned!" said Harms. "That logic stuff does work, don't it? I figured it was all baloney. That's why I looked you up just now, to see what kind of monkey business you were up to. But you know there's one thing you forgot."

"What?" said Carlson.

"Well, now, these logics and premises and factuals and reasonables is all right in books. You use 'em, and you get the answer, and it's fine. But you use 'em in murder, and the answer is liable to get pretty mad about it and come after you with an ice pick."

Carlson shivered a little. "I—I found that out," he agreed, without his usual aggressive self-confidence. "The perfect combination, I am convinced, would be an unprejudiced coöperation of theory and practice."

To Break the Wall

EVAN HUNTER

"To Break the Wall," which originally appeared in 1953 in discovery no. 2, *a literary magazine in paperback form, was Evan Hunter's first major short story. "[It] was my first attempt to voice some of my feelings about the vocational high school," he wrote in a preface to his collection,* The Jungle Kids *(1956). "Many months later, I expanded this story into* The Blackboard Jungle, *using it—with minor revisions—as the climactic chapter." The story, like the novel, is every bit as powerful today as it was thirty years ago. Hunter, who once worked as a teacher in a vocational high school similar to the one in these pages, is one of America's most popular novelists, whether writing under his own name or his 87th Precinct nom de plume, Ed McBain.*

THE DOOR to Room 206 was locked when Richard Dadier reached it for his fifth period English class. He tried the knob several times, peered in through the glass panel, and motioned for Serubi to open the door. Serubi, sitting in the seat closest the door, shrugged his shoulders innocently and grinned. Richard felt again the mixed revulsion and fear he felt before every class.

Easy, he told himself. Easy does it.

He reached into his pocket and slipped the large key into the keyhole. Swinging the door open, he slapped it fast against the prongs that jutted out from the wall, and then walked briskly to his desk.

A falsetto voice somewhere in the back of the room rapidly squeaked, "Daddy-oh!" Richard busied himself with his Delaney book, not looking up at the class. He still remembered that first day, when he had told them his name.

"Mr. Dadier," he had said, and he'd pronounced it carefully. One of the boys had yelled, "Daddy-oh," and the class had roared approval. The name had stuck since then.

Quickly, he glanced around the room, flipping cards over as he took the attendance. Half were absent as usual. He was secretly glad. They were easier to handle in small groups.

He turned over the last card, and waited for them to quiet down. They never would, he knew, never.

Reaching down, he pulled a heavy book from his briefcase and rested it on the palm of his hand. Without warning, he slammed it onto the desk.

"Shut up!" he bellowed.

The class groaned into silence, startled by the outburst.

Now, he thought. Now, I'll press it home. Surprise plus advantage plus seize your advantage. Just like waging war. All day long I wage war. Some fun.

"Assignment for tomorrow," Richard said flatly.

A moan escaped from the group. Gregory Miller, a large boy of seventeen, dark-haired, with a lazy sneer and hard, bright eyes said, "You work too hard, Mr. Daddy-oh."

The name twisted deep inside Richard, and he felt the tiny needles of apprehension start at the base of his spine.

"Quiet, Mueller," Richard said, feeling pleasure at mispronouncing the boy's name. "Assignment for tomorrow. In *New Horizons . . .*"

"In what?" Ganigan asked.

I should have known better, Richard reminded himself. We've only been using the book two months now. I can't expect them to remember the title. No.

"In *New Horizons,*" he repeated impatiently, "the blue book, the one we've been using all term." He paused, gaining control of himself. "In the blue book," he continued softly, "read the first ten pages of *Army Ants in the Jungle.*"

"Here in class?" Hennesy asked.

"No. At home."

"Christ," Hennesy mumbled.

"It's on page two seventy-five," Richard said.

"What page?" Antoro called out.

"Two seventy-five."

"What page?" Levy asked.

"Two seventy-five," Richard said. "My God, what's the matter with you?" He turned rapidly and wrote the figures on the board in a large hand, repeating the numerals slowly. "Two, seven-ty, five." He heard a chuckle spread maliciously behind him, and he whirled quickly. Every boy in the class wore a deadpan.

"There will be a short test on the homework tomorrow," he announced grimly.

"Another one?" Miller asked lazily.

"Yes, Mailler," Richard said, "another one." He glared at the boy heatedly, but Miller only grinned in return.

"And now," Richard said, "the test I promised you yesterday."

A hush fell over the class.

Quick, Richard thought. Press the advantage. Strike again and again. Don't wait for them. Keep one step ahead always. Move fast and they won't know what's going on. Keep them too busy to get into mischief.

Richard began chalking the test on the board. He turned his head and barked over his shoulder, "All books away. Finley, hand out the paper."

This is the way to do it, he realized. I've figured it out. The way to control these monsters is to give them a test every day of the week. Write their fingers off.

"Begin immediately," Richard said in a businesslike voice. "Don't forget your heading."

"What's that, that heading?" Busco asked.

"Name, official class, subject class, subject teacher," Richard said wearily.

Seventy-two, he thought. I've said it seventy-two times since I started teaching here two months ago. Seventy-two times.

"Who's our subject teacher?" Busco asked. His face expressed complete bewilderment.

"Mr. Daddy-oh," Vota said quite plainly. Vota was big and rawboned, a muscular, rangy, seventeen-year-old. Stringy blond hair hung over his pimply forehead. There was something mannishly sinister about his eyes, something boyishly innocent about his smile. And he was Miller's friend. Richard never forgot that for a moment.

"Mr. Dadier is the subject teacher," Richard said to Busco. "And incidentally, Vito," he glared at Vota, "anyone misspelling my name in the heading will lose ten points."

"What!" Vota complained, outraged.

"You heard me, Vota," Richard snapped.

"Well, how do you spell Daddy-oh?" Vota asked, the innocent smile curling his lips again.

"You figure it out, Vota. I don't need the ten points."

Richard bitterly pressed the chalk into the board. It snapped in two, and he picked up another piece from the runner. With the chalk squeaking wildly, he wrote out the rest of the test.

"No talking," he ordered. He sat down behind the desk and eyed the class suspiciously.

A puzzled frown crossed Miller's face. "I don't understand the first question, teach'," he called out.

Richard leaned back in his chair and looked at the board. "It's very simple, Miltzer," he said. "There are ten words on the board. Some are spelled correctly, and some are wrong. If they're wrong, you correct them. If they're right, spell them just the way they're written."

"Mmmmm," Miller said thoughtfully, his eyes glowing. "How do you spell the second word?"

Richard leaned back again, looked at the second word and began, "D-I-S . . ." He caught himself and faced Miller squarely. "Just the way you want to. You're taking this test, not me."

Miller grinned widely. "Oh. I didn't know that, teach'."

"You'll know when you see your mark, Miller."

Richard cursed himself for having pronounced the boy's name correctly. He made himself comfortable at the desk and looked out over the class.

Di Pasco will cheat, he thought. He will cheat and I won't catch him. He's uncanny that way. God, how I wish I could catch him. How does he? On his cuff? Where? He probably has it stuffed in his ear. Should I search him? No, what's the use? He'd cheat his own mother. An inborn crook. A louse.

Louse, Richard mused. Even I call them that now. All louses. I must tell Helen that I've succumbed. Or should I wait until after the baby is born? Perhaps it would be best not to disillusion her yet. Perhaps I should let her think I'm still trying to reach them, still trying. What was it Solly Klein had said?

"This is the garbage can of the educational system."

He had stood in the teachers' lunchroom, near the bulletin board, pointing his stubby forefinger at Richard.

"And it's our job to sit on the lid and make sure none of this garbage spills over into the street."

Richard had smiled then. He was new, and he still thought he could teach them something, still felt he could mold the clay.

Lou Savoldi, an electrical wiring teacher, had smiled too and said, "Solly's a great philosopher."

"Yeah, yeah, philosopher." Solly smiled. "All I know is I've been teaching machine shop here for twelve years now, and only once did I find anything valuable in the garbage." He had nodded his head emphatically then. "Nobody knowingly throws anything valuable in with the garbage."

Then why should I bother? Richard wondered now. Why should I teach? Why should I get ulcers?

"Keep your eyes on your own paper, Busco," he cautioned.

Everyone is a cheat, a potential thief. Solly was right. We have to keep them off the streets. They should really hire a policeman. It would be funny, he thought, if it weren't so damned serious. How long can you handle garbage without beginning to stink yourself? Already, I stink.

"All right, Busco, bring your paper up. I'm subtracting five points from it," Richard suddenly said.

"Why? What the hell did I do?"

"Bring me your paper."

Busco reluctantly slouched to the front of the room and tossed his paper onto the desk. He stood with his thumbs looped in the tops of his dungarees as Richard marked a large –5 on the paper in bright red.

"What's that for?" Busco asked.

"For having loose eyes."

Busco snatched the paper from the desk and examined it with disgust. He wrinkled his face into a grimace and slowly started back to his seat.

As he passed Miller, Miller looked to the front of the room. His eyes met Richard's, and he sneered, "Chicken!"

"What!" Richard asked.

Miller looked surprised. "You talking to me, teach'?"

"Yes, Miller. What did you just say?"

"I didn't say nothing, teach'." Miller smiled.

"Bring me your paper, Miller."

"What for?"

"Bring it up!"

"What for, I said."

"I heard what you said, Miller. And *I* said bring me your paper. Now. Right this minute."

"I don't see why," Miller persisted, the smile beginning to vanish from his face.

"Because I say so, that's why."

Miller's answer came slowly, pointedly. "And supposing I don't feel like?" A frown was twisting his forehead.

The other boys in the room were suddenly interested. Heads that were bent over papers snapped upright. Richard felt every eye in the class focus on him.

They were rooting for Miller, of course. They wanted Miller to win. They wanted Miller to defy him. He couldn't let that happen.

He walked crisply up the aisle and stood beside Miller. The boy looked up provokingly.

"Get up," Richard said, trying to control the modulation of his voice.

My voice is shaking, he told himself. I can feel it shaking. He knows it, too. He's mocking me with those little, hard eyes of his. I must control my voice. This is really funny. My voice is shaking.

"Get up, Miller."

"I don't see, Mr. Daddy-oh, just why I should," Miller answered. He pronounced the name with great care.

"Get up, Miller. Get up and say my name correctly."

"Don't you know your own name, Mr. Daddy-oh?"

Richard's hand snapped out and grasped Miller by the collar of his shirt. He pulled him to his feet, almost tearing the collar. Miller stood a scant two inches shorter than Richard, squirming to release himself.

Richard's hand crushed tighter on the collar. He heard the slight rasp of material ripping. He peered into the hateful eyes and spoke quietly. "Pronounce my name correctly, Miller."

The class had grown terribly quiet. There was no sound in the room now. Richard heard only the grate of his own shallow breathing.

I should let him loose, he thought. What can come of this? How far can I go? *Let him loose!*

"You want me to pronounce your name, sir?" Miller asked.

"You heard me."

"Go to hell, Mr. Daddy . . ."

Richard's fist lashed out, catching the boy squarely across the mouth. He felt his knuckles scrape against hard teeth, saw the blood leap across the upper lip in a thin crimson slash, saw the eyes widen with surprise and then narrow immediately with deep, dark hatred.

And then the knife snapped into view, sudden and terrifying. Long and shining, it caught the pale sunlight that slanted through the long schoolroom windows. Richard backed away involuntarily, eying the sharp blade with respect.

Now what, he thought? Now the garbage can turns into a coffin. Now the garbage overflows. Now I lie dead and bleeding on a schoolroom floor while a moron slashes me to ribbons. Now.

"What do you intend doing with that, Miller?"

My voice is exceptionally calm, he mused. I think I'm frightened, but my voice is calm. Exceptionally.

"Just come a little closer and you'll see," Miller snarled, the blood in his mouth staining his teeth.

"Give me that knife, Miller."

I'm kidding, a voice persisted in Richard's mind. I must be kidding. This is all a big, hilarious joke. I'll die laughing in the morning. I'll die . . .

"Come and get it, Daddy-oh!"

Richard took a step closer to Miller and watched his arm swing back and forth in a threatening arc. Miller's eyes were hard and unforgiving.

And suddenly, Richard caught a flash of color out of the corner of his eye. Someone was behind him! He whirled instinctively, his fist smashing into a boy's stomach. As the boy fell to the floor Richard realized it was Miller's friend Vota. Vota cramped into a tight little ball that writhed and moaned on the floor, and Richard knew that any danger he might have presented was past. He turned quickly to Miller, a satisfied smile clinging to his lips.

"Give me that knife, Miller, and give it to me now."

He stared into the boy's eyes. Miller looked big and dangerous. Perspiration stood out on his forehead. His breath was coming in hurried gasps.

"Give it to me now, Miller, or I'm going to take it from you and beat you black and blue."

He was advancing slowly on the boy.

"Give it to me, Miller. Hand it over," his voice rolled on hypnotically, charged with an undercurrent of threat.

The class seemed to catch its breath together. No one moved to help Vota who lay in a heap on the floor, his arms hugging his waist. He moaned occasionally, squirming violently. But no one moved to help him.

I've got to keep one eye on Vota, Richard figured. He may be playing possum. I have to be careful.

"Hand it over, Miller. Hand it over."

Miller stopped retreating, realizing that he was the one who held the weapon. He stuck the spring-action knife out in front of him, probing the air with it. His back curved into a large C as he crouched over, head low, the knife always moving in front of him as he advanced. Richard held his ground and waited. Miller advanced cautiously, his eyes fastened on Richard's throat, the knife hand moving constantly, murderously, in a swinging arc. He grinned terribly, a red-stained, white smile on his face.

The chair, Richard suddenly remembered. There's a chair. I'll take the chair and swing. Under the chin. No. Across the chest. Fast though. It'll have to be fast, one movement. Wait. Not yet, wait. Come on Miller. Come on. *Come on!*

Miller paused and searched Richard's face. He grinned again and began speaking softly as he advanced, almost in a whisper, almost as if he were thinking aloud.

"See the knife, Mr. Daddy-oh? See the pretty knife? I'm gonna slash you up real good, Mr. Daddy-oh. I'm gonna slash you, and then I'm gonna slash you some more. I'm gonna cut you up real fine. I'm gonna cut you up so nobody'll know you any more, Mr. Daddy-oh."

All the while moving closer, closer, swinging the knife.

"Ever get cut, Mr. Daddy-oh? Ever get sliced with a sharp knife? This one is sharp, Mr. Daddy-oh, and you're gonna get cut with it. I'm gonna cut you now, and you're never gonna bother us no more. No more."

Richard backed away down the aisle.

Thoughts tumbled into his mind with blinding rapidity. I'll make him think I'm retreating. I'll give him confidence. The empty seat in the third row. Next to Ganigan. I'll lead him there. I hope it's empty. Empty when I checked the roll. I can't look, I'll tip my hand. Keep a poker face. Come on, Miller, follow me. Follow me so I can crack your ugly skull in two. Come on, you louse. One of us goes, Miller. And it's not going to be me.

"Nossir, Mr. Daddy-oh, we ain't gonna bother with you no more. No more tests, and no more of your noise. Just your face, Mr. Daddy-oh. Just gonna fix your face so nobody'll wanna look at you no more."

One more row, Richard calculated. Back up one more row. Reach. Swing. One. More. Row.

The class followed the two figures with fascination. Miller stalked Richard down the long aisle, stepping forward on the balls of his feet, pace by pace, waiting for Richard to back into the blackboard. Vota rolled over on the floor and groaned again.

And Richard counted the steps. A few more. A . . . few . . . more . . .

"Shouldn't have hit me, Mr. Daddy-oh," Miller mocked. "Ain't nice for teachers to hit students like that, Mr. Daddy-oh. Nossir, it ain't nice at . . ."

The chair crashed into Miller's chest, knocking the breath out of him. It came quickly and forcefully, with the impact of a striking snake. Richard had turned, as if to run, and then the chair was gripped in his hands tightly. It sliced the air in a clean, powerful arc, and Miller covered his face instinctively. The chair crashed into his chest, knocking him backward. He screamed in surprise and pain as Richard leaped over the chair to land heavily on his chest. Richard pinned Miller's shoulders to the floor with his knees and slapped him ruthlessly across the face.

"Here, Miller, here, here, here," he squeezed through clenched teeth. Miller twisted his head from side to side, trying to escape the cascade of blows that fell in rapid onslaught on his cheeks.

The knife, Richard suddenly remembered! Where's the knife? What did he do with the . . .

Sunlight caught the cold glint of metal, and Richard glanced up instantly. Vota stood over him, the knife clenched tightly in his fist. He grinned boyishly, his rotten teeth flashing across his blotchy, thin face. He spat vehemently at Richard, and then there was a blur of color: blue steel, and the yellow of Vota's hair, and the blood on Miller's lip, and the brown wooden floor, and the gray tweed of Richard's suit. A shout came up from the class, and a hiss seemed to escape Miller's lips.

Richard kicked at Vota, feeling the heavy leather of his shoes crack against the boy's shins. Miller was up and fumbling for Richard's arms. A sudden slice of pain started at Richard's shoulder, careened down the length of his arm. Cloth gave way with a rasping scratch, and blood flashed bright against the gray tweed.

From the floor, Richard saw the knife flash back again, poised in Vota's hand ready to strike. He saw Miller's fists, doubled and hard, saw the animal look on Vota's face, and again the knife threatening and sharp, drenched now with blood, dripping on the brown, cold, wooden floor.

The noise grew louder and Richard grasped in his mind for a picture of the Roman arena, tried to rise, felt pain sear through his right arm as he put pressure on it.

He's cut me, he thought with panic. Vota has cut me.

And the screaming reached a wild crescendo, hands moved

with terrible swiftness, eyes gleamed with molten fury, bodies squirmed, and hate smothered everything in a sweaty, confused, embarrassed embrace.

This is it, Richard thought, this is it.

"Leave him alone, you crazy jerk," Serubi was shouting.

Leave who alone, Richard wondered. Who? I wasn't . . .

"Lousy sneak," Levy shouted. "Lousy, dirty sneak."

Please, Richard thought. Please, quickly. Please.

Levy seized Miller firmly and pushed him backward against a desk. Richard watched him dazedly, his right arm burning with pain. He saw Busco through a maze of moving, struggling bodies, Busco who was caught cheating, saw Busco smash a book against Vota's knife hand. The knife clattered to the floor with a curious sound. Vota's hand reached out and Di Pasco stepped on it with the heel of his foot. The knife disappeared in a shuffle of hands, but Vota no longer had it. Richard stared at the bare, brown spot on the floor where the knife had been.

Whose chance is it now, he wondered? Whose turn to slice the teacher?

Miller tried to struggle off the desk where Levy had him pinned. Brown, a Negro boy, brought his fist down heavily on Miller's nose. He wrenched the larger boy's head back with one hand, and again brought his fist down fiercely.

A slow recognition trickled into Richard's confused thoughts. Through dazzled eyes, he watched.

Vota scrambled to his feet and lunged at him. A solid wall seemed to rise before him as Serubi and Gomez flung themselves against the onrushing form and threw it back. They tumbled onto Vota, holding his arms, lashing out with excited fists.

They're fighting for me! No, Richard reasoned, no. But yes, *they're fighting for me!* Against Miller. Against Vota. For me. For me, oh my God, for me.

His eyes blinked nervously as he struggled to his feet.

"Let's . . . let's take them down to the principal," he said, his voice low.

Antoro moved closer to him, his eyes widening as they took in the livid slash that ran the length of Richard's arm.

"Man, that's some cut," he said.

Richard touched his arm lightly with his left hand. It was soggy and wet, the shirt and jacket stained a dull brownish-red.

"My brother got cut like that once," Ganigan offered.

The boys were still holding Miller and Vota, but they no longer seemed terribly interested in the troublemakers.

For an instant, Richard felt a twinge of panic. For that brief, terrible instant he imagined that the boys hadn't really come to his aid at all, that they had simply seen an opportunity for a good fight and had seized upon it. He shoved the thought aside, began fumbling for words.

"I . . . I think I'd better take them down to Mr. Stemplar," he said. He stared at the boys, trying to read their faces, searching for something in their eyes that would tell him he had at last reached them, had at last broken through the wall. He could tell nothing. Their faces were blank, their eyes emotionless.

He wondered if he should thank them. If only he knew. If he could only hit upon the right thing to say, the thing to cement it all.

"I'll . . . I'll take them down. Suppose . . . you . . . you all go to lunch now."

"That sure is a mean cut," Julian said.

"Yeah," Ganigan agreed.

"You can all go to lunch," Richard said. "I want to take Miller and Vota . . ."

The boys didn't move. They stood there with serious faces, solemnly watching Richard.

". . . to . . . the . . . principal," Richard finished.

"A hell of a mean cut," Gomez said.

Busco chose his words carefully, and he spoke slowly. "Maybe we better just forget about the principal, huh? Maybe we oughta just go to lunch?"

Richard saw the smile appear on Miller's face, and a new

weary sadness lumped into his throat.

He did not pretend to understand. He knew only that they had fought for him and that now, through some unfathomable code of their own, had turned on him again. But he knew what had to be done, and he could only hope that eventually they would understand why he had to do it.

"All right," he said firmly, "let's break it up. I'm taking these two downstairs."

He shoved Miller and Vota ahead of him, fully expecting to meet the resistance of another wall, a wall of unyielding bodies. Instead, the boys parted to let him through, and Richard walked past them with his head high. A few minutes ago, he would have taken this as a sign that the wall had broken. That was a few minutes ago.

Now, he was not at all surprised to hear a high falsetto pipe up behind him, "Oh, Daddy-oh! You're a *hee*-ro!"

When Greek Meets Greek

GRAHAM GREENE

Having graduated from Oxford, Graham Greene is no stranger to that prestigious university, and he has used his own college, Balliol, as part of this story's background. Greene's work ranges from crime fiction such as The Confidential Agent *(1939) and* Our Man in Havana *(1958)—termed "entertainments" by their author—to such psychological novels as* The Power and the Glory *(1940) and* The Comedians *(1966); and he is considered to be one of our most important contemporary authors. His ability to create memorable backgrounds, as well as his unfailing touch with eccentric characters, is evident in "When Greek Meets Greek"—a story that proves the old adage that "there's one born every minute."*

1

WHEN THE CHEMIST had shut his shop for the night he went through a door at the back of the hall that served both him and the flats above, and then up two flights and a half of stairs carrying an offering of a little box of pills. The box was stamped with his name and address: Priskett, 14, New End Street, Oxford. He was a middle-aged man with a thin moustache and scared evasive eyes: he wore his long white coat even when he was off duty as if it had the power of protecting him like a King's uniform from his enemies. So long as he wore it he was free from summary trial and execution.

On the top landing was a window: outside Oxford spread through the spring evening: the peevish noise of innumerable bicycles, the gasworks, the prison, and the grey spires, beyond the bakers and confectioners, like paper frills. A door was marked with a visiting-card Mr Nicholas Fennick, B.A.: the chemist rang three short times.

The man who opened the door was sixty years old at least, with snow-white hair and a pink babyish skin. He wore a mulberry velvet dinner jacket, and his glasses swung on the end of a wide black ribbon. He said with a kind of boisterousness, 'Ah, Priskett, step in, Priskett. I had just sported my oak for a moment . . .'

'I brought you some more of my pills.'

'Invaluable, Priskett. If only you had taken a degree—the Society of Apothecaries would have been enough—I would have appointed you resident medical officer of St Ambrose's.'

'How's the college doing?'

'Give me your company for a moment in the common-room, and you shall know all.'

Mr Fennick led the way down a little dark passage cluttered with mackintoshes: Mr Priskett, feeling his way uneasily from mackintosh to mackintosh, kicked in front of him a pair of girl's shoes. 'One day,' Mr Fennick said, 'we must build . . .' and he made a broad confident gesture with his glasses that seemed to press back the walls of the common-room: a small round table covered with a landlady's cloth, three or four shiny chairs and a glass-fronted bookcase containing a copy of *Every Man His Own Lawyer*. 'My niece Elisabeth,' Mr Fennick said, 'my medical adviser.' A very young girl with a lean pretty face nodded perfunctorily from behind a typewriter. 'I am going to train Elisabeth,' Mr Fennick said, 'to act as bursar. The strain of being both bursar and president of the college is upsetting my stomach. The pills . . . thank you.'

Mr Priskett said humbly, 'And what do you think of the college, Miss Fennick?''

'My name's Cross,' the girl said. 'I think it's a good idea. I'm surprised my uncle thought of it.'

'In a way it was—partly—my idea.'

'I'm more surprised still,' the girl said firmly.

Mr Priskett, folding his hands in front of his white coat as though he were pleading before a tribunal, went on: 'You see, I said to your uncle that with all these colleges being taken over by the military and the tutors having nothing to do they ought to start teaching by correspondence.'

'A glass of audit ale, Priskett?' Mr Fennick suggested. He took a bottle of brown ale out of a cupboard and poured out two gaseous glasses.

'Of course,' Mr Priskett pleaded, 'I hadn't thought of all this—the common-room, I mean, and St Ambrose's.'

'My niece,' Mr Fennick said, 'knows very little of the set-up.' He began to move restlessly around the room touching things with his hand. He was rather like an aged bird of prey inspecting the grim components of its nest.

The girl said briskly, 'As I see it, Uncle is running a swindle called St Ambrose's College, Oxford.'

'Not a swindle, my dear. The advertisement was very carefully worded.' He knew it by heart: every phase had been carefully checked with his copy of *Every Man His Own Lawyer* open on the table. He repeated it now in a voice full and husky with bottled brown ale. 'War conditions prevent you going to Oxford. St Ambrose's—Tom Brown's old college—has made an important break with tradition. For the period of the war only it will be possible to receive tuition by post wherever you may be, whether defending the Empire on the cold rocks of Iceland or on the burning sands of Libya, in the main street of an American town or a cottage in Devonshire . . .'

'You've overdone it,' the girl said. 'You always do. That hasn't got a cultured ring. It won't catch anybody but suckers.'

'There are plenty of suckers,' Mr Fennick said.

'Go on.'

'Well, I'll skip that bit. "Degree-diplomas will be granted at the end of three terms instead of the usual three years." ' He explained, 'That gives a quick turnover. One can't wait for money these days. "Gain a real Oxford education at Tom Brown's old college. For full particulars of tuition fees, battels, etc., write to the Bursar." '

'And do you mean to say the University can't stop that?'

'Anybody,' Mr Fennick said with a kind of pride, 'can start a college anywhere. I've never said it was part of the University.'

'But battels—battels mean board and lodgings.'

'In this case,' Mr Fennick said, 'it's quite a nominal fee—to keep your name in perpetuity on the books of the old firm—I mean the college.'

'And the tuition . . .'

'Priskett here is the science tutor. I take history and classics. I thought that you, my dear, might tackle—economics?"

'I don't know anything about them.'

'The examinations, of course, have to be rather simple—within the capacity of the tutors. (There is an excellent public library here.) And another thing—the fees are returnable if the diploma is not granted.'

'You mean . . .'

'Nobody will ever fail,' Mr Priskett brought breathlessly out with scared excitement.

'And you are really getting results?'

'I waited, my dear, until I could see the distinct possibility of at least six hundred a year for the three of us before I wired you. And today—beyond all my expectations—I have received a letter from Lord Driver. He is entering his son at St Ambrose's.'

'But how can he come here?'

'In his absence, my dear, on his country's service. The Drivers have always been a military family. I looked them up in Debrett.'

'What do you think of it?' Mr Priskett asked with anxiety and triumph.

'I think it's rich. Have you arranged a boat-race?'

'There, Priskett,' Mr Fennick said proudly, raising his glass of audit ale, 'I told you she was a girl of the old stock.'

2

Directly he heard his landlady's feet upon the stairs the elderly man with the grey shaven head began to lay his wet tea-leaves round the base of the aspidistra. When she opened the door he was dabbing the tea-leaves in tenderly with his fingers. 'A lovely plant, my dear.'

But she wasn't going to be softened at once: he could tell that: she waved a letter at him. 'Listen,' she said, 'what's this Lord Driver business?'

'My name, my dear: a good Christian name like Lord George Sanger had.'

'Then why don't they put Mr Lord Driver on the letter?'

'Ignorance, just ignorance.'

'I don't want any hanky-panky from my house. It's always been honest.'

'Perhaps they didn't know if I was an esquire or just a plain mister, so they left it blank.'

'It's sent from St Ambrose's College, Oxford: people like that ought to know.'

'It comes, my dear, of having such a good address. W.I. And all the gentry live in Mewses.' He made a halfhearted snatch at the letter, but the landlady held it out of reach.

'What are the likes of you writing to Oxford College about?'

'My dear,' he said with strained dignity, 'I may have been a little unfortunate: it may even be that I have spent a few years in chokey, but I have the rights of a free man.'

'And a son in quod.'

'Not in quod, my dear. Borstal is quite another institution. It is—a kind of college.'

'Like St Ambrose's.'

'Perhaps not quite of the same rank.'

He was too much for her: he was usually in the end too much for her. Before his first stay at the Scrubs he had held a number of positions as manservant and even butler: the way he raised his eyebrows he had learned from Lord Charles Manville: he wore his clothes like an eccentric peer, and you might say that he had even learned the best way to pilfer from old Lord Bellen who had a penchant for silver spoons.

'And now, my dear, if you'd just let me have my letter?' He put his hand tentatively forward: he was as daunted by her as she was by him: they sparred endlessly and lost to each other; interminably the battle was never won—they were always afraid. This time it was his victory. She slammed the door. Suddenly, ferociously, when the door had closed, he made a little vulgar noise at the aspidistra. Then he put on his glasses and began to read.

His son had been accepted for St Ambrose's, Oxford. The great fact stared up at him above the sprawling decorative signature of the President. Never had he been more thankful for the coincidence of his name. 'It will be my great pleasure,' the President wrote, 'to pay personal attention to your son's career at St Ambrose's. In these days it is an honour to welcome a member of a great military family like yours.' Driver felt an odd mixture of amusement and of genuine pride. He'd put one over on them, but his breast swelled within his waistcoat at the idea that now he had a son at Oxford.

But there were two snags—minor snags when he considered how far he'd got already. It was apparently an old Oxford custom that fees should be paid in advance, and then there were the examinations. His son couldn't do them himself: Borstal would not allow it, and he wouldn't be out for another six months. Besides the whole beauty of the idea was that he should receive the gift of an Oxford degree as a kind of welcome home. Like a chess player who is always several moves ahead he was already seeing his way around these difficulties.

The fees he felt sure in his case were only a matter of bluff: a peer could always get credit, and if there was any trouble after the degree had been awarded, he could just tell them to sue and be damned. No Oxford college would like to admit that it had been imposed on by an old lag. But the examinations? A funny little knowing smile twitched the corners of his mouth: a memory of the Scrubs five years ago and the man they called Daddy, the Reverend Simon Milan. He was a short time prisoner—they were all short time prisoners at the Scrubs: no sentence of over three years was ever served there. He remembered the tall lean aristocratic parson with his iron-grey hair and his narrow face like a lawyer's which had gone somehow soft inside with too much love. A prison, when you came to think of it, contained as much knowledge as a University: there were doctors, financiers, clergy. He knew where he could find Mr Milan: he was employed in a boarding-house near Euston Square, and for a few drinks he would do most things—he would certainly make out some fine examination papers. 'I can just hear him now,' Driver reminded himself ecstatically, 'talking Latin to the warders.'

3

It was autumn in Oxford: people coughed in the long queues for sweets and cakes, and the mists from the river seeped into the cinemas past the commissionaires on the look-out for people without gas-masks. A few undergraduates picked their way through the evacuated swarm; they always looked in a hurry: so much had to be got through in so little time before the army claimed them. There were lots of pickings for racketeers, Elisabeth Cross thought, but not much of a chance for a girl to find a husband: the oldest Oxford racket had been elbowed out by the black markets in Woodbines, toffees, tomatoes.

There had been a few days last spring when she had treated St Ambrose's as a joke, but when she saw the money actually coming in, the whole thing seemed less amusing. Then for some weeks she was acutely unhappy—until she realized that of all the war-time rackets this was the most harmless. They were not reducing supplies like the Ministry of Food, or destroying confidence like the Ministry of Information: her uncle paid income-tax, and they even to some extent educated people. The suckers, when they took their diploma-degrees, would know several things they hadn't known before.

But that didn't help a girl to find a husband.

She came moodily out of the matinée, carrying a bunch of papers she should have been correcting. There was only one 'student' who showed any intelligence at all, and that was Lord Driver's son. The papers were forwarded from 'somewhere in England' via London by his father; she had nearly found herself caught out several times on points of history, and her uncle she knew was straining his rusty Latin to the limit.

When she got home she knew that there was something in the air: Mr Priskett was sitting in his white coat on the edge of a chair and her uncle was finishing a stale bottle of beer. When something went wrong he never opened a new bottle: he believed in happy drinking. They watched her in silence. Mr Priskett's silence was gloomy, her uncle's preoccupied. Something had to be got round—it couldn't be the university authorities: they had stopped bothering him long ago—a lawyer's letter, an irascible interview, and their attempt to maintain 'a monopoly of local education'—as Mr Fennick put it—had ceased.

'Good evening,' Elisabeth said. Mr Priskett looked at Mr Fennick and Mr Fenneck frowned.

'Has Mr Priskett run out of pills?'

Mr Priskett winced.

'I've been thinking,' Elisabeth said, 'that as we are now in the third term of the academic year, I should like a rise in salary.'

Mr Priskett drew in his breath sharply, keeping his eyes on Mr Fennick.

'I should like another three pounds a week.'

Mr Fennick rose from his table; he glared ferociously into the top of his dark ale, his frown beetled. The chemist scraped his chair a little backward. And then Mr Fennick spoke.

'We are such stuff as dreams are made on,' he said and hiccupped slightly.

'Kidneys,' Elisabeth said.

'Rounded by a sleep. And these our cloud-capped towers . . .'

'You are misquoting.'

'Vanished into air, into thin air.'

'You've been correcting the English papers.'

'Unless you allow me to think, to think rapidly and deeply, there won't be any more examination papers,' Mr Fennick said.

'Trouble?'

'I've always been a Republican at heart. I don't see why we want a hereditary peerage.'

'*À la lanterne,*' Elisabeth said.

'This man Lord Driver: why should a mere accident of birth . . . ?'

'He refuses to pay?'

'It isn't that. A man like that expects credit: it's right that he should have credit. But he's written to say that he's coming down tomorrow to see his boy's college. The old fat-headed sentimental fool,' Mr Fennick said.

'I knew you'd be in trouble sooner or later.'

'That's the sort of damn fool comfortless thing a girl would say.'

'It just needs brain.'

Mr Fennick picked up a brass ash-tray—and then put it down again carefully.

'It's quite simple as soon as you begin to think.'

'Think?'

Mr Priskett scraped a chair-leg.

'I'll meet him at the station with a taxi, and take him to—say Balliol. Lead him straight through into the inner quad, and there you'll be, just looking as if you'd come out of the Master's lodging.'

'He'll know it's Balliol.'

'He won't. Anybody who knew Oxford couldn't be stupid enough to send his son to St Ambrose's.'

'Of course it's true. These military families are a bit crass.'

'You'll be in an enormous hurry. Convocation or something. Whip him round the Hall, the Chapel, the Library, and hand him back to me outside the Master's. I'll take him out to lunch and see him into his train. It's simple.'

Mr Fennick said broodingly, 'Sometimes I think you're a terrible girl, terrible. Is there nothing you wouldn't think up?'

'I believe,' Elisabeth said, 'that if you're going to play your own game in a world like this, you've got to play it properly. Of course,' she said, 'if you are going to play a different game, you go to a nunnery or to the wall and like it. But I've only got one game to play.'

4

It really went off very smoothly. Driver found Elisabeth at the barrier: she didn't find him because she was expecting something different. Something about him worried her; it wasn't his clothes or the monocle he never seemed to use—it was something subtler than that. It was almost as though he were afraid of her, he was so ready to fall in with her plans. 'I don't want to be any trouble, my dear, any trouble at all. I know how busy the President must be.' When she explained that they would be lunching together in town, he even seemed relieved. 'It's just the bricks of the dear old place,' he said. 'You mustn't mind my being a sentimentalist, my dear.'

'Were you at Oxford?'

'No, no. The Drivers, I'm afraid, have neglected the things of the mind.'

'Well, I suppose a soldier needs brains?'

He took a sharp look at her, and then answered in quite a different sort of voice, 'We believed so in the Lancers.' Then he strolled beside her to the taxi, twirling his monocle, and all the way up from the station he was silent, taking little quiet sideways peeks at her, appraising, approving.

'So this is St Ambrose's,' he said in a hearty voice just before the porter's lodge and she pushed him quickly by, through the first quad, towards the Master's house, where on the doorstep with a B.A. gown over his arm stood Mr Fennick permanently posed like a piece of garden statuary. 'My uncle, the President,' Elisabeth said.

'A charming girl, your niece,' Driver said as soon as they were alone together. He had really only meant to make conversation, but as soon as he had spoken the old two crooked minds began to move in harmony.

'She's very home-loving,' Mr Fennick said. 'Our famous elms,' he went on, waving his hands skywards. 'St Ambrose's rooks.'

'Crooks?' Driver exclaimed.

'Rooks. In the elms. One of our great modern poets wrote about them. "St Ambrose elms, oh St Ambrose elms," and about "St Ambrose rooks calling in wind and rain".'

'Pretty. Very pretty.'

'Nicely turned, I think.'

'I meant your niece.'

'Ah, yes. This way to the Hall. Up these steps. So often trodden, you know, by Tom Brown.'

'Who was Tom Brown?'

'The great Tom Brown—one of Rugby's famous sons.' He

added thoughtfully, 'She'll make a fine wife—and mother.'

'Young men are beginning to realize that the flighty ones are not what they want for a lifetime.'

They stopped by mutual consent on the top step: they nosed towards each other like two old blind sharks who each believes that what stirs the water close to him is tasty meat.

'Whoever wins her,' Mr Fennick said, 'can feel proud. She'll make a fine hostess . . .'

'I and my son,' Driver said, 'have talked seriously about marriage. He takes rather an old-fashioned view. He'll make a good husband . . .'

They walked into the hall, and Mr Fennick led the way round the portraits. 'Our founder,' he said, pointing at a full-bottomed wig. He chose it deliberately: he felt it smacked a little of himself. Before Swinburne's portrait he hesitated: then pride in St Ambrose's conquered caution. 'The great poet Swinburne,' he said, 'we sent him down.'

'Expelled him?'

'Yes. Bad morals.'

'I'm glad you are strict about those.'

'Ah, your son is in safe hands at St Amb's.'

'It makes me very happy,' Driver said. He began to scrutinize the portrait of a 19th-century divine. 'Fine brushwork,' he said. 'Now religion—I believe in religion. Basis of the family.' He said with a burst of confidence, 'You know our young people ought to meet.'

Mr Fennick gleamed happily. 'I agree.'

'If he passes . . .'

'Oh, he'll certainly pass,' Mr Fennick said.

'He'll be on leave in a week or two. Why shouldn't he take his degree in person?'

'Well, there'd be difficulties.'

'Isn't it the custom?'

'Not for postal graduates. The Vice-Chancellor likes to make a small distinction . . . but Lord Driver, in the case of so distin-guished an alumnus, I suggest that I should be deputed to present the degree to your son in London.'

'I'd like him to see his college.'

'And so he shall in happier days. So much of the college is shut now. I would like him to visit it for the first time when its glory is restored. Allow me and my niece to call on you.'

'We are living very quietly.'

'Not serious financial trouble, I hope?'

'Oh, no, no.'

'I'm so glad. And now let us rejoin the dear girl.'

5

It always seemed to be more convenient to meet at railway stations. The coincidence didn't strike Mr Fennick who had fortified himself for the journey with a good deal of audit ale, but it struck Elisabeth. The college lately had not been fulfilling expectations, and that was partly due to the laziness of Mr Fennick: from his conversation lately it almost seemed as though he had begun to regard the college as only a step to something else—what she couldn't quite make out. He was always talking about Lord Driver and his son Frederick and the responsibilities of the peerage. His Republican tendencies had quite lapsed. 'That dear boy,' was the way he referred to Frederick, and he marked him 100% for Classics. 'It's not often Latin and Greek go with military genius,' he said. 'A remarkable boy.'

'He's not so hot on economics,' Elisabeth said.

'We mustn't demand too much book-learning from a soldier.'

At Paddington Lord Driver waved anxiously to them through the crowd; he wore a very new suit—one shudders to think how many coupons had been gambled away for the occasion. A little behind him was a very young man with a sullen mouth and a scar on his cheek. Mr Fennick bustled forward; he wore a black raincoat over his shoulder like a cape and carrying his hat in his hand he disclosed his white hair venerably among the porters.

'My son—Frederick,' Lord Driver said. The boy sullenly took off his hat and put it on again quickly: they wore their hair in the army very short.

'St Ambrose's welcomes her new graduate,' Mr Fennick said.

Frederick grunted.

The presentation of the degree was made in a private room at Mount Royal. Lord Driver explained that his house had been bombed—a time bomb, he added, a rather necessary explanation since there had been no raids recently. Mr Fennick was satisfied if Lord Driver was. He had brought up a B.A. gown, a mortar-board and a Bible in his suitcase, and he made quite an imposing little ceremony between the book-table, the sofa and the radiator, reading out a Latin oration and tapping Frederick lightly on the head with the Bible. The degree-diploma had been expensively printed in two colours by an Anglo-Catholic firm. Elisabeth was the only uneasy person there. Could the world, she wondered, really contain two such suckers? What was this painful feeling growing up in her that perhaps it contained four?

After a little light lunch with bottled brown beer—'almost as good, if I may say so, as our audit ale,' Mr Fennick beamed—the President and Lord Driver made elaborate moves to drive the two young people together. 'We've got to talk a little business,' Mr Fennick said, and Lord Driver hinted, 'You've not been to the movies for a year, Frederick.' They were driven out together into bombed shabby Oxford Street while the old men rang cheerfully down for whisky.

'What's the idea?' Elisabeth said.

He was good-looking; she liked his scar and his sullenness; there was almost too much intelligence and purpose in his eyes. Once he took off his hat and scratched his head: Elisabeth again noticed his short hair. He certainly didn't look a military type. And his suit, like his father's, looked new and ready-made. Hadn't he had any clothes to wear when he came on leave?

'I suppose,' she said, 'they are planning a wedding.'

His eyes lit gleefully up. 'I wouldn't mind,' he said.

'You'd have to get leave from your C.O., wouldn't you?'

'C.O.?' he asked in astonishment, flinching a little like a boy who has been caught out, who hasn't been prepared beforehand with that question. She watched him carefully, remembering all the things that had seemed to her odd since the beginning.

'So you haven't been to the movies for a year,' she said.

'I've been on service.'

'Not even an Ensa show?'

'Oh, I don't count those.'

'It must be awfully like being in prison.'

He grinned weakly, walking faster all the time, so that she might easily have been pursuing him through the Hyde Park gates.

'Come clean,' she said. 'Your father's not Lord Driver.'

'Oh yes, he is.'

'Any more than my uncle's President of a College.'

'What?' He began to laugh—it was an agreeable laugh, a laugh you couldn't trust but a laugh which made you laugh back and agree that in a crazy world like this all sorts of things didn't matter a hang. 'I'm just out of Borstal,' he said. 'What's yours?'

'Oh, I haven't been in prison yet.'

He said, 'You'll never believe me, but all that ceremony—it looked phoney to me. Of course Dad swallowed it.'

'And my uncle swallowed you . . . I couldn't quite.'

'Well, the wedding's off. In a way I'm sorry.'

'I'm still free.'

'Well,' he said, 'we might discuss it,' and there in the pale Autumn sunlight of the Park they did discuss it—from all sorts of angles. There were bigger frauds all round them: officials of the Ministries passed carrying little portfolios; controllers of this and that purred by in motor-cars, and men with the big blank faces of advertisement hoardings strode purposefully in khaki with scarlet tabs down Park Lane from the Dorchester. Their fraud was a small one by the world's standard, and a harmless one: the boy from Borstal and the girl from nowhere at all—from the draper's counter and the semi-detached villa. 'He's got a few hundred stowed away, I'm sure of that,' said Fred. 'He'd make a settlement if he thought he could get the President's niece.'

'I wouldn't be surprised if Uncle had five hundred. He'd put it all down for Lord Driver's son.'

'We'd take over this college business. With a bit of capital we could really make it go. It's just chicken-feed now.'

They fell in love for no reason at all, in the park, on a bench to save twopences, planning their fraud on the old frauds they knew they could outdo. Then they went back and Elisabeth declared herself before she'd got properly inside the door. 'Frederick and I want to get married.' She almost felt sorry for the old fools as their faces lit up, suddenly, simultaneously, because everything had been so easy, and then darkened with caution as they squinted at each other. 'This is very surprising,' Lord Driver said, and the President said, 'My goodness, young people work fast.'

All night the two old men planned their settlements, and the two young ones sat happily back in a corner, watching them fence, with the secret knowledge that the world is always open to the young.

Charles

SHIRLEY JACKSON

Can there be terrors even in kindergarten? Shirley Jackson's excellent story "Charles" poses this question—and leaves it to the reader to find the answer. Ms. Jackson (1919–1965) was one of the masters of horror and suspense fiction, who produced such acclaimed novels as The Haunting of Hill House *(1960) and* We Have Always Lived in the Castle *(1963), in addition to short stories, a play, juvenile fiction, and various nonfiction books and essays. Her short story collection* The Lottery *(1949) is considered to be one of the finest in the genre.*

THE DAY MY SON Laurie started kindergarten he renounced corduroy overalls with bibs and began wearing blue jeans with a belt; I watched him go off the first morning with the older girl next door, seeing clearly that an era of my life was ended, my sweet-voiced nursery-school tot replaced by a long-trousered, swaggering character who forgot to stop at the corner and wave good-bye to me.

He came home the same way, the front door slamming open, his cap on the floor, and the voice suddenly become raucous shouting, "Isn't anybody *here*?"

At lunch he spoke insolently to his father, spilled his baby sister's milk, and remarked that his teacher said we were not to take the name of the Lord in vain.

"How *was* school today?" I asked, elaborately casual.

"All right," he said.

"Did you learn anything?" his father asked.

Laurie regarded his father coldly. "I didn't learn nothing," he said.

"Anything," I said. "Didn't learn anything."

"The teacher spanked a boy, though," Laurie said, addressing his bread and butter. "For being fresh," he added, with his mouth full.

"What did he do?" I asked. "Who was it?"

Laurie thought. "It was Charles," he said. "He was fresh. The teacher spanked him and made him stand in a corner. He was awfully fresh."

"What did he do?" I asked again, but Laurie slid off his chair, took a cookie, and left, while his father was still saying, "See here, young man."

The next day Laurie remarked at lunch, as soon as he sat down, "Well, Charles was bad again today." He grinned enormously and said, "Today Charles hit the teacher."

"Good heavens," I said, mindful of the Lord's name, "I suppose he got spanked again?"

"He sure did," Laurie said. "Look up," he said to his father.

"What?" his father said, looking up.

"Look down," Laurie said. "Look at my thumb. Gee, you're dumb." He began to laugh insanely.

"Why did Charles hit the teacher?" I asked quickly.

"Because she tried to make him color with red crayons," Laurie said. "Charles wanted to color with green crayons so he hit the teacher and she spanked him and said nobody play with Charles but everybody did."

The third day—it was Wednesday of the first week—Charles bounced a see-saw on to the head of a little girl and made her bleed, and the teacher made him stay inside all during recess. Thursday Charles had to stand in a corner during story-time because he kept pounding his feet on the floor. Friday Charles was deprived of blackboard privileges because he threw chalk.

On Saturday I remarked to my husband, "Do you think kindergarten is too unsettling for Laurie? All this toughness, and bad grammar, and this Charles boy sounds like such a bad influence."

"It'll be all right," my husband said reassuringly. "Bound to be people like Charles in the world. Might as well meet them now as later."

On Monday Laurie came home late, full of news. "Charles," he shouted as he came up the hill; I was waiting anxiously on the front steps. "Charles," Laurie yelled all the way up the hill, "Charles was bad again."

"Come right in," I said, as soon as he came close enough. "Lunch is waiting."

"You know what Charles did?" he demanded, following me through the door. "Charles yelled so in school they sent a boy from first grade to tell the teacher she had to make Charles keep quiet, and so Charles had to stay after school. And so all the children stayed to watch him."

"What did he do?" I asked.

"He just sat there," Laurie said, climbing into his chair at the table. "Hi, Pop, y'old dust mop."

"Charles had to stay after school today," I told my husband. "Everyone stayed with him."

"What does this Charles look like?" my husband asked Laurie. "What's his other name?"

"He's bigger than me," Laurie said. "And he doesn't have any rubbers and he doesn't ever wear a jacket."

Monday night was the first Parent-Teachers meeting, and only the fact that the baby had a cold kept me from going; I wanted passionately to meet Charles's mother. On Tuesday Laurie remarked suddenly. "Our teacher had a friend come to see her in school today."

"Charles's mother?" my husband and I asked simultaneously.

"Naaah," Laurie said scornfully. "It was a man who came and made us do exercises, we had to touch our toes. Look." He climbed down from his chair and squatted down and touched his toes. "Like this," he said. He got solemnly back into his chair and said, picking up his fork, "Charles didn't even *do* exercises."

"That's fine," I said heartily. "Didn't Charles want to do exercises?"

"Naaah," Laurie said. "Charles was so fresh to the teacher's friend he wasn't *let* do exercises."

"Fresh again?" I said.

"He kicked the teacher's friend," Laurie said. "The teacher's friend told Charles to touch his toes like I just did and Charles kicked him."

"What are they going to do about Charles, do you suppose?" Laurie's father asked him.

Laurie shrugged elaborately. "Throw him out of school, I guess," he said.

Wednesday and Thursday were routine; Charles yelled during story hour and hit a boy in the stomach and made him cry. On Friday Charles stayed after school again and so did all the other children.

With the third week of kindergarten Charles was an institution in our family; the baby was being a Charles when she cried all afternoon; Laurie did a Charles when he filled his wagon full of mud and pulled it through the kitchen; even my husband, when he caught his elbow in the telephone cord and pulled telephone, ashtray, and a bowl of flowers off the table, said, after the first minute, "Looks like Charles."

During the third and fourth weeks it looked like a reformation in Charles; Laurie reported grimly at lunch on Thursday of the third week, "Charles was so good today the teacher gave him an apple."

"What?" I said, and my husband added warily, "You mean Charles?"

"Charles," Laurie said. "He gave the crayons around and he picked up the books afterward and the teacher said he was her helper."

"What happened?" I asked incredulously.

"He was her helper, that's all," Laurie said, and shrugged.

"Can this be true, about Charles?" I asked my husband that night. "Can something like this happen?"

"Wait and see," my husband said cynically. "When you've got a Charles to deal with, this may mean he's only plotting."

He seemed to be wrong. For over a week Charles was the teacher's helper; each day he handed things out and he picked things up; no one had to stay after school.

"The P.T.A. meeting's next week again," I told my husband one evening. "I'm going to find Charles's mother there."

"Ask her what happened to Charles," my husband said. "I'd like to know."

On Friday of that week things were back to normal. "You know what Charles did today?" Laurie demanded at the lunch table, in a voice slightly awed. "He told a little girl to say a word and she said it and the teacher washed her mouth out with soap and Charles laughed."

"What word?" his father asked unwisely, and Laurie said, "I'll have to whisper it to you, it's so bad." He got down off his chair and went around to his father. His father bent his head down and Laurie whispered joyfully. His father's eyes widened.

"Did Charles tell the little girl to say *that*?" he asked respectfully.

"She said it *twice*," Laurie said. "Charles told her to say it *twice*."

"What happened to Charles?" my husband asked.

"Nothing," Laurie said. "He was passing out the crayons."

Monday morning Charles abandoned the little girl and said the evil word himself three or four times, getting his mouth washed out with soap each time. He also threw chalk.

My husband came to the door with me that evening as I set out for the P.T.A. meeting. "Invite her over for a cup of tea after the meeting," he said. "I want to get a look at her."

"If only she's there," I said prayerfully.

"She'll be there," my husband said. "I don't see how they could hold a P.T.A. meeting without Charles's mother."

At the meeting I sat restlessly, scanning each comfortable matronly face, trying to determine which one hid the secret of Charles. None of them looked to me haggard enough. No one stood up in the meeting and apologized for the way her son had been acting. No one mentioned Charles.

After the meeting I identified and sought out Laurie's kindergarten teacher. She had a plate with a cup of tea and a piece of chocolate cake; I had a plate with a cup of tea and a piece of marshmallow cake. We maneuvered up to one another cautiously, and smiled.

"I've been so anxious to meet you," I said, "I'm Laurie's mother."

"We're all so interested in Laurie," she said.

"Well, he certainly likes kindergarten," I said. "He talks about it all the time."

"We had a little trouble adjusting, the first week or so," she said primly, "but now he's a fine little helper. With occasional lapses, of course."

"Laurie usually adjusts very quickly," I said. "I suppose this time it's Charles's influence."

"Charles?"

"Yes," I said, laughing, "you must have your hands full in that kindergarten, with Charles."

"Charles?" she said. "We don't have any Charles in the kindergarten."

The Ten O'Clock Scholar

HARRY KEMELMAN

While the oral examination for the doctoral degree is a harrowing experience, it is seldom an occasion that provokes murder; but in "The Ten O'Clock Scholar," Harry Kemelman demonstrates what can happen when academic passions run amok. The hero of this tale, Nicky Welt, is a professor of English language and literature and appears in a series of short stories first published in Ellery Queen's Mystery Magazine. *Professor Welt's methods of investigation are those befitting an intellectual, as he employs the finest principles of logic. In addition to these stories, Kemelman is the author of the well-known novels featuring Rabbi David Small, the first of which,* Friday the Rabbi Slept Late, *won the Mystery Writers of America Edgar for Best First Novel of 1964.*

I DO NOT THINK it was a strong sense of justice that prompted Nicky Welt to come to my assistance on occasion, after I left the Law Faculty to become County Attorney. Rather, I think, it was a certain impatience of mind—like that of the skilled mechanic who chafes as he watches the bungling amateur and at last takes the wrench from his hand with a "Here, let me do it."

Nevertheless, I felt that he enjoyed these brief excursions from the narrow routine of lecturing and grading papers, and when he invited me to attend a doctoral examination, I felt that it was his way of thanking me and reciprocating.

I was busy at the time and loath to accept, but it is hard for me to refuse Nicky. A three-hour doctor's oral can be very dull if you are not yourself the candidate, or at least a member of the examining committee. So I temporized.

"Who is the candidate, Nicky?" I asked. "One of your young men? Anyone I know?"

"A Mr. Bennett—Claude Bennett," he replied. "He has taken some courses with me, but he is not working in my field."

"Anything interesting about his dissertation?" I continued.

Nicky shrugged his shoulders. "Since this is a preliminary examination according to the New Plan, we don't know what the dissertation subject is. In the last half-hour of the examination the candidate will announce it and outline what he hopes to prove. I understand from other members of the committee, however, that Mr. Bennett's interest is primarily in the eighteenth century, and that he is planning to do some work in the Byington Papers."

And now I thought I saw light. I suppose no university is really complete without a faculty feud. Ours was localized to the English Department, and the principals were our two eighteenth century specialists, Professor George Korngold, biographer of Pope, and Professor Emmett Hawthorne, discoverer and editor of the Byington Papers. And so bitter was the conflict between the two men that Professor Hawthorne had been known to walk out of meetings of learned societies when Korngold rose to speak, and Korngold had once declared in a sectional meeting of the Modern Language Association that the Byington Papers were a nineteenth century forgery.

I smiled knowingly. "And Korngold is on the committee?" Professor Hawthorne, I knew, was at the University of Texas for the semester, as an exchange professor.

Nicky's lips twisted into a most unscholarly smirk. "They're both on the committee, Korngold and Hawthorne."

I looked puzzled. "Is Hawthorne back?"

"We had a wire from him saying that he had made arrangements to return north early, ostensibly to check proof on the new edition of his book. But I consider it most significant that we got the wire shortly after Bennett's examination date was posted in the *Gazette,* and equally significant that he is due to arrive the night before the examination. Of course, we invited him to participate and he wired his acceptance." Nicky rubbed his hands with pleasure.

And although in the nature of things I did not expect to enjoy the proceedings quite as much as Nicky would, I thought it might be interesting.

Like many an anticipated pleasure, however, the actuality proved disappointing. The candidate, Claude Bennett, failed to appear.

The examination was scheduled for ten o'clock Saturday morning, and I arrived in good time—about a quarter of—so as not to miss any part of the fun. The committee had already assembled, however, and I could detect from the general atmosphere, and more particularly from the way the members were grouped as they stood around and gossiped, that Korngold and Hawthorne had already had an exchange or two.

Professor Korngold was a large, stout man, with a fringe of reddish hair. His naturally ruddy complexion was exaggerated by a skin disorder, a form of eczema from which he suffered periodically. He smoked a large curved-stem pipe which was rarely out of his mouth, and when he spoke, the burbling of the pipe was a constant overtone to the deep rumble of his voice.

He came over to me when I entered the room and offering his hand, he bellowed, "Nicky said you were coming. Glad you could make it."

I took his outstretched hand with some reluctance for he was wearing a soiled cotton glove on the other to protect, or perhaps only to conceal, the broken skin where the eczema had penetrated. I withdrew my hand rather quickly, and to cover any awkwardness that might have resulted, I asked, "Has the candidate arrived yet?"

Korngold shook his head. He tugged at his watch chain and brought forth a turnip of a watch. He squinted at the dial and then frowned as he snapped the case shut. "Getting on to ten o'clock," he rumbled. "Bennett better not funk it again."

"Oh, he's been up before, has he?"

"He was scheduled to come up at the beginning of the semester, and a day or two before, he asked for a postponement."

"Does that count against him?"

"It's not supposed to," he said, and then he laughed.

I sauntered over to the other side of the room where Professor Hawthorne was standing. Hawthorne was a small, tidy man, with more than a touch of the dandy about him. He had pointed mustaches, and he was one of the few men in the university who wore a beard, a well-trimmed imperial. He also went in for pince-nez on a broad black ribbon, and even sported a cane, a slim ebony wand with a gold crook. All this since his discovery of the Byington Diary some few years ago, during a summer's study in England. He had been an ordinary enough figure before that, but the discovery of the Byington Papers had been hailed by enthusiasts as of equal importance to the deciphering of the Pepys Diary, and honors had come to him: a full professorship, an editorial sinecure with a learned publication, and even an honorary degree from a not too impossible Western college. And with it had come the imperial and the cane and the pince-nez on a ribbon.

"George Korngold being amusing at my expense?" he asked with seeming negligence.

"Oh, no," I said quickly. "We were talking about the candidate. George said something about his having funked the examination once before."

"Yes, I suppose Professor Korngold would regard Bennett's request for a postponement as funking it," Hawthorne said ironically, raising his voice so that it was just loud enough to be heard across the room. "I happen to know something about it. And so does Professor Korngold, for that matter. It so happens that Bennett was working on the Byington Papers. Our library acquired the manuscript just a few days before Bennett was scheduled to stand for examination. As a real scholar, naturally he wanted a chance to study the original manuscript. So he asked for a postponement. That's what Korngold calls funking an exam."

From across the room the voice of George Korngold boomed out, "It's ten o'clock, Nicky."

Hawthorne glanced at his watch and squeaked, "It's only five of."

Korngold laughed boisterously, and I realized that he had only been baiting Hawthorne.

When five minutes later the clock in the chapel chimed the hour, Korngold said, "Well, it's ten o'clock now, Nicky. Do we wait till noon?"

Hawthorne waved his stick excitedly. "I protest, Nicky," he cried. "From the general attitude of one member of this committee the candidate has already been prejudged. I think in all fairness that member should disqualify himself. As for the candidate, I am sure he will be along presently. I stopped by at his hotel on my way down and found that he had already gone. I suppose he has dropped in at the library for a last-minute checkup of some point or other. I urge that in all decency we should wait."

"I think we can wait a while, Emmett," said Nicky soothingly.

By a quarter past, however, the candidate had still not arrived, and Hawthorne was in a panic of anxiety. He wandered from one window to another looking out over the campus toward the library. Korngold, on the other hand, was elaborately at ease.

I think we all felt a little sorry for Hawthorne, and yet relieved, somehow, when Nicky finally announced, "It's half-past ten. I think we have waited long enough. I suggest we adjourn."

Hawthorne started to protest, and then thought better of it and remained silent, gnawing on his mustache in vexation. As we all moved to the door, Korngold rumbled loud enough for all to hear, "That young man had better not plan on standing again for examination in this university."

"He may have an adequate excuse," Nicky ventured.

"The way I feel right now," said Korngold, "it would have to be something more than just an adequate excuse. Only a matter of life and death would justify this cavalier treatment of the examining committee."

Nicky had some work to do at the library, so I went back to my office. I had been there less than an hour when I was informed of the reason for Bennett's seeming negligence. He had been found dead in his room—murdered!

My first reaction, I recall, was the idiotic thought that now Bennett had an excuse that would satisfy even Professor Korngold.

I felt that Nicky ought to be notified, and my secretary tried to reach him several times during the afternoon but without success. When, at four o'clock, Lieutenant Delhanty, our Chief of Homicide, accompanied by Sergeant Carter who had also been working on the case, came to report on his progress, she still had had no luck.

Carter remained outside in the anteroom, in case he should be needed, while I led Delhanty into my office. Delhanty is a systematic man. He brought forth his notebook and placed it carefully on my desk, so that he could refer to it when necessary. Then he carefully drew up a chair and after squinting through his eyeglasses he began to read.

"At ten-forty-five we were notified by James Houston, manager of the Avalon Hotel, that one of his guests, a Claude Bennett, twenty-seven, unmarried, graduate student at the university, had been found dead by the chambermaid, a Mrs. Agnes Underwood. He had obviously been murdered. The call was taken by Sergeant Lomasney who ordered Houston to close and lock the door of the room and to await the arrival of the police.

"The Medical Examiner was notified and came out with us. We arrived at ten-fifty." He looked up from his notes to explain. "The Avalon is that little place on High Street across from the university gymnasium. It's more of a boardinghouse than a hotel, and practically all the guests are permanent, although occasionally they take a transient. There was a car parked in front of the entrance, a Ford coupe, 1957, registration 769214. The key was in the ignition switch." He looked up again. "That turned out to be important," he said. He made a deprecatory gesture with his hand. "It's the sort of thing a policeman would notice—a parked car with the key in the switch. It's practically inviting someone to steal it. I made inquiries of the manager, Houston, and it turned out to be Bennett's car.

"Bennett's room was one flight up, just to the right of the stairs. The shades were drawn when we entered, and Houston explained that they had been found that way. Bennett was lying on the floor, his head bashed in by half a dozen blows from some blunt instrument. The Medical Examiner thought the first one might have done the trick, and the rest were either to make sure or were done out of spite. Near the body was a long dagger, the haft of which was covered with blood. A few strands of hair adhered to the sticky haft and were readily identified as the victim's."

He reached down and drew from the briefcase he had brought with him a long, slim package. He carefully unfolded the waxed-paper wrapper and exposed to view a dagger in a metal sheath. It was about a foot and a half long. The haft, which was stained with dried blood, was about a third of the overall length, about an inch wide and half an inch thick, with all the edges nicely rounded off. It appeared to be made of bone or ivory, and was engraved with swastikas.

"That was the weapon, I suppose," I said with a smile.

He grinned back at me. "Not much doubt about that," he said. "It fits the wounds just right."

"Any fingerprints?" I asked.

Delhanty shook his head. "None on the weapon, and only the ones you'd expect in the room."

I picked up the dagger gingerly by the sheath.

"Why, it's weighted in the haft," I said.

Delhanty nodded grimly. "It would have to be," he replied, "to have done the job it did on Bennett."

I put it down again. "Well, a dagger like that shouldn't be too hard to trace," I said hopefully.

Delhanty smiled. "We had no trouble with that. It belonged to Bennett."

"The chambermaid identified it?"

"Better than that. The mate to it was right there hanging on the wall. Here, let me show you." Once again he reached into his briefcase and this time came up with a large photograph showing one side of a room. There was a desk against the wall and a typewriter on a small table beside it. But it was the wall above the desk that attracted my attention, for arranged symmetrically on hooks was a veritable arsenal of weapons, each with a little card, presumably of explanation, tacked underneath. By actual count, there were two German sabers, three pistols, two weapons that looked like policemen's night-sticks (at my puzzled look, Delhanty murmured, "Taken from guards of a concentration camp—nasty weapons—almost as thick as my wrist") and one dagger, the twin of the weapon lying on my desk. But there was another card and an empty hook where the other dagger should have been, and it was just possible to discern its outline as a darker area in the faded wallpaper.

Delhanty chuckled. "G.I. trophies. My boy brought home enough stuff to equip a German regiment."

He drew a pencil from his breast pocket and pointed with it to the desk in the photograph.

"Now I call your attention to this stuff on the desk to the right of this pile of books. It's hard to make out in the picture, but I itemized it."

He referred to his notes again. "Loose change to the sum of twenty-eight cents, a key to the room, a pen and pencil set, a jackknife, a clean handkerchief, and a billfold. It's the usual stuff that a man keeps in his pockets and transfers every time he changes his suit. One thing struck me as funny: the billfold was empty. It had his license and registration and a receipted bill for his room rent and a little book of stamps, but I mean there wasn't a dollar in the money compartment."

"Nothing odd in that," I remarked. "Students are not noted for their wealth."

Delhanty shook his head stubbornly. "Usually you carry some money with you. The change on the desk didn't even amount to lunch money. We searched the place carefully and found no money and no bankbook. But in the wastebasket we did find this."

Once again he ducked down to rummage in his briefcase. This time he brought forth a long government-franked envelope.

"That's the kind they send checks in," he remarked. "And do you notice the postmark? He must have received it yesterday. So we checked with the local banks and the first one we tried admitted they had cashed a government check for Bennett for one hundred dollars. The teller couldn't be sure, of course, but unless Bennett asked for bills of a particular denomination, he would probably give him the money in three twenties, two tens, three fives, and five ones."

"Well," Delhanty went on, "a young man in Bennett's circumstances wouldn't be likely to spend all that in a day. So that suggested to me that robbery might be the motive. And then I thought of the car parked outside with the ignition key still in the switch. It wasn't left there overnight because it would have been tagged. That meant that it was delivered there this morning, either by a friend who had borrowed it, or, more likely, by some garage. We had luck on that too. We found that the car had been left at the High Street Garage for lubrication and was delivered around nine-thirty this morning. When I asked about the key in the switch, the manager of the garage was as puzzled as I had been. They always deliver the keys to the owner, he said, or make arrangements with him to leave them somewhere.

"I asked to look at their records to see who delivered the car. Well, it's only a small place and they didn't keep any such records, but the manager knew that it was a young apprentice mechanic they had there—fellow named Sterling. James Sterling. He does most of the lubricating work and delivers cars when necessary. The manager couldn't be sure, but he thought Sterling had delivered Bennett's car to him several times before. I considered that important because it would show that Sterling knew Bennett's room number and would be able to go right on up without making inquiries."

"I take it," I said, "that there wouldn't be any trouble getting into the hotel without being noticed."

"Oh, as to that, the place is wide open. It's not really a hotel, you see. There's no desk clerk. The outer door is kept open during the day, and anyone could come in and out a dozen times without being seen.

"I asked to speak to Sterling," Delhanty went on, "and learned that he had gone home sick. I got his address and was just leaving, when I noticed a row of steel lockers which I figured were used by the mechanics for their work clothes. I asked the manager to open Sterling's and, after a little fuss, he did. And what do you think I found there, tucked away behind the peak of his greasy work cap? Three twenties, two tens, and three fives. No ones—I suppose he figured he could have those on him without exciting suspicion."

"You went to his home?"

"That's right, sir. He may have been sick before, but he was a lot sicker when he saw me. At first he said he didn't know anything about the money. Then he said he won it shooting crap.

And then he said he had found it in Bennett's car, tucked down between the seat and the back cushion. So I told him we had found his fingerprints on the billfold. We hadn't, of course, but sometimes a little lie like that is enough to break them. His answer to that was that he wanted a lawyer. So we locked him up. I thought I'd talk to you before we really put him through the wringer."

"You've done an excellent job, Delhanty," I said. "Quick work and good, straight thinking. I suppose Sterling thought that leaving the key in the switch would indicate that he hadn't seen Bennett to deliver it to him personally. And you went him one better and figured that his leaving the key in the switch was in itself an indication that something was wrong. Finding the money clinches it, of course. But it would be nice if we found someone who had seen him. You questioned the residents, of course?"

"Naturally, we questioned everybody at the hotel," Delhanty said. He chuckled. "And it just goes to show how sometimes too much investigating can hinder you by leading you off on a tangent. I questioned them before I got a line on Sterling, and for a while I thought I had the logical suspect right there in one of the residents of the hotel. You see we had gone through all the residents, and Houston, the manager, had drawn a perfect blank: no one had seen anything; no one had heard anything. Then we called in the chambermaid. We had left her for the last because she had been kind of upset and hysterical, what with finding the body and all. Well, she *had* seen something.

"She had started to work on that floor at half-past eight. She's sure of the time because the chapel clock was just chiming. She was just going into the room at the other end of the corridor from Bennett's when she saw Alfred Starr, who occupies the room next to Bennett, leave his room and knock on Bennett's door. She watched, and saw him enter. She waited a minute or two and then went on with her work."

"Why did she watch?" I asked.

"I asked the same question," said Delhanty, "and she said it was because Starr and Bennett had had a fearful row a couple of days before, and she wondered about his going in now. When I had questioned Starr earlier, he had said nothing about having gone into Bennett's room. So I called him in again and asked him about it. At first he denied it. That's normal. Then when he realized that someone had seen him, he admitted that he had visited Bennett that morning, but insisted that it was only to wish him luck on his exam. Then I mentioned the row he had had a couple of days before. He didn't try to dodge it. He admitted he had had a fight with Bennett, but he claimed he had been a little tight at the time. It appears he had brought his girl down from Boston for a dance at the Medical School a couple of weeks ago. He had been tied up in the morning and had asked Bennett to entertain her. Then he had found out that after she had gone back to Boston, Bennett had written her a couple of times. That was what the fight was about, but he had later realized that he had been foolish. Bennett's coming up for his exam gave him an opportunity to apologize and to wish him luck. He hadn't said anything about it because he didn't want to get mixed up in anything, especially now with final exams on."

Delhanty shrugged his shoulders. "For a while, I thought I had my whole case right there: jealousy over a girl as the motive; weapon and opportunity right at hand; and even some indication of guilt in his not telling a straight story from the beginning. And then the whole case collapsed. The time element was off. The Medical Examiner had figured the murder had taken place about nine o'clock. That didn't bother me too much since the best they can give you is only an approximate time. But Starr was on his way to play squash at the gym, and they have a time-clock arrangement there because there's a fee for the use of the squash courts. Well, according to that clock, Starr was ready to start playing at eight-thirty-three. That would give him only three minutes from the time he entered Bennett's room to the time when he started playing, and it just isn't enough. So there you are. If the time at both ends hadn't been so exact, we would have felt that Starr was the star suspect."

He laughed at his pun, and I managed a smile. Then a thought occurred to me.

"Look here," I said, "there's something wrong with the time even as it stands. I know the arrangement for the squash courts; I've played there often enough. The lockers are at the other end of the building from the courts. You change into your gym clothes first and then you go down to the squash courts and get stamped in. Starr would not have had a chance to change if those times are correct as given."

Delhanty was apologetic. "He didn't change in the gym. I should have mentioned that. The hotel is just across the street, you see. He was wearing shorts and a sweatshirt and had his racket with him when he went to Bennett's room. The chambermaid told us that."

I nodded, a little disappointed. Strictly speaking, criminal investigation is not my job. The police report to me because as County Attorney it is my function to indict, and if a true bill is found, to try the case in court. But it is only natural to seize the opportunity of showing the professional where he might have slipped up.

There was a discreet knock and my secretary opened the door just wide enough to put her head in and say, "Professor Welt is outside."

"Have him come in," I said.

Nicky entered and I introduced him to Delhanty.

"A sad business, Lieutenant," Nicky said, shaking his head. Then he noticed the dagger on the desk. "This the weapon?" he asked.

I nodded.

"Bennett's, I suppose."

"That's right," said Delhanty, his tone showing surprise. "How did you know?"

"I'm only guessing of course," Nicky replied, with an amused shrug of the shoulders. "But it's fairly obvious. A dagger like that isn't anything that a man would normally carry around with him. And if you went calling on someone with the intent of bludgeoning him to death, it is hardly the sort of thing you would select to take with you. There are a thousand things that are readily available and are so much better for the purpose—a wrench, a hammer, a piece of pipe. But, of course, if you had no intention of killing when you set out, and then found it necessary or expedient, and this was the only thing to hand—"

"But it wasn't," I said. "Show him the photograph, Lieutenant."

Delhanty handed over the photograph with some reluctance, I thought. I got the impression that he was not too pleased with Nicky's characteristic air of amused condescension.

Nicky studied the photograph intently. "These books on the desk here," he said, pointing with a lean forefinger, "are probably the texts he was planning to take to the examination with him. Notice that they all have paper markers. I don't see any notes. Did you find a package of notes anywhere in the room, Lieutenant?"

"Notes?" Delhanty shook his head. "No notes."

"Notes and texts at an examination, Nicky?" I asked.

"Oh, yes, in accordance with the New Plan, you remember, the candidate outlines his dissertation in the last half-hour, indicating what he hopes to prove, listing a partial bibliography and so forth. He is permitted to make use of any texts and notes that he cares to bring with him for that part of the examination."

"Is that so?" said Delhanty politely. "History student was he? I noticed the top book was History of Cal—Cali—something."

"No, he was an English Literature student, Lieutenant," I said. "But that involves the study of a lot of history. The two fields are interrelated." I remembered that there had been a brief vogue of Moslem influence among eighteenth century writers. "Was it *History of the Caliphate?*" I suggested.

He sampled the title, and then shook his head doubtfully.

I shrugged my shoulders and turned again to Nicky. "Well, why didn't Bennett's assailant select one of the bludgeons instead of the dagger?'' I asked. ''Excellent weapons for the purpose according to the Lieutenant here—each as thick as his wrist.''

''But he didn't use the dagger—at least not to kill with,'' Nicky replied.

We both stared at him.

''But there is blood on the haft, and some of Bennett's hair. And the Medical Examiner found that it fitted the wounds just right.''

Nicky smiled, a peculiarly knowing and annoying smile. ''Yes, it would fit, but it is not the weapon.'' He spread his hands. ''Consider, here is a large variety of weapons ready to hand. Would a man select a dagger to bludgeon with when there are actually two bludgeons handy? Besides, hanging there on the wall, how would he know that the haft of the dagger was weighted and could be used as a bludgeon at all?''

''Suppose he planned to stab him, but that Bennett turned before he could draw the blade from the sheath, or say it stuck,'' Delhanty suggested.

''Then there would be fingerprints showing,'' Nicky retorted.

''He might have worn gloves,'' I offered.

''In this weather?'' Nicky scoffed. ''And attracted no notice? Or are you suggesting that Bennett obligingly waited while the assassin drew them on?''

''He could have wiped the prints off,'' said Delhanty coldly.

''Off the sheath, yes, but not off the haft. When you draw a dagger, you grip the haft in one hand and the sheath in the other. Now if your victim turns at just that moment and you have to club him with the weighted haft, his prints would be nicely etched in the resultant blood. And you couldn't wipe those off unless you also wiped off the blood or smeared it. That would mean that the murderer would have to have worn at least one glove, and that would be even more noticeable than a pair.''

A faint, elusive thought flickered across my mind that was connected somehow with a man wearing a single glove, but Delhanty was speaking and it escaped me.

"I'll admit, Professor," he was saying, "that I'd expect he would have taken one of the bludgeons—but the fact is, he didn't. We know he used the dagger because it was right there. And it was covered with blood which matches Bennett's and with hair that matches his, and most of all, it fits the wounds."

"Of course," Nicky retorted scornfully. "That's why it was used. It had to fit the wounds in order to conceal the real weapon. The bludgeons wouldn't do because they were too thick. Suppose you had just crushed somebody's skull with a weapon that you felt left a mark which could be traced to you. What would you do? You could continue bashing your victim until you reduced his head to a pulp—in the hope of obliterating the marks; but that would be an extremely bloody business and would take some time. If there was something lying around that would fit the wound nicely, however, you could use it once or twice to get blood and hair on it, and then leave it for the police to find. Having a weapon at hand which apparently fits, they would not think to look for another."

"But there was nothing distinctive about the mark of the weapon," Delhanty objected.

"If you are thinking of something like a branding iron, of course not. But if we assume that the dagger haft was selected because it fitted the original wound, it automatically gives us the shape of the real weapon. Since it was the edge of the haft that was used, I should surmise that the real weapon was smooth and rounded, or round, and about half an inch in diameter. It would have to be something that the attacker could have with him without exciting comment."

"A squash racket!" I cried.

Nicky turned sharply. "What are you talking about?" he asked.

I told him about Starr. "He was dressed in his gym clothes and he had his squash racket with him. The frame of a squash racket would about fit those dimensions. And it would excite no comment from Bennett since Starr was in shorts and sweatshirt."

Nicky pursed his lips and considered. "Is there any reason for supposing that the mark of a squash racket would implicate him?" he asked.

"He was seen by the chambermaid to go into the room."

"That's true enough," Nicky conceded, "although I gathered from your story that he did not know he had been seen."

Before I could answer, Delhanty spoke up. "Of course," he said sarcastically, "I'm nothing but a cop, and all these theories are a little over my head. But I've made an arrest and it was done through ordinary police work on the basis of evidence. Maybe I shouldn't have wasted my time, and my men's time, with legwork, and just sat back and dreamed the answer. But there's pretty good proof that Bennett was robbed of a hundred dollars this morning, and I've got a man in a cell right now who had that hundred dollars on him and who hasn't been able to give any explanation that would satisfy a child as to how it got there." He sat back with an air of having put Nicky, and me too, I suspect, in our places.

"Indeed! And how did you go about finding this individual?"

Delhanty shrugged his shoulders in a superior sort of way and did not answer. So I explained about the envelope and billfold clues, and how they had been tracked down.

Nicky listened attentively and then said quietly, "The mechanic arrived around nine-thirty. Have you considered the possibility, Lieutenant, that Bennett was already dead at the time, and that Sterling's crime was not of having killed, but only of having robbed? Much more likely, I assure you. The man would be an idiot to kill, especially for so small a sum, when he knows that he would be suspected almost immediately—after all, his employer knew where he was going and the approximate time that he would arrive. But if he found the man already dead and he saw the money in the wallet, it would be fairly safe to take it. Even if the police were to discover that a sum of money was missing, which was unlikely in the first place, they would normally assume that it had been taken by the murderer. So he probably took the money and then went back to the shop prepared to say, if he should be asked, that he had knocked on Bennett's door to deliver the keys and Bennett had not answered."

"That sounds reasonable, Nicky," I said. Then noticing the look on Delhanty's face, I quickly added, "But it's only a theory. And we know that criminals are guilty of idiotic acts as well as criminal ones. Now if we knew exactly when Bennett was killed, we'd know whether Sterling could be completely eliminated, or if he was still a suspect."

"You could always get the Medical Examiner to swear that it couldn't have happened after nine," Delhanty murmured sarcastically.

I ignored the remark. Besides, it occurred to me that we had overlooked a possible piece of evidence.

"Look, Nicky," I said, "do you remember Emmett Hawthorne saying that he called on Bennett on his way down to the exam? Bennett must already have been dead, which is why he didn't answer and why Emmett concluded that he had gone on ahead. Maybe Emmett remembers what time it was. If it was before nine-thirty, it would at least clear Sterling."

Nicky gave me a nod of approval, and I felt inordinately pleased with myself. It happened so seldom.

I reached for the telephone. "Do you know where he's staying, Nicky? I'll ring him."

"He's staying at the Ambassador," Nicky answered, "but I doubt if he's there now. He was in his cubicle in the library stacks when I left, and there's no phone connection except at the center desk of the Reading Room. If you had a messenger, you might send him over and ask him to come here. I don't think he'd mind. I'm sure he'd be interested in our discussion."

"Sergeant Carter is outside chinning with your secretary," said Delhanty grudgingly. "I could have him go. Where is it?"

"It's a regular rabbit warren of a place," I said. I looked at Nicky. "Perhaps you could go out and give him directions—"

"Perhaps I'd better," said Nicky, and crossed the room to the door.

I smiled inwardly while we waited for him to return. I did not see how Starr's alibi could be broken, but I was sure that Nicky did. When he returned a minute or two later, however, his first words were discouraging.

"Your idea of Starr and the squash racket," he said, "is not entirely devoid of ingenuity, but it won't do. Consider: the original quarrel was about a girl and it occurred a couple of days ago. Now if the two young men are living in the same house—on the same floor, in fact—and Bennett was probably around most of the time, since he was preparing for his exam, why didn't Starr seek him out earlier? It is most unlikely that he would have brooded over the matter for two whole days, and then bright and early on the morning of the third day, on his way to play squash, have stopped off and killed him. Absurd! It would not be beyond the bounds of possibility if Starr had dropped in to warn him off or to threaten him, and then in the course of the quarrel that might have followed, killed him. But in that event there would have been voices raised in anger, and the noise would have been heard by the chambermaid, who was listening for it. There would have been some sign of a struggle—and there was none."

He shook his head. "No, no, I'm afraid you don't grasp the full significance of the dagger and the necessity for its use.

"Look at it this way," he continued. "Suppose the attacker had not used the dagger as a red herring. Suppose that after having bludgeoned Bennett with the weapon he had brought with him, he had departed. What line of investigation would the police have pursued then? On the basis of the wound, the Medical Examiner would describe the weapon as a blunt instrument, round or rounded, and about half an inch in diameter. A length of narrow pipe, or a heavy steel rod would fit, but the assailant couldn't walk around or come into Bennett's room carrying something like that without exciting comment and suspicion. Of course, he could carry it concealed—up his coat sleeve, perhaps. It would be awkward, but it could be managed. And it would be still more awkward to draw out without Bennett seeing and making an outcry. But again, with luck it could be managed. All this if the attacker set out with the deliberate idea of murdering. But sooner or later, the police would consider the possibility of the crime having been committed on the spur of the moment. And then it would occur to them that the weapon would have to be something that the attacker had with him, something he could carry openly without exciting the slightest suspicion. And that could only be—"

"A *cane!*" I exclaimed.

"Precisely," said Nicky. "And when you think of a cane, Professor Hawthorne is the first person who comes to mind."

"Are you serious, Nicky?"

"Why not? It's an important part of the rather theatrical costume he designed to go with the new personality he acquired since becoming a great man. You can readily see that in his mind, at least, the mark of his cane would identify him as surely as if he had branded the young man with his initials."

"But why would he want to kill his protégé?"

"Because he wasn't—wasn't his protégé, I mean. You remember the young man was scheduled to come up for examination at the beginning of the semester and did not. Hawthorne told us that it was because our library had acquired the original Byington Papers and that Bennett wanted a chance to study them. But the Byington Papers had been published in full, and it is only a short summary of his dissertation that the candidate expounds at the exam. So that even if the original manuscript were to furnish additional proof of his thesis, it would not justify postponing the exam. Hence, we must conclude that Bennett had got an idea for an entirely new dissertation. Naturally, he told Hawthorne about it. But Hawthorne had to go down to Texas, so he probably got Bennett to say nothing of his discovery until his return. Then when announcement was made of the new edition of Hawthorne's book, Bennett decided to stand for examination again. Hawthorne came back as soon as he found out. He arrived last night and this morning was his first chance to see Bennett. I am quite sure he did not come intending to kill him. He would have brought another weapon if he had. He came to beg him to hold off again until they could work out something together—a paper on which they would collaborate, perhaps. I don't think it occurred to Hawthorne that Bennett might refuse. But he did, probably because he felt that after the announcement of a new edition of the Byington Papers he could no longer trust Hawthorne.

"To Hawthorne, this refusal meant the loss of everything he held dear—his academic standing, his reputation as a scholar, his position in the university. So he raised his cane and struck."

"But what discovery could Bennett have made that would justify Hawthorne's killing him?" I asked.

Nicky's eyebrows rose. "I should think you could guess that. We know that Bennett's dissertation subject had something to do with the original manuscript. My guess would be that the book that you noticed on his desk, Lieutenant, was *A History of Calligraphy*—two 'l's,' Lieutenant—a history of handwriting." (The look of sudden recognition that lit up Delhanty's face confirmed the guess.) "I fancy the other books were probably concerned with paper and the chemistry of ink—that sort of thing. In any case, I am quite certain that Bennett had discovered some proof—scientific proof, not internal criticism like Korngold's which is always subject to different interpretations—but proof of handwriting styles and ink and paper that the Byington Papers were a forgery."

The telephone exploded into sound and when I lifted the instrument to my ear, I heard the excited, panicky voice of Sergeant Carter.

"He just shot himself," he cried. "Professor Hawthorne just shot himself here at the hotel!"

I glanced at the two men in the room and saw that they had heard. Delhanty had risen and was reaching for his hat.

"Stay there," I said into the phone. "Lieutenant Delhanty will be there in a minute. What happened?"

"I don't know," Carter answered. "I went to the library but he had just gone. I caught him at the hotel here and I gave him Professor Welt's message. He just nodded and went into the next room, and a couple of seconds later there was a shot."

"All right, stand by." I cradled the phone.

Delhanty was already at the door. "That's it," I said to him.

"Guess so," he muttered, and closed the door behind him.

I turned to Nicky. "What message did you ask Carter to give him?"

He smiled. "Oh, that? I merely suggested to the Sergeant that he ask Hawthorne to bring Bennett's notes with him."

I nodded moodily. For a minute or two I was silent, staring at the desk in front of me. Then I looked up.

"Look here, Nicky, did you expect that your request would have the effect it did?"

He pursed his lips as if to take thought. Then he shrugged his shoulders. "I did not consider it beyond the bounds of possibility. However, my primary concern was my responsibility to poor Bennett. I thought that if there was any merit in his idea, I ought to expand his notes into a paper which I would publish in his name." His little blue eyes glittered and his lips relaxed in a frosty smile. "Naturally, I wanted to begin as soon as possible."

The Problem of the Little Red Schoolhouse

EDWARD D. HOCH

The one-room country schoolhouse was still a common American institution in the mid-1920s, when this story takes place. Although its author, Edward D. Hoch, was born in 1930 and thus has no personal knowledge of the era, his fine touch with the period piece has enabled him to re-create those times for his reader. Hoch has the distinction of being one of the few of today's mystery writers to concentrate almost exclusively on the short story. Although he has written five novels, including The Shattered Raven *(1969) and* The Fellowship of the Hand *(1976), he prefers the short story form and feels it lends itself best to the formal detective story he likes to write. Since 1955, his stories, including the Edgar-winning "The Oblong Room" (1968), have appeared in such publications as* Ellery Queen's Mystery Magazine, Alfred Hitchcock's Mystery Magazine, *and* The Saint.

"SURE, WE HAD one-room schoolhouses back in my day," Dr. Sam Hawthorne said. " 'Fact, one of my most bafflin' cases involved a kidnapin' at a little red schoolhouse. This was in the fall of 1925, you realize—nearly seven years before the Lindbergh case put kidnapin' on the front pages and got a law passed makin' it a federal crime. Here, let me pour you—ah—a small libation and tell you what happened . . ."

My position as one of the few doctors in the area (Dr. Sam Hawthorne began) was what got me into the case in the first place. I had a call from Mrs. Deasey, the widow up on Turk Hill, who said her little boy was just home from school and actin' strange. We'd had a bit of polio back in the summer that year, and though I knew the frost had lessened the danger it still seemed like a good idea for me to ride out and see what the trouble was. I told my nurse April where I'd be, then collected my bag and started up to Turk Hill in my yellow Pierce-Arrow Runabout.

Turk Hill had originally been called Turkey Hill, back in the days when there were still wild turkeys to be seen around Northmont. It had always been the back end of town, the area that well-to-do people avoided. Even the farming land was second-rate on Turk Hill, and in that autumn of '25 there were only three houses still lived in up there. Mrs. Deasey tried her best to farm the land her husband had left her, but the other two made no pretense of farmin'. One was a hermit nobody ever saw, an' the other was a young French-Canadian everyone suspected of making illegal whiskey in a hidden still.

As I turned my car into the rutted driveway of her farm, Mrs. Deasey came out to meet me. "I swear I don't know what's got into that child, Dr. Sam. He come home from school today all frightened of somethin'. He won't talk to me about it, whatever it is. I don't know if he's sick or what."

Robert was her only child—an undersized boy of nine who'd

already had the usual assortment of childhood illnesses. I found him around the back of the barn, throwing rocks at some target invisible to me. "Hello, Robert," I called to him. "Feelin' a bit under the weather?"

He turned away from me. "I'm okay."

But he was pale, and when I touched the clammy skin of his face he shivered a little. "What's the trouble? You've had a fright, haven't you? Something on the way back from school?" I knew his route home took him past the other two occupied houses on Turk Hill, and there might be something at either place to frighten a lad of nine. Then too, I was remembering his father's mental problems before he died. Was Robert beginnin' to imagine things too?

"It's nothin'," the boy mumbled and went back to throwing stones.

"Did somebody scare you? Threaten you?"

"No." He hesitated. "It's Tommy Belmont."

I tried to touch him again but he broke free and ran away, heading out into the field. I knew I could never catch him, so I turned back to the farmhouse where his mother was waiting.

"He appears to have had a bad fright," I told her. "But he should get over it. Boys his age usually do. See how he is in the mornin'. If there's still some problem, call me on the telephone." The farms on Turk Hill had been linked to town by a party line just the year before, though it was common knowledge Old Josh the hermit had taken a shotgun to the telephone men when they approached his place.

"Thank you for comin', Dr. Sam. It relieves my mind to know it's nothin' serious." She fumbled in her apron pocket. "How much am I owin' you?"

"Nothin' yet. Let's make sure he's all right."

Robert had appeared around the corner of the barn, prob'ly to see if I was gone yet, and I waved goodbye as I climbed into my car. There was nothing more to be done here, but I had the feeling I should talk to young Tommy Belmont.

Unlike Mrs. Deasey and her son, the Belmonts lived in the

wealthier part of Northmont, on a hundred-acre dairy farm. Herb Belmont was the town equivalent of a gentleman farmer, spending much of his time with area dairymen and Boston bankers while paid employees fed and milked the cows.

The Belmonts had two sons and a daughter, but the older son was away at school in Boston and the girl was only four. There was just Tommy to attend the one-room schoolhouse at the edge of town.

Tommy was a frisky lad of ten, with flaming red hair and freckles to match, who looked for all the world as if he'd escaped from a book by Mark Twain. I almost expected to see him whitewashin' a fence as I pulled up and parked, but instead all I saw was the familiar black police car belonging to Sheriff Lens.

As I went up the walk to the front door, the sheriff himself appeared. "What you doin' here, Dr. Sam?" he asked. "Somebody call you?"

"No. Is something the matter, Sheriff?"

"You'd better come in. Mebbe you can help with Mrs. Belmont."

I walked into the living room and found the woman in tears, hunched in a big flowered chair and being comforted by her husband. "What is it?" I asked Herb Belmont. "Has something happened to Tommy?"

The boy's father stared at me. "He's been kidnaped."

"Kidnaped!"

"He disappeared from the schoolhouse yard, right under the eyes of Mrs. Sawyer. And now there's been a demand for ransom."

"A note?"

"A call on the telephone—a voice I never heard before, sayin' they want $50,000 or they'll kill Tommy!" His voice broke and there was renewed sobbing from Mrs. Belmont.

"Tarnation!" Sheriff Lens thundered. "Ain't nothin' like this ever happened in Northmont afore!"

"When do you have to deliver the money?" I asked, trying to calm them with conversation.

"They said they'd telephone again."

I turned to the sheriff. "It should be no trouble tracin' that call. Jinny down at the switchboard must know who made it."

He nodded agreement. "I'll go check on it."

"And I'll go talk to Mrs. Sawyer at the schoolhouse," I said. "I want to find out more about this disappearance."

Some neighbors came in to stay with the Belmonts, and I went off in my automobile to the schoolhouse on the hill. I didn't know if Mrs. Sawyer would still be there at four in the afternoon, but her house was within walking distance and I figured I'd find her at one place or the other.

Though there was a newer high school built just after the war at the other end of town, the grammar-school pupils still went to the traditional little red schoolhouse set off by itself on a rise of ground not far from Turk Hill. Mrs. Sawyer, a widow who'd lost her husband in France, presided over the 38 students with a firm grip on the realities of New England life, instructing them on the sort of life that might await those who ventured to Boston or even to New York. She held daily fingernail inspection for all the children, and kept a chart of health chores they had to perform.

When I reached the school she was still there, straining to close a balky window with a wooden window pole bent dangerously close to the breaking point.

"Here, let me do that for you," I said as I entered.

"Dr. Sam! You startled me." She flushed a bit and handed me the pole. She was still an attractive woman, though the years without her husband were beginning to tell on her.

I closed the window and returned the pole to the corner. "I came about Tommy Belmont," I said.

"Tommy! Have they found him?"

"No. Somebody called the Belmont house to say he'd been kidnaped."

"Oh, surely not! Not that—not in Northmont!" She collapsed onto the nearest chair. "I swear he wasn't out of my sight for more than a few seconds. It just couldn't be!"

"Suppose you tell me what happened."

"Nothing happened—that's just it! During the recess Tommy was out playin' with the other boys. They avoided the girls—you know how it is at that age—but they seemed to be having a fine old time, just like any other noon recess. They'd been down the hill to Mr. Tilley's wagon for treats and they were back up swingin' and chasin' around as boys will do. I remember seeing Tommy on the swing, going up higher than I'd ever seen him go before. It looked as if he were going all the way to heaven. I glanced away for just a few seconds, when I rang the bell to summon them all back inside, and when I looked back the swing was empty, movin' gently back and forth as if someone had just left it. When they all trooped in, Tommy wasn't among them. He wasn't anywhere, Dr. Sam!"

"Perhaps he went down the hill for more treats."

"No, no. Mr. Tilley had been gone a good ten minutes by that time, and there was no one else on the road. I can see in both directions from up here—look for yourself. There's not even a tree except the big oak the two swings are attached to."

"Was anyone else swinging?"

"No, Tommy was alone. I looked behind the tree, and in the outhouse, and around the other side of the school building. I sent all the children to look for him—but he wasn't anywhere."

"He must have just wandered off."

She stamped her foot. "He *couldn't* have, Dr. Sam! I tell you he was on that swing an' off it, all in a few seconds. I was here in the doorway. There was noplace he could have gotten to without my seein' him! And as for kidnapin', well, who could have taken him? There wasn't another adult on this hill all day, and none of the other children was missin'. He didn't leave by himself and nobody came to get him. He just—vanished."

I walked outside and stared up at the oak tree, then tugged on the ropes that held the swings side by side. "Could he have gone up in the tree?"

"How? The nearest limb is at least fifteen feet up."

"You said he was swinging high."

"He didn't sail off that swing into the tree, Dr. Sam. And he didn't climb the rope, either. I'd have seen him. The other children would have seen him."

"What did you do when you decided he was missin'?"

"When he didn't come back after an hour or so, I sent Mary Lou Phillips over to the Belmont house to tell his folks. We don't have a telphone here."

"What about Robert Deasey?"

"That little boy? What about him?"

"Was he acting strangely?"

"I suppose all the children were very upset. I didn't rightly notice."

"What about strangers? Has anybody been lurking around the schoolhouse lately?"

"No one—no one at all."

"Come on," I said. "I'll give you a ride home."

She accepted with thanks, though her house was no more than a few yards away. I had a reason for wanting to go there, because it was the closest structure of any sort to the red schoolhouse. I thought Tommy Belmont just might be there, but I was disappointed. The place was empty when I escorted her inside, and Tommy Belmont was still among the missing.

Sheriff Lens had gotten back to the Belmont farm before me. I parked behind his car and hurried inside. "We traced the call," he told me grimly. "Jinny on the switchboard remembers it came from the Leotard place—that French-Canadian up on Turk Hill. She remembered it especially 'cause he don't make that many calls an' he never made one afore to the Belmont place."

"You think the boy is there?"

"Where else? I don't want to risk goin' up there in daylight, so we'll wait a couple hours till dark. Then me an' my deputies will storm the farmhouse an' rescue the lad."

"Sounds simple," I agreed, but the thought of it troubled me.

Could kidnapers be that foolish, to telephone the ransom demand from their own home?

But the news seemed to have bolstered the spirits of the Belmonts, and for that I was thankful. In fact, I was preparing to leave them again when the telephone gave its characteristic double ring.

Tommy's father grabbed the receiver. "Hello? Hello?"

The receiver wasn't quite pressed to his ear, so I could hear the child's terrified, high-pitched voice. I darted forward, reaching Belmont's side before either his wife or Sheriff Lens. But now the child's voice had been replaced by another, harsher tone. "That was to show you we've really got him. We'll deal with him the way Loeb and Leopold did with Bobby Franks, unless you come up with the fifty thousand dollars in a hurry!"

"I—the bank won't be open till morning."

"It'll open special for you. Have the money in your house tonight, and we'll telephone again with instructions."

The telephone went dead. Belmont waited a moment and then replaced the receiver. "My God!" he mumbled. "They'll kill him!"

"We'll see to it they won't, Mr. Belmont," the shriff told him. "Now, don't you worry none."

I took a deep breath. "You still think they've got him at the Leotard farm?"

"Sure do! But I'll just check with Jinny." He picked up the telephone and had the operator in a moment. "Jinny? Where'd that last call come from?" He listened to her reply and then said, "Fine, Jinny. You done good work."

"Leotard again?" I asked.

Sheriff Lens nodded. "She listened in this time an' heard the boy."

"But did she recognize Leotard's voice?"

"You heard him—he had it disguised."

"I don't know. It all seems too easy."

"He mentioned Loeb an' Leopold, didn't he? And his name's

*Leo*tard, ain't it? The guy imagines himself another thrill killer like Leopold."

"Not a killer," Mrs. Belmont gasped. "No, not that!"

"Sorry," Sheriff Lens mumbled. "Figure o' speech."

I could see that Tommy's mother was only moments away from fainting. I led her into the sitting room where there was a couch and got her to lie down. "I've got some sleeping powder here if you think it would help you," I suggested.

"No, no, I have to be awake for Tommy!"

"There's nothing you can do right now, Mrs. Belmont."

Even under extreme stress she was a handsome woman. Her son's flaming red hair had obviously come from her. "There's *surely* nothing I can do if I'm unconscious!"

There was no point in arguin' with her. "Try to rest anyway. You may need your strength later, after Tommy is released."

"Do you think he will be released? Do you think I'll ever see him alive again?"

"I'm sure of it," I said, trying to sound confident. "Now answer a couple of questions for me. What was Tommy wearing today?"

"Brown pants, striped shirt, and a necktie, just like all the other boys. That Mrs. Sawyer insists they wear neckties, 'cept in the hot weather."

"Who were his closest friends at school?"

"There weren't any really close, but sometimes after classes he played with that Deasey boy up on Turk Hill."

"I see." I checked her pulse one more time and then rose to leave. "You take it easy, Mrs. Belmont. We'll get Tommy back for you. I promise you."

I left the Belmont farm and drove around the back roads for a half hour till finally I spotted Mr. Tilley's wagon. Tilley was a peddler who'd become a familiar figure on the county roads, hawking household goods and candy for the kids and even doin' a little repair work for farm wives while their husbands were busy in the fields. The sides of his horse-drawn wagon carried only his name—*Tilley*—but everyone knew what he had to sell. Besides, a list of all the things he carried in the wagon wouldn't fit on the sides.

Tilley had a son about Tommy Belmont's age, though no one ever heard tell of a Mrs. Tilley anywhere. As I drove up to the wagon in my car, I could see the Tilley boy up on the seat next to his father. He hopped down when he saw me stop and came runnin' over to examine my yellow Pierce-Arrow, as boys always did.

" 'Evenin', Mr. Tilley," I called out, strolling over to the wagon. It was not yet dark, but anytime after six was considered evenin' in Northmont. "Had a good day?"

"Middlin'," the peddler said, climbing down from his rig. "This time o' year one day's pretty much like another."

"You hear about the Belmont boy?"

He nodded. "I was just up on Turk Hill an' Mrs. Deasey told me. Turrible thing for the town. People come out here to get away from all that big-city crime."

"Your boy is at school with Tommy Belmont, isn't he?"

"Sure is." The peddler scratched his day-old growth of beard. "Frank, come over here an' talk to the man. Did you see Tommy Belmont today before he disappeared?"

"Sure did. So did you—he bought some penny candy off'n the wagon at lunchtime."

"I remember him now. Red-haired boy. Stands out in a crowd."

I turned to Frank Tilley. "Any other redheads in the class?"

"Not like Tommy. His hair's like a fire engine."

"So he bought some penny candy from you?" I asked Tilley.

"Sure did."

"Then what?"

"Him an' Frank went runnin' back up the hill. I watched them a bit till they started swingin'. Then I got old Daisy here movin' along."

"So you weren't there when he disappeared?"

"No, I was long gone."

"Did you see anyone else on the road? Another wagon maybe?"

"Not a one."

"Mr. Tilley, I been up talkin' to the teacher, Mrs. Sawyer. She claims Tommy was swingin' on the swings and then he just disappeared. She claims there was noplace he could have gone where she wouldn't have seen him."

The peddler shrugged. "Mebbe he went to the outhouse."

"She looked there. She looked everywhere. And if he'd run down the hill she'd have seen him. She's positive."

"Well, he sure wasn't kidnaped by no aeroplane!"

"No," I agreed. I was staring through the twilight at the houses up on Turk Hill, thinking about Sheriff Lens and his plan to raid the Leotard place. Suddenly I had an idea. "Mr. Tilley, do you ever call on the hermit up there?"

"Ain't seen him in months. Don't think he lives there any more."

"Could we ride up and take a look?"

"Right now?"

"Right now."

I got up on the seat next to Mr. Tilley, while young Frank opened the rear doors and climbed into the back of the wagon. My car would be safe where it was, and I knew I'd attract far less attention approaching Turk Hill on Tilley's wagon.

By the time we reached the hermit's place it was growing dark. Tilley clanged his bell and called out, "Household goods, candy, pots an' pans. Knives sharpened, repairs made, electrical gadgets put in order!"

This last seemed unnecessary, since there were no electrical lines running into the hermit's house. The hermit had a name, Old Josh, but hardly anyone ever called him that. He was just the hermit of Northmont and word was he might have been a deserter hiding out since the Spanish-American War.

Now I ran around the far side of Mr. Tilley's wagon and into the tall grass. I didn't want to get a shotgun blast from one of the windows, either from the hermit or the kidnapers I thought might be there. I made a wide careful circle to the back door and was surprised to find it unlocked. Opening it slowly, I went in on my hands and knees. An odor of rank must hit my nostrils, but there was no sound.

With barely enough twilight left to see my way around, I rose quickly to my feet and made my way through the rooms cluttered with broken-down furniture, dirty plates, and dusty newspapers. One paper I picked up was more than a year old, and it seemed unlikely that the hermit of Turk Hill had received any recent visitors.

I opened the door to the cellar steps, and that was when the odor hit me. I'd been a doctor long enough to recognize it as that of a body long dead. Old Josh was crumpled at the bottom of the stairs, where he'd fallen and died months ago. There were no kidnapers here—only a lonely old man who'd died alone.

Outside, Tilley had started ringing his bell again—as if to summon me. I went out and he came runnin' up. "There's somethin' goin' on at the Leotard place. I thought I heard a shot."

"Stay here," I told him. "I'll go see."

It was only a short distance across the fields to the Leotard house, and before I was halfway there I could make out the sheriff's car in the rutted driveway. There was some sort of commotion, and a good deal of shoutin', but Sheriff Lens seemed to have matters firmly in hand. He was standin' in the light from his car's headlamps, holding a long-barreled revolver pointed straight at Marcel Leotard. The young French-Canadian stood with his hands raised above his head.

"Hello, Dr. Sam," the sheriff greeted me. "You're just in time."

"Did you find the boy?"

"Well, no. But my men are still searchin' the outbuildings. He's gotta be here somewhere. We already uncovered a couple of cases o' bootleg whiskey."

Leotard tried to lower his hands. "This is an insult! I know nothing of any kidnaping. I did not even know the boy was missing!''

''The kidnapers used your telephone,'' Sheriff Lens informed him.

''Impossible!''

''Why'd you take a shot at me when we drove up?''

''I—I thought it was someone after the whiskey.''

A deputy came back from the barn, swingin' a glowin' lantern. ''Nothin' back there, Sheriff, 'cept some copper tubing and big vats. Looks like he does a bit o' moonshinin' at times.''

Leotard took a step forward and Lens jabbed him with the barrel of his gun. ''You just hold it there if you don't want to be a dead man! We're takin' you into town for questionin'.''

When the deputies had the handcuffs on him, I told Lens about my discovery at the hermit's house. ''Think somebody killed him?'' the sheriff asked.

''No sign of it. A man his age probably got dizzy and fell down the stairs. Then he couldn't get up. Not a pleasant way to die, all alone like that.''

''What took you over there?''

''Leotard's place seemed too obvious. I got to thinkin' the kidnapers could be somewhere nearby, cutting into the Leotard telephone line for their messages. The hermit's place seemed the most likely, but I was wrong.''

Sheriff Lens snorted. ''Got any other fine ideas?''

''Just one.''

''What's that?''

''Maybe Jinny on the switchboard lied about those calls.''

Sheriff Lens sent a couple of deputies over to the hermit's house, and I retrieved my car and followed behind him as he drove Leotard into town. He locked him in a cell, promising to return soon, and then the two of us walked down the block to the wooden telephone exchange building where Jinny was on duty.

She was one of those stocky middle-aged women given to loud talk and too much beer. I liked her, and she'd been a patient of mine off and on, but right now I had to treat her like a suspect. "We have to know about that call, Jinny," I said. "It didn't come from the Leotard place."

"It darn well did!" she answered indignantly.

"I'm not saying you lied, and neither is the sheriff. But maybe you made a mistake."

"No mistake. It came from Leotard's. Look, it just lit up agin!"

I stared in fascinated disbelief at the switchboard. A tiny red light was glowing above the name *Leotard*. "Answer it."

She plugged in and I picked up the earphones. It was the same harsh voice. "Give me the Belmont house."

"One moment," Jinny said, her hand trembling to make the connection.

I could hear only the breathing of the kidnaper. Then Herb Belmont came on the line. "Hello?"

"Do you have the fifty thousand?"

"Yes, I have it. Is Tommy all right? Let me talk to him."

"I want no more raids by Sheriff Lens, or your son dies. Understand that?"

"Yes."

"Put the fifty thousand dollars—in unmarked bills—into a Gladstone bag or a small suitcase. I want that doctor, Sam Hawthorne, to deliver it at midnight tonight. He's to come alone to the red schoolhouse and leave the bag of money by the door. Then he's to drive away. If anyone tries to interfere, the boy dies. Understand?"

"Yes. But is he all right?"

The connection was broken without an answer from the kidnaper. Sheriff Lens, who'd been listening too, looked at me. "I guess you're elected, Doc."

But at the moment I was more interested in who'd made the call—and from where. "Jinny, is it possible these name tags were switched? Could this be someone else's line?"

"No, it's Leotard's, all right. The only other phone on Turk Hill is at the Deasey place."

I remembered Robert Deasey. I shouldn't have forgotten him

for so long. "The Deasey place . . ."

"You want to go up there?" Sheriff Lens asked.

"First we'd better check in at the Belmont farm and tell them what's been happening."

Mrs. Sawyer, the teacher, had joined the anxious circle at the Belmont house by the time we arrived. I could see she was trying to comfort the missing boy's mother, but she was having a difficult time of it.

"I hold myself responsible," Mrs. Sawyer said. "Something happened there that I didn't see, didn't notice. The kidnapers got to him somehow "

"You can't blame yourself," I said.

"But I do!"

"Try to think," I said. "Was there anything you forgot to tell me, anything about those last minutes when you saw Tommy on the swing?"

"No."

"Was he looking at you?"

"No, he was facing the other way."

"Is there a cellar under the school where he might have hidden?"

"No."

"A nearby cave where the children played?"

"There's nothing like that, Dr. Sam—nothing at all!"

"And yet the kidnaper wants the money delivered back at the school. He must have some way of getting it."

While we talked, Herb Belmont had been busy packing bundles of currency into a black Gladstone bag. "I'm about ready with this, Dr. Sam."

"It's only ten o'clock. We've got two hours yet."

"You got another idea?" Sheriff Lens asked.

"Just one—the Deasey place."

I drove up Turk Hill as I had that afternoon, stopping in front of Mrs. Deasey's farmhouse. She heard the car and came to the door to see who it was.

"Oh, Dr. Sam! I wasn't expectin' you again tonight."

"How's Robert? Is he asleep?"

"I put him to bed, but he's still awake."

"I'd like to see him again if I could."

"Dr. Sam, you don't think he's been—well, imaginin' things, do you?"

"We'll see." I followed her to the small back bedroom on the ground floor. Robert sat up in bed as soon as we entered the room.

"What is it?" he asked.

"Only Dr. Sam again, honey. He wants to see how you're feelin'."

"Leave me alone with him," I suggested, and she returned to the living room.

"Am I really sick, Dr. Sam?" the boy asked.

"That's something you've got to tell me."

"I can't sleep."

"Maybe if you told me what happened today—"

"No!"

"You said earlier it was about Tommy Belmont, but you couldn't have known then he'd been kidnaped. What was it about Tommy that frightened you so?"

He turned his face to the pillow. "Nuthin'."

"Did you see him disappear?"

"No."

"Well, what then?"

"My mom always says I imagine things. She says if I keep imaginin' things I'll end up in an insane asylum like my dad."

"And that's why you don't want to tell anyone what you saw?"

He nodded, his bobbing head caught by the moonlight streaming through the window. I took his hand and held it tight. "I promise no one's going to send you away for telling me what you saw, Robert. You believe me, don't you?"

"I guess so, Dr. Sam."

"Then tell me. Did you see Tommy disappear?"

"You won't believe me when I tell you."

"Try me anyway."

I could feel his hand tighten in mine. "You see, Dr. Sam, it wasn't that Tommy disappeared at all. It was that I saw two of him."

"Two of him," I repeated.

"Do you believe me, Dr. Sam?"

"I believe you, Robert."

At ten minutes before midnight I parked the Pierce-Arrow at the foot of the little hill and lifted the Gladstone bag from the seat next to me. In the darkness I could barely make out the shape of the little red schoolhouse ahead. Even the moon had sought shelter behind a cloud, and I dared not risk using the lantern I'd brought in the car.

There seemed to be no one around when I reached the door of the one-room schoolhouse and dropped my satchel. I hesitated only an instant and then headed back down the hill. This was the tricky phase of it, when a rash move on my part could endanger the boy's life.

I climbed back into my car and started the motor. "How'd it go?" Sheriff Lens asked in a whisper. He was crouched down in the passenger's seat, half on the floor.

"No sign of anybody."

"He'll come. He ain't goin' to let that fifty grand just sit there."

Then I saw it—a flash of movement on the hill. The moon had come out from behind the clouds, bathing the landscape in a pale unnatural light. "It's a child!" I said.

Lens was up beside me, his pistol out. "Damned if it ain't the Belmont kid! They sent him to collect his own ransom!"

"Go after him, Sheriff, but be careful."

He jumped out of the car. "What about you?"

"I've got bigger game." I gunned the Pierce-Arrow forward, bumping over the dirt road and rounding a bend.

Ahead of me, targeted in the headlamps, I saw what I'd expected. Pulled up out of sight, under a sheltering willow tree, was Mr. Tilley's wagon. Tilley himself had heard my car approaching. He jumped down from the wagon, taking aim at me with a shotgun.

I jammed the accelerator to the floor and headed straight at him. The roar of the shotgun exploded in front of me, blasting away the right side of my windshield. But then the car hit him, pinning him against his own wagon.

I leaped out and grabbed the shotgun before he could reload. "Damn!" he screamed. "You near killed me with that car! My leg—"

"Shut up and be glad you're alive. I'll take care of your leg."

Sheriff Lens came over the hill then, gripping the red-haired lad with an iron fist and carrying the Gladstone bag with his other hand. "This ain't the Belmont boy!" he called out.

"I know," I told him. "It's Tilley's son Frank, wearin' a bright red wig. Unless I'm mistaken, we're goin' to find Tommy Belmont tied up in this wagon."

It was one o'clock in the mornin' back at the Belmont farm, but it might as well have been high noon from the number of people around the place. Tommy had been in the wagon, all right, bound and gagged, and drugged with sleeping powders. He was still drowsy, but I knew he'd be okay.

His father and Sheriff Lens and Mrs. Sawyer all had questions. Finally I just held up my hands and quieted them. "Calm down now and I'll tell you the whole thing from the beginning."

"I want to know how he vanished from my schoolhouse yard," Mrs. Sawyer said, "before I go out of my mind."

"Tommy was actually kidnaped about ten minutes before you noticed him missing from the swing. He was kidnaped when he went down the hill with the other children to buy candy from Mr. Tilley's wagon. Tilley drugged him with a piece of candy and put him in the back of the wagon. Then Tilley's son Frank took his place, wearing a red wig and with a few freckles painted on his face."

"And nobody saw this happen?"

"Mrs. Deasey's son Robert saw it, but he was afraid to tell anyone there'd been two Tommy Belmonts down by that wagon. The false Tommy ran up the hill and began to swing, while the real Tommy was taken away in Tilley's wagon."

"But it was *Tommy* on the swing!" Mrs. Sawyer protested.

I shook my head. "It was a boy dressed like the others, more or less, and with bright red hair. You saw the hair and not the face. Tommy was your only red-haired pupil, so you assumed the boy you saw was Tommy. But you should have known better. When I talked to you earlier you told me Tommy had been swinging higher than you'd ever seen him go before. Why? Because it wasn't Tommy."

"But how'd he disappear?"

"In the simplest way possible. When you turned your head and called the children back into the schoolhouse, Frank Tilley made sure no one was looking, took off the wig, and stuffed it under his shirt. Maybe he wiped off his painted freckles too, with his handkerchief."

"All right," Sheriff Lens conceded. "But what about those telephone calls?"

"Tilley knew all about electrical repairs, remember? He knew about telephones too. He tapped into the line from near the Leotard place to make his calls. He worked right from his wagon all the time, while Tommy was tied up and drugged in the back of it. When he needed a boy to scream into the telephone, he used his son to imitate Tommy."

"How'd you know it was Tilley?" Lens asked.

"His wagon was up around Turk Hill when the ransom calls were made. And I was suspicious when he said he watched Tommy and his son run back up the schoolhouse hill and start swingin' together. Mrs. Sawyer had already told me Tommy was swingin' alone, and she had no reason to lie about it. Once I decided Tommy must have been kidnaped earlier than she realized, Tilley was the only suspect. No one else had come near the school at noon. No one else had a wagon to carry the boy away.

The whole business of the mysterious vanishin' was just a ruse to change the *time* of the kidnapin' so we wouldn't think about Tilley, so Tilley could be away from the scene of the crime."

"How'd he expect to get away with it?"

"By tappin' into the telephone lines for his ransom calls, he figured to keep us chasin' around the countryside till he had the money. Then he'd high-tail it out of here fast before Tommy could tell us what happened." I didn't raise the possibility that Tilley might have planned to kill Tommy to keep him from talkin'.

"What'll happen to Tilley's son?" Herb Belmont asked.

"That's for the courts to decide," I replied.

"They found a foster home for the Tilley boy in the next town (Dr. Sam concluded), and with a normal family life he turned out right well. His father drew a long sentence, comin' so soon after Leopold and Loeb, and he died in prison.

"I thought that would be enough crime for the year 1925, but I thought wrong. Next time you come by—another small, ah, libation before you go?—I'll tell you about the strange things that happened at the town church—and on Christmas Day, at that!"

The Disappearance of Maggie

TALMAGE POWELL

The central plot element of "The Disappearance of Maggie" is the same as that of the previous story by Edward D. Hoch: the seemingly impossible disappearance of a child from under the watchful eyes of a teacher. We chose to include both stories here, back to back, because Talmage Powell's handling and explanation of the subject are wholly different from Hoch's; and to demonstrate how writers, working independently of each other, sometimes hit on a similar idea and yet make of it dissimilar stories. Powell has been a professional writer for five decades (he made his first sale, to a pulp, in 1943) and has a long and impressive list of accomplishments that include five hundred published stories and sixteen novels. Among his books are five featuring a well-drawn Tampa private detective named Ed Rivers, perhaps the best of which is The Girl's Number Doesn't Answer *(1960).*

"SHERIFF, the child simply *disappeared*," Miss Crimm said, in her helplessness to arrive at any other explanation.

Responding to her call, David Landsburg had met with the teacher in the privacy of an anteroom off the principal's office of Edney Elementary School. The window beside him overlooked the playground, where noisy children were making the most of a morning recess on a perfect spring day.

"Miss Crimm, little girls, like little boys, are pretty rugged creatures—hardly subject to disappearance."

"Of course!" the diminutive, graying, worried figure snapped. Then Miss Crimm sighed. "It's just that I'm so concerned for Maggie Malone. A teacher should retain complete objectivity, but in Maggie's case it's been difficult. So fine a little girl . . . saddled with such parents . . . she knows the meaning of hardship, Sheriff, the kind that really hurts."

"Let's get back to the beginning," David said, "to the schoolbus that Maggie Malone rides. It arrived on schedule this morning."

"Precisely. As usual."

"You had parked in the teacher's parking area and were crossing the schoolground. You saw the bus stop, the door open. You watched the children get off. You noted that Maggie Malone was not among the arrivals."

"Hers is the first face I look for, Sheriff, sometimes wondering what the hours have held for the child since I last saw her. She did not get off that bus—and I wondered if she was going without breakfast while attending a hungover mother."

"You attached no special significance to her absence at the time?"

"No, nothing special. She misses a lot of school, through no fault of her own. She likes school, books, learning. Very intelligent. Keeps up her work if she has only half a chance. But not bookish. She's friendly, affectionate, outgoing, popular with her classmates. Lively spirit, and Lord knows how . . . a rare child, Sheriff."

Miss Crimm's frosty blue gaze flickered to the window as though searching for a nonexistent figure among the boisterous playground games. "I marked it down in my mind as another bad day for Maggie, and started classes. During rollcall I omitted Maggie's name, and Stephanie Smith said, 'Did you send Maggie someplace, Miss Crimm?' And I said, 'No, dear, how could I send her when she isn't here?' To that, Stephanie muttered, 'She was on the bus,' somewhat as if Maggie and I had conspired to let her skip class."

Miss Crimm nervously tucked in an errant wisp of gray at her temple. "I put Stephanie's remark down to a childish mistake, but it stayed on my mind, and just before recess I simply had to say a word about it. I asked Stephanie why she had fibbed, and she flashed back that she hadn't, because Maggie *had* been on the schoolbus. Several of the children backed up Stephanie's statement. Gary London had ridden beside her. He said Maggie had dropped her pencil and told him to get his big feet out of the way so she could scrounge under the seat."

Miss Crimm turned from the view of the schoolground. "I tried to pass the incident off as the children filed out. But in the teacher's lounge I found I didn't want my usual coffee during the break. I was getting more upset by the minute. Jumping at shadows perhaps . . . but I decided it would be better to call you, Sheriff, and cry wolf than not to call and discover later that something inexplicable, perhaps dreadful, had really happened."

"You did the right thing," David said. "I wish everyone would stitch-in-time with the sheriff's office."

He took Miss Crimm's hand in his. "Don't worry. We'll probably discover that she slipped out of the pack for the truant freedom of a rare, lovely day."

Miss Crimm's attractive elderly head snapped a movement of absolute negative. "She did not sneak off. I saw the loaded bus as it pulled in. I saw the door open. I witnessed the emergence of every single child. I watched the empty bus trundle off to the county garage. Maggie Malone had been on that schoolbus—but she did not get off. I would back the statement with my life, Sheriff."

David believed her.

Carly Tillons was hosing down a schoolbus when David pulled into the sprawling complex where county vehicles were serviced.

A lanky, rawboned figure in poplin pants and shirt, Carly glanced over his shoulder. The reddish cast of his lean face and curly hair made David think of rust.

" 'Morning, Sheriff."

"Got a minute, Carly?"

"Sure." Carly twisted the hose nozzle, turning off the stream of water. He tossed the hose aside, wiped his palms on his poplin-covered thighs, and fished a partially smoked cigar from his shirt pocket.

"What can I do for you, Sheriff?" Carly's blue eyes held that vague look that always came into them when he looked at David. He'd voted for David, but that didn't mean he liked David's image. David was young, lean, and always dressed in a conservative business suit—crisp and cool, as though he never sweated. Sheriffs were supposed to be big-gutted and rumpled, equipped with amber eyeshades, a tough snarl, and a gravelly voice. It was easier to imagine David doing a television commercial for aftershave.

"You drove Number Sixteen this morning, Carly?"

"Sure, just like always."

"Was Maggie Malone a passenger?"

"Sure was." Carly struck a match and looked at David through the first puff of cigar smoke. "How come you ask?"

"I want you to be very certain, Carly."

"Am I certain you're standing here?"

"I would hope so."

"Then," Carly said, "you can take my word that Maggie

Malone got on the bus this morning and rode to school. I can't be mistaken. She didn't board at the usual stop. She came running to the corner, jumping up and down to make sure I saw her. I stopped and let her on. Told her the corner was a no-no, not a regular stop, and she knew better than to pull a prank like that. She thanked me with a shy little smile. Some kid, that Maggie."

Carly, David knew, meant that Maggie Malone was a darling little girl; but words like "darling" weren't in Carly's vocabulary.

"Which corner, Carly? Pinpoint the location where she got on the bus."

"Corner of Henderson and Macon."

"Then what?"

"What do you mean, then what?"

"Anything unusual occur?"

"Nope," Carly said. "Maggie just squeezed along the aisle and sat down. Kids their usual selves—laughing, talking, couple rapscallions sticking out their tongues at people in passing cars, like always."

"Did Maggie get off the bus between the corner and Edney Elementary?"

"Hell, nobody got off the bus. The schoolground itself was the next stop for Number Sixteen."

"Emergency door open at any time?"

"Now what the hell kind of question is that?"

"Okay," David said, a new tightness creeping into his tone. "We can guarantee that Maggie Malone got on the bus and the bus was sealed until you pulled into the schoolground and opened the door for the kids to get off."

"You've spelled it, Sheriff. Look, why the questions? What's going on?"

"That's what I intend to find out," David said. "Did you see Maggie get off the bus?"

"They all got off. Gang of kids. Poured out of the bus. Bill Ramey had pulled his bus in behind mine. We passed a word,

Bill and me, while the buses emptied. I got back behind the wheel of Number Sixteen and looked the crate over to make sure it was empty and I didn't have a straggler. Then I drove her over here and went and had myself a morning coffee at Ownby's Diner."

"Where is Sixteen, Carly?"

Carly pointed with a jerk of his head. "Third grillwork along the row."

David crossed from the concrete apron to the line of parked buses. He entered Number Sixteen, shoulders slightly stooped because of his height, while Carly watched from the door.

"Looking for something, Sheriff?"

"One of her classmates told Miss Crimm that Maggie dropped a pencil. Where was Maggie sitting?"

"Toward the back. About where you're standing."

David bent his knees and body. The seats were thin cushions on tubular frames, with about a dozen inches separating the cushions from the floor. Crouched very low, David fished a hand beneath the seat. His fingers bumped a small rattle from a pencil. He coaxed the pencil with his fingertips and stood up, holding it.

"Didn't get her pencil, I see," Carly said, leaning in the open door. He shook his head. "You'd be surprised, the stuff we find under them seats."

At such a tense moment David didn't feel he would be very much surprised by anything.

Armed with useless school-record statistics concerning Maggie Malone, David turned off Henderson into the littered sprawl of Walker View, a public housing development.

Looking for a number, he cruised the narrow, pot-holed driveways that webbed the barrackslike buildings together. He pulled over in front of Building H. He got out, his senses assaulted by the aura of hopeless poverty, and mounted the low stoop of apartment H-2.

The buzzer button had long since been ripped out, leaving two thin wires dangling. David made a fist and banged on the door.

Carelessly latched, the door creaked ajar under the impact of his knuckles. He poked his head in. "Mrs. Malone?"

He heard the steady drip of water from a leaky faucet. The apartment smelled stale, sour.

"Anybody home?"

A human voice garbled a sound. David took it as an invitation and stepped inside. The living room held a closed-in twilight and a few pieces of broken-down furniture were scattered about. There was a crawly feeling of dust. A few flies buzzed about food remains on the dinette table.

"Hey, Mrs. Malone! Important! Sheriff David Landsburg. It's about Maggie."

"Go 'way."

He trailed the thick, barely coherent sound to the open bedroom doorway.

A young woman was wriggling against the unkempt bed, fumbling to pull a limp, dingy pillow over her head. David looked at the too-thin lines of the body in the faded jeans and dirty halter top, the small pale face, the matted brunette hair. Motherhood. He caught a vision of Maggie's mother five years ago, very pretty; five years from now, a premature hag.

Wondering what she was zonked on, he pulled the pillow from her thin, clutching fingers.

"Le' me alone! Le' me alone!" Her daintily boned, slightly dirty bare feet kicked in a tantrum.

David took a heavy breath, knowing that, for now, he might as well try talking to the dripping faucet. There was a telephone on the beside table. He picked up the receiver and dialed the number for a rescue squad ambulance.

Arch Malone was resting on the back barstool, winding up a joke for a guffawing prenoon beer drinker as David entered the gloomy hops-and-yeast smell of My Father's Mustache.

Malone felt the new presence at the end of the bar and turned his head. He raised his buttocks from the barstool, standing up slowly, suspiciously. The business suit, white shirt, and necktie were not common to the habitués of Mustache.

"Looking for somebody, fella?"

"You Arch Malone?"

"Right on."

"I'd like to talk to you for a minute."

Malone lifted a brow, shrugged, and came along the inside of the bar, tossing his grayish barcloth carelessly across his shoulder.

About thirty, David guessed. Strapping husky. A pair of shoulders and biceps in the tight, knitted shirt. A macho face beneath the tousle of curly black hair. An unconscious swagger in the gait.

David flipped open his I.D. and Malone's eyes went deliberately blank at the sight of the small gold badge. He stood with bravado, spread-legged, twisting his bar towel into a thick rope and slapping it in slow rhythm across his other palm.

David might have been amused, but the circumstances were wrong. He thrust out his hand and caught the towel, then jerked it loose and tossed it down the bar.

Malone looked at the crumpled rag, touching his teeth with his tongue tip. "That bitch send you, Sheriff? I told her I'd break her stinking neck if she tried taking out any papers on me."

"Maggie is the focus of my interest, Mr. Malone."

"So Hazel went and did it! Okay, okay! So serve your child-support paper and I'll talk to His Honor. I'll settle that junkie's hash for good!"

"When did you last see Maggie?"

"Not since I threw the bitch and brat out. I'm not the dumb sucker Hazel played me for. All that time, buying groceries for a kid Hazel said was mine. Suspected it, pally, from the brat's first bleat. Kept after Hazel, and when she finally admitted the truth . . ." Malone jerked a thumb across his shoulder. "That cut it. And when old Arch makes up his mind, his mind is made up for good."

"Maggie has disappeared, Mr. Malone."

"So? What business is it of mine? Maybe she got smart and ran away. Last I heard, Hazel had moved into public housing and was freeloading with the brat at the taxpayer's trough. So, okay. I could care less. I don't want to see her or that brat ever again. Got my own thing to do, and it don't include taking care of some s.o.b.'s leavings."

"You're quite a man, Arch," David said. He reached across the bar and laid his hand on Malone's arm with bruising finger pressure. "Favor me by running afoul of the law sometime."

Miss Crimm was lunching at a corner table in the Edney Elementary cafeteria. David made his way across the lunchroom, which was busy with the noisy clatter of dishes and silver. He sat down across from Miss Crimm, and shook his head in negative response to the question in the teacher's eyes.

"Got an All Points Bulletin out on Maggie, a mother under guard at the drug center, and a papa who claims he isn't. At least . . ."

"Yes, Sheriff?"

"No young bodies have turned up today."

Miss Crimm reached over. "You'll find her, I know you will! The child surely deserves it. She has had so little."

David looked at the small hand covering his own on the table top.

"Maggie boarded the bus at Henderson and Macon," he said. "Have you any idea why that corner? What was she doing in that neighborhood? Why did she get on the bus at that particular location?"

"She probably had been at Laura Parker's house, Sheriff."

"Who is Laura Parker?"

"A friend of Maggie's. They met one afternoon in the park.

Sometimes Mrs. Parker would drive Maggie to school. On those mornings, I'm sure, she'd given Maggie a decent breakfast."

"How well do you know Laura Parker?"

"Not very. We've chatted a time or two, whenever she'd bring Maggie to school. Nice person. Quiet. Lovely. And very fond of Maggie."

"She must live near the Henderson-Macon intersection," David said. "Do you know the address?"

"Sorry, I don't."

"Well, there's always the city directory."

As David started to rise, Miss Crimm looked up sharply. "There is one thing . . . Mrs. Parker mentioned one morning that if she didn't hurry along she was going to be late for work at *Mountaintops*."

The magazine was an excellent regional publication.

David did his telephoning from the principal's office. Laura Parker, he learned, was a features editor, and when he got past the receptionist-secretary, David said, "Mrs. Parker, David Landsburg the sheriff here. I would like to speak to you about Margaret Malone."

"Yes, of course." A sudden tautness in the added words: "Has something happened?"

"I'd rather discuss it in person."

"I was on the point of leaving for lunch. I usually snack at home. Will you meet me there right away?"

"What is the address?"

"Seven-sixteen Hollybrook. Just off Macon."

The house was an unpretentious rancher reflecting friendliness in its brown tones and white shutters, its comfortably informal living room, its slightly jumbled bookcase, the hibachi dusted in gray charcoal ash set in the fireplace.

Laura Parker had opened the front door as David parked behind her modest station wagon. The anxious look in her eyes drew him inside. He guessed she was about thirty. Hard to tell.

She was one of those tallish, attractive women with even features and a flawless complexion, who age like a fine wine.

In the middle of the living room, David said, "Let me tell you about it before you start asking questions. Maggie Malone boarded a schoolbus this morning at the corner. Nothing unusual happened on the bus. Yet when the bus pulled in at Edney Elementary, Maggie had vanished."

He saw a fearful darkness tinge her eyes. He thought: Surrogate mother. More real than the woman who births because she's accidentally and unintentionally pregnant.

"How could that be? What could have happened to Maggie?"

"I'm trying to find out," David said.

He saw the sudden fine sweat against the smooth skin of her forehead. Don't think of the monsters that sometimes seem to fill the world, he thought. Don't let in the images of little girls, and boys, found dead, mangled, violated . . .

As if sharing the thought, she asked in a voice of forced steadiness, "Have you any evidence that Maggie has been harmed?"

"No, none whatever." No evidence—not yet.

She sank onto the edge of the tweedy couch.

"Maggie left this house today to catch the bus?" David asked.

"Yes." She heard the muffled quality of the word. She cleared her throat, looked up at him. "Yes. She was here for breakfast . . . and dinner last night. She spent the night here. We did her homework, played Atari . . . talked about the job I've been offered in Atlanta."

"Then she comes here often."

"Yes . . . as if it were her real home. You see . . . she is like my own, in a manner of speaking."

"I see."

Laura Parker drew a breath. "I lost my own daughter two years ago—and my husband. It was a weekend on the lake. A wind came up. The boat—it capsized."

"I understand," David said, sparing her the telling of further details.

Her gaze slipped away, glistening with tears. "Maggie and I met on a beautiful day in Henderson Park. She'd been racing in a game of tag. Had fallen. Skinned her knee, badly. Brave little girl. She refused to cry. When I learned she was in the park alone, we walked over here and I dressed the knee. I offered her cookies and milk, and the child was famished. We had a good dinner and I took her home. She asked me if she could come see me again. Gradually, there was a . . . a belonging . . ."

Laura Parker gazed about the room, hearing the echoes of a little girl's voice. "She was a part of this place, when she was able."

"When wasn't she able, Mrs. Parker?"

"Her mother had a senseless hatred of me," Laura Parker said.

"Rage of the have-nots for the haves," David said. "In this case, having the love of a child."

"But her mother didn't want her. Why should she care where Maggie turned?"

"Perhaps she couldn't face the fact that Maggie was worthy of love. Who knows?"

"Worthy?" Laura stood up. "This morning I thrashed it out with myself. I decided not to take the job in Atlanta. Faced with it, I knew I would miss Maggie too much. But now the question is quite irrelevant, isn't it? Will I ever have the chance to tell Maggie?"

"I believe you will. I think I'm beginning to understand what happened to Maggie Malone this morning," David said. "Does Maggie have a key to this house?"

"She knows where the spare key is hidden in the carport."

"And your natural daughter's room? Have you changed it very much since she was taken from you? Is it still essentially a child's room? Maggie's room?"

She turned her hard gaze away from his face. She went into the hallway, reaching the bedroom door a step ahead of David.

He saw the flash of small sneakers disappearing under the bed. He flopped to his hands and knees, flipped back the side of the counterpane, and looked directly into a small, snub-nosed face that was white with fear and anger.

"You come out from under there, young lady!" He reached a hand to drag Maggie out. She squirmed away, moving toward the farther side of the bed.

When David stood, Maggie had her arms locked about Laura Parker's waist. She threw a stricken look in David's direction. "Don't let the hookey man get me! I just wanted to be here and go to Atlanta."

Laura sat on the edge of the bed, drawing Maggie to eye-level beside her. "Hush that wailing," Laura delivered the order in a voice that was shaky with relief after the dose of fright. "You're a big girl now, not a crybaby. Anyhow, he isn't a truant officer. He's our sheriff and he's been looking for you because you scared us to death."

"You mean," Maggie ventured, "he isn't going to send me to juvenile hall for playing hookey?"

"Of course not, but I wouldn't blame him if he gave you a sound spanking!" Laura looked at David. "How did she manage it?"

"With aplomb, intelligence, and innate creativity," David said. "She got on the bus thinking about Atlanta. Before she reached school, the prospect of separation had become overpowering. She'd dropped a pencil, and bending down to retrieve it, the space beneath the schoolbus seat beckoned. Such a hiding place! In the hustle of all the other kids getting off, she lingered, fetching her pencil. Only the pencil didn't matter any longer. She hid under the seat, and nobody at the time had any reason to think of looking for her. The driver boarded the bus, saw it apparently empty, and drove to the parking lot. While the driver was off having a cup of coffee in Ownby's Diner, Maggie had the chance to disembark without being seen. She headed for seven-sixteen Hollybrook, and the spare key that would let her into the house, into the room on which she'd laid claim."

Laura swept a wisp of sweaty dark brown hair from Maggie's forehead. "Sheriff, what would be the reaction of your office to a woman who set about having a mother declared unfit and adopting a child?''

''Adoption is a civil matter, but on behalf of a woman like that, my office would be glad to provide evidence of unfitness,'' David said. ''You can count on that.''

''I will,'' Laura Parker said.

Turning his car out of the driveway of seven-sixteen Hollybrook, David thought about the business of being sheriff. You saw the blood from the knifings, the shootings, the auto smash-ups. You went into dark alleys with drawn gun and heart in your throat. You took a little longer getting to sleep at night now and then because the screams of a rape victim or a mugger's target were too close in time, too fresh in mind.

But there were other times.

Small moments.

Like today.

A Matter of Scholarship

ANTHONY BOUCHER

First published in Ellery Queen's Mystery Magazine *in 1955, this clever academic vignette was conceived as an exercise to prove that a full-bodied crime story could, indeed, be written in no more than a few hundred words. Its author, Anthony Boucher (1911–1968), was a true Renaissance man: a master of several languages, a dedicated opera lover and critic, an incisive book reviewer, a creative editor and anthologist, a poker player non-pareil, and of course a fine writer. Among his novels are* The Case of the Seven of Calvary *(1937),* The Case of the Baker Street Irregulars *(1940), and* Rocket to the Morgue *(1942, as H. H. Holmes). A long-overdue collection of his short crime fiction was published in 1983, under the title* Exeunt Murderers.

No scholar can pretend to absolute completeness, but every scholarly work must be as nearly complete as possible; any omission of available data because of carelessness, inadequate research, or (most damning of all) personal motives—such as the support of a theory which the data might contradict—is the blackest sin against scholarship itself . . .

Such were my thoughts as I sat working on my definitive MURDEROUS TENDENCIES IN THE ABNORMALLY GIFTED: A STUDY OF THE HOMICIDES COMMITTED BY ARTISTS AND SCHOLARS. The date was October 21, 1951. The place was my office in Wortley Hall on the campus of the University.

My conclusions seemed unassailable: Murder had been committed by eminent scholars (one need only allude to Professor Webster of Harvard) and by admirable artists (François Villon leaps first to the mind). But in no case had the motivation been connected with the abnormal gift; my study of the relationship between homicidal tendencies and unusual endowments established, in the best scholarly tradition, that no such relationship existed.

It was then that Stuart Danvers entered my office. "Professor Jordan?" he asked. His speech was blurred and he swayed slightly. "I read your piece in the *Atlantic* on Villon [it sounded like *villain*] and I said to myself, 'There's the guy to help you.' " And before I could speak he had placed a large typewritten manuscript on my desk. "Understand," he went on, "I'm no novice at this. I'm a pro. I've sold fact-crime pieces to all the top editors." He hiccuped. "Only now it strikes me it's time for a little hard-cover prestige."

I stared at the title page, which read GENIUS IN GORE, and then began flipping through the book. The theme was my own. The style was lurid, the documentation inadequate. He had taken seriously the pretensions to learning of such frauds as Aram and Rulloff; he had omitted such a key figure as the composer

Gesualdo da Venosa. But I had read enough in the field to know that his abominable work was what is called "commercial." He would have no trouble in finding a publisher immediately; and my own book was scheduled by the University Press for, at best, "some time" in 1953.

"Little nip?" he suggested, and as I shook my head he drank from his flask. "Like it? Thought maybe you could help—well, sort of goose it with a couple of footnotes . . . *you* know."

I looked at this drunken, unscholarly lout. I saw myself eclipsed in his shadow, the merest epigone to his attack upon my chosen Thebes. And then he said, "Of course that's just a rough first draft, you understand."

"Do you keep a carbon of first drafts?" I asked idly. And when he shook his addled skull, I split that skull's forehead with my heavy paperweight. He stumbled back against the wall, lurched forward, and then collapsed. His head struck the desk. I tucked his obscene manuscript away, wrapped the paperweight in a handkerchief, carried it down the hall, washed it, flushed the handkerchief down the toilet, returned to my room, and called the police. A stranger had wandered into my office drunk, stumbled, and cracked his head against my desk.

The crime, if such it can be considered, was as nearly perfect as any of which I have knowledge. It is also unique in being the only instance of a crime committed by an eminent scholar which was *motivated* by his scholarship . . .

[*Excerpt from* MURDEROUS TENDENCIES IN THE ABNORMALLY GIFTED *(University Press, 1953), State's Exhibit A in the trial for murder of the late Professor Rodney Jordan.*]

Final Exam

BILL PRONZINI and BARRY N. MALZBERG

The collaborative team of Bill Pronzini and Barry N. Malzberg has consistently produced works of high quality, including the novels The Running of Beasts *(1976),* Acts of Mercy *(1977),* Night Screams *(1979), and* Prose Bowl *(1980). In addition, Pronzini and Malzberg have coedited a number of anthologies—among them* Shared Tomorrows *(1979), which brings together a dozen collaborative science fiction stories—and coauthored some forty short stories. "Final Exam" takes place not in a traditional academic setting, but rather in a Faginesque "school of the streets." In it, we see one man's unusual manner of testing a student's progress in his equally unusual subject. (M. M.)*

FOR HIS FINAL EXAM I take the Kid to Candlestick Park.

It is a bright and brisk fall Sunday, typical football weather in San Francisco. The 49ers are playing the Colts and the game is a sellout—fifty thousand fans, at least half of whom will soon be drunk on beer and all of whom will be deeply involved with the game and such matters as the point spread. It is an ideal location and the one where I always hold my finals.

"I want to start getting the money right now, Old Man," the Kid says to me after we pass through the turnstiles. He calls me the Old Man and I call him the Kid. This is part of our professional relationship, although I like to think that there are undertones of genuine affection between us. The Kid is my most recent and greatest student and every now and then, watching him operate, I see the 24-year-old me when the world was mine for the taking. But I sometimes suspect he pictures me as being over the hill and himself as the new king of the hill, which is why I am putting him through a final exam. I have had such brash and eager students before and some have not, it has turned out, properly learned their lessons; I am hoping the Kid is not one of these and that I will not be forced to fail him as a result.

I say in answer to his question, "Remember what I've taught you, Kid. No more than two marks pre-game and no more than two during the half-time ceremonies. Save your major operations for the post-game exodus."

"Sure," the Kid says. "Whatever you say."

When we approach the tunnel to our section I nudge him and gesture to where a big man in a grey suit is lounging against the wall pretending to read a program. "See that fellow over there?" I say.

"What about him?"

"His name is Harrahan. He is one of Candlestick's security chiefs and also very difficult on people in our profession. Avoid him and anyone who looks like him—anyone who seems to be an easy mark. Easy-looking marks often turn out to be security officers or undercover cops."

"Right," the Kid says. "Nothing comes easy in this business, right? You always got to work hard for the money."

"Good," I say, and nod my approval.

I steer him away from Harrahan and the tunnel and over toward the crowded concession stands. The Kid eyes a fat man who is paying for a hot dog with money from an equally fat wallet, but I shake my head. The fat man is not a good mark because he is with a fat woman who has eyes like a television camera: they see everything and record it in detail. The Kid looks half annoyed and half disappointed, but says nothing.

After five minutes I select his first mark—a moustachioed gentleman with a preoccupied expression and an expensive camel's-hair coat folded across one arm. The Kid dips him deftly, so deftly that I almost miss the operation even though I am watching each of the Kid's moves. He has the greatest left-hand snag hook I have ever seen, and in his right thumb and forefinger there is magic. I once saw him lift a lady's pocketbook on a crowded bus while at the same time tipping his hat to a clergyman.

I allow him a second score, from a white-haired man with a hip flask, and give him a fatherly smile after he executes another perfect dip. He grins. "A piece of cake, Old Man," he says. "Let's go count up the swag."

"Patience, Kid," I say. "The game will be starting pretty soon. It's time to take our seats."

We go through our tunnel and come out into the seats near the thirty-yard line, midway up. The 49ers and the Colts are already on the field and the referees are about to reenact the coin flip. The Kid and I sit down, after which I unfold the blanket I am carrying and spread it over our laps. The wind at Candlestick Park is always cool and blustery on fall days and I have to be careful of my rheumatism. It is the rheumatism, of course, which has necessitated my retirement from active service and my new profession as teacher of young hopefuls.

The 49ers lose the coin toss and prepare to kick off to the Colts. While the teams are lining up, the Kid takes out the two wallets he has dipped and opens them under the blanket. His face quirks in disgust. "Forty-six dollars, total," he mutters to me. "Damn lousy take so far."

"Not to worry," I tell him, "We have a long afternoon ahead of us."

"Yeah, I guess so. But hell, Old Man, I want to get the money—the *real* money. That fat dude at the concession stand must have had two, three hundred in his wallet."

I give him a reproachful look. "The most important thing at this point in your career," I say, "is artistry. Haven't I explained that often enough? The act is its own reward; even in a rain forest Jean-Pierre Rampal would still play the flute."

"What's a rain forest?" the Kid says. "Who the hell is Jean-Pierre Rampal?"

Brilliant in many ways, he is ignorant of matters cultural. But this does not bother me; like wine and age, the command of the intellect will develop. Still, I seem to have detected a note of belligerence in his voice. Belligerence, ofttimes, is a sign of ingratitude; this will have to be watched more carefully as the day progresses.

The game has already begun and I give my attention to the conflict below. The 49ers intercept a pass, cannot move the ball, and settle for a 37-yard field goal. The Colts score a touchdown on a fifty-yard pass play to their wide receiver. The 49ers score a touchdown on a 22-yard pass play to their tight end. The first quarter ends with San Francisco leading 10–7.

The Kid, I have noticed, is uninterested in the game. He fidgets in his seat and his eyes roam the crowd in a restless way. "Relax," I say to him. "Enjoy the contest. Half time will arrive soon enough."

"I don't like football," the Kid says. "I don't give a damn for it. All I want is to get the money."

"That is all any of us want," I agree. "Nevertheless, too much anticipation can lead to mistakes. You're an artist, Kid, and there is no need for an artist to be overeager. The money will be there when the time comes."

"O.K., O.K." But I detect the note of belligerence in his voice again, along with something which sounds like annoyance. This makes me wonder if the Kid is no longer listening to my advice, if he feels he knows more than I do about the business. An unhappy prospect. I have never had such a brilliant student and to have to fail him would depress me a great deal.

Little happens in the second quarter of the game. The Colts manage to make a field goal to tie the score at 10–10 with three minutes remaining, and that is the tally when the teams leave the field for half time. As soon as the gun sounds, the Kid pushes the blanket aside and stands. His eyes are bright and determined and I watch his nimble fingers flex eagerly, as if they are already plucking wallets from the pockets of marks.

"I'm going to work, Old Man," he says.

I have already informed him that on this second part of his final exam—the half-time score, as it were—he will be on his own; I will wait here and he will choose his own marks. I nod. "Remember," I say, "no more than two. And make sure to watch out for—"

"Yeah, yeah, I know," the Kid says shortly. "Watch out for Harrahan and his boys, and watch out for pickings that look too easy. You think I'm stupid, Old Man? I don't need to be told things a hundred times." He pushes past me and hurries up the stairs to the tunnel.

I sigh, rearrange the blanket, and place my once-great hands beneath it to keep them warm. The half-time ceremonies at 49er games are usually interesting, but today I am unable to enjoy the marching bands and the dancing girls. My mind is occupied with the Kid and how he is doing on his exam.

He is gone for twenty minutes; the teams are already back on the field when he returns. He does not look at me as he slides past, sits down, and sips at a cup of beer.

I say, "All went well?"

"So-so. No sweat with the operations, but this is a goddamn cheap crowd, let me tell you. A hundred and six bucks and that's it."

This makes me frown. "Then you've already made an accounting," I say.

"Yeah. In one of the johns."

"Your instructions were to bring everything straight back here to me—"

"The hell with my instructions. I did it my own way for a change."

I say, tight-lipped, "What else did you do your own way, Kid? How many operations? It wasn't just two, was it?"

"No, and the hell with that too. I told you, it's a cheap crowd. Five scores and barely more than a C-note."

The belligerence is unveiled in his voice now and it is accompanied by a certain contempt. I feel sadness inside me, for there seems to be little doubt that I am going to have to fail the Kid. It is not too late for him to redeem himself—he may yet pass—but in my heart I sense that he is beyond redemption.

Neither of us has anything to say during the second half. I have lost my taste for football and I am not even cheered when the 49ers score a last-second touchdown on a run by O. J. Simpson to win the game 24–23. As before, the Kid is on his feet the instant the gun sounds. I watch him as he moves quickly up the aisle and see he has forgotten or chosen to ignore everything I have taught him. He does not even wait until he is inside the tunnel before he makes his first dip. But he is good, very good, and no one is aware of the operation, least of all the mark.

I follow him through the tunnel and around to the concession area. He works fast, with utter confidence and utter carelessness: four marks, five, six, seven. Wallets disappear into his pockets, along with a folder of traveler's checks, a money clip, and a digital calendar watch. It is a virtuoso performance, begun and completed within the space of eight minutes, and in one sense I am awed by the artistry of it. But in the last analysis, of course, I feel even more saddened and depressed because, for all its brilliance, it is the performance of a failure.

The Kid has hopelessly failed the exam.

But I determine to give him one last chance. Despite all his shortcomings, I am still impressed by his talents and am not quite able to shed the remnants of my fatherly affection for him. I approach him near the main turnstiles and place my hand on his arm. He tries to shrug me away, scowling, but I say, "We're going to have a talk, Kid, right here and now. If you make a scene, it will only call attention to you."

He accepts the wisdom of that, and allows me to lead him over to one of the concession stands, out of the flow of departing fans. "You've done everything wrong today," I tell him, "ignored everything I tried to teach you. Why, Kid? Why?"

"Because you're an old fool," he says, "you're small potatoes. I want the big money, and I sure as hell can't get it doing things your way."

I wince at this; it hurts to hear him say these things to me. "You could have been caught," I say. "Then neither of us would have gotten the money."

"I'm too good to get caught," he says cockily. "I'm the best there is, Old Man."

"The fact remains that you jeopardized the entire operation. I'm going to have to penalize you for that."

"Penalize? What the hell you talking about?"

"Our arrangement was for an even split of the proceeds," I say. "Instead, I intend to take sixty percent."

His lip curls. "Is that so? Well, I've got another idea. How about if I take a *hundred* percent?"

I look at him sadly. "You'd do that to me, Kid? After all I've done for you?"

"You ain't done nothing for me," he says. "You gave me a few pointers, that's all—maybe smoothed off a couple of rough edges. I been giving you half my scores for three months now and that's plenty. I'm in the big time now; I'm an artist, just like you said. You want any more money, Old Man, go out and work for it just like I been doing."

"You have to pay your dues in this business," I say. "Don't you understand that? Nothing comes easy, nothing comes free. You've got to pay off, Kid, one way or another. There's plenty of money to be had, more than enough for everybody, but you've got to learn to honor your commitments and make your splits."

"I ain't making no splits with you or anybody else," the Kid says. "Now get out of my way, Old Man. I want to make another score or two while there's still a crowd around."

He shoves past me roughly and heads toward the nearest tunnel, out of which people are still emptying. I shake my head. I had thought that the Kid was different from most, but it was not so—he was my greatest student, but now he is my greatest disappointment. Sad, very sad—but what is to be done? The final exam is over and he has failed, and as his teacher I have no choice except to flunk him out of school.

I drift over to where Harrahan is waiting and watching the Kid from his position by the bathrooms; and I give him the high sign. He nods and moves in quickly, just as the Kid is about to dip an elderly gentleman in sunglasses and straw hat. Harrahan, who is as good at his job as I used to be at mine, has him handcuffed and is leading him away before the Kid quite realizes what has happened.

If only the Kid had listened to me. If only he had listened and if only I could have trusted him from the beginning.

Because then there would not have been any need for a final exam; trust would have superseded such a hard necessity. And because then I would have been able to tell him about my longstanding working arrangement with Harrahan, a humble crook like myself who knows that one must always pay the price—here in Candlestick Park if not to all of the world.

As it is, the Kid will bother me. He had all of the tools, all of the genius; he could have continued my life's work and granted me a kind of immortality.

He will bother me for a long, long time.

Broken Pattern

GEORGE C. CHESBRO

A number of George C. Chesbro's works feature protagonists from the halls of academia. His well-known series character, Dr. Robert Fredrickson *(familiarly called Mongo), is both a college professor and a dwarf who doubles as a private investigator.* Mongo *has appeared in three excellent novels:* An Affair of Sorcerers *(1980),* City of Whispering Stone *(1981), and* Shadow of a Broken Man *(1981). Chesbro, who began publishing in the late 1960s, has been acclaimed as a short story writer as well as a novelist; some of his short fiction has been in the science fiction field, other stories are in the psychological suspense mode. In "*Broken Pattern,*" he introduces another academician, this time on the junior high school level.*

EMILY FINISHED GRADING the last of the homework papers, fastened them together with a large clip and placed them carefully in her briefcase. She closed the case, rose and walked to the window. She loved this room, with its view overlooking the school's vast athletic field. Below her, to the right, was a small stand of blue spruce. At the far end of the field the ninth-grade football team was just finishing practice. Sometimes when she was very upset, when the old feelings caught her by surprise, she would stop whatever she was doing and come to stand by this window. Usually a moment was enough, and she could turn back to her class without a scream in her throat.

Already the first month had passed, and she was happy for the first time in more years than she could remember. This time everything was going to be all right; she just knew everything was going to be all right.

"Mrs. Terrault?"

Emily wheeled and choked off a cry when she saw the two students standing by her desk. Heath Eaton stood a few inches taller than Kathy, his twin. Both children had blond hair, fair skin, and bodies that had been flattered by the onset of puberty. Their physical appearance was marred only by blue eyes that seemed too bright and did not, in Emily's opinion, blink often enough.

"You startled me," Emily said in a voice that was not as steady as she would have liked. "I didn't hear you come in." She paused and smiled. The children stared at her impassively. "What are you doing in the school so late?"

"Kathy asked her counselor for permission to come and speak to you about her grades," the boy said. "I got permission to come with her."

The boy's tone was flat, a perfect cover for the strange hint of insolence that was forever peering around its edges. Emily had noticed this before, in class, but now it seemed especially pronounced. She turned her attention to the girl.

"So, speak." She had meant the words to be light and cheerful; they came out heavy and tired.

"You failed me on this paper, Mrs. Terrault," Kathy said, taking a neatly folded paper from her purse and handing it to Emily.

"Yes, Kathy, I know," Emily said, keeping her hands at her sides. She found it somewhat unnerving that the small hand with the folded paper remained stretched out toward her. "But I didn't 'fail you,' as you put it. You failed yourself. I gave you what you earned."

"I'd like you to change it please, Mrs. Terrault."

"Kathy, you know I can't do that."

"You mean you won't."

"Kathy!" Emily glanced sideways at Heath. The boy was studying his hands, seemingly oblivious to the entire conversation. "I've never heard you talk like this before."

"This is the third paper I've failed this term, Mrs. Terrault. Besides that, my work in class hasn't been what it should. I know that. I'm going to fail if you don't change my marks."

Emily turned quickly to the window. Heath was already there, staring out, tapping his fingers on a desk. She turned back as the girl spoke.

"I'm bright, Mrs. Terrault, very bright. You know that, if you've bothered to look at my record. I've been upset the past few weeks. You know very well I could get good grades if I tried, and I *am* going to try. It's not as if you were *giving* me something."

"I don't know about your other courses, Kathy, but in this subject you will get exactly what you earn. No more, and no less." Emily's tone had been very soft, masking the tension under it. Kathy's matched it.

"Both Heath and I plan on getting into good colleges," the girl said evenly. "Since we're both in a home, an institution, that means we'll have to depend on scholarships—good scholarships. And *that* means we're going to have to be at the top of our class. Either Heath or I—we haven't decided which one as yet—is going to be valedictorian. The other is going to be salutatorian. But we have to start now, in the ninth grade. You know that too, I can't afford to fail even a single subject, especially Social Studies."

"Kathy . . . Kathy, I don't know what to say to you. I do think, though, that there's someone else you should speak to. I'm going to make an appointment—"

"Hey, Kathy," Heath said loudly from his place near the window, "I've got things to do." Emily did not turn. She heard the boy's footsteps coming across the room, around the desks, and then he was standing in front of her. "Change the mark, Mrs. Terrault," the boy said. "If you don't, we'll kill you."

The room was suddenly silent, the stillness grazed only by the sound of Emily's heavy breathing. She wanted desperately to look out the window, but she was afraid to move.

"You're very impatient," Kathy said to her brother.

"I told you I've got things to do. Sister Joseph gave us permission to watch the Knicks on TV, but we have to start study period an hour earlier."

"My brother's telling the truth, Mrs. Terrault," Kathy said to Emily. "If you don't change the mark, we will kill you. We've killed people before. Just last month we killed Margie Whitehead, and—"

"Shut up, Kathy," the boy said.

"But she should know that we're not fooling, Heath."

"I think she knows, don't you, Mrs. Terrault?" The boy's eyes were steady on her. "There isn't going to be any problem. Mrs. Terrault is going to take care of you this term, and then you're going to promise to do the work you're capable of. Right, Kathy?"

"Right. Take the paper, Mrs. Terrault, and change it in the grade book too."

Emily started to run toward the open door, stumbled and fell to the floor. The two children remained where they were. She slowly pulled herself to her feet and turned to face the children. Now she was grateful she had tripped; she had almost allowed two desperately sick children to stampede her. But she couldn't panic, couldn't run, not again. Not ever again.

The problem remained as to what to do if the children actually attacked her. There was a letter opener in the desk, but that was too far away. No, she would have to rely on her authority; she was the teacher, they were the students. She took a very deep breath.

"Come with me, Heath and Kathy," Emily said, grateful that her voice did not quiver. "Did you hear me? I want you to come with me."

The children exchanged glances. "Where do you want us to go, Mrs. Terrault?" Kathy said.

"You know very well. We're all going down to see Mr. Atkins."

"You're going to do that old office number?" The boy laughed, quickly and without humor.

For one long, terrible moment Emily did not think they would obey her. Then the boy shrugged and started across the room. Kathy followed.

The custodians had already shut off the lights in the corridor and dusk seeped through the skylights, painting the lockers, the walls and the air a murky gray. Emily walked at a steady pace, shoulders back and head high. The children's footsteps echoed on the floor behind her. She would not run, and she dared not turn. She knew she must not, for a moment, show fear.

Somehow she made it down the stairway to the ground floor. Behind her, the children marched in step. She rounded the last corner, stopped and burst into tears. The office area was dark and deserted.

Kathy stepped around in front of her. Heath remained behind, very close. Emily was afraid—very afraid. She closed her eyes and put her hands to her face.

"Well, it's just as well nobody's here, Mrs. Terrault," Kathy said easily. "Believe me, it wouldn't have gone well for you."

Emily slowly took her hands away from her face. The girl was smiling up at her, supremely confident. In that moment their roles had been reversed; Emily was the child, the child was the teacher.

"What did you say?"

"Mr. Atkins would never believe you. Nobody would believe you. Heath and I came all the way back to school for extra help. You started to talk and act funny. It wouldn't be the first time, would it?"

"I don't know what you mean," Emily said in a strangled voice.

"Yes you do, Mrs. Terrault," Heath said, stepping forward to stand next to his sister. "You know how teachers sometimes talk to each other in the halls and classrooms without bothering to see who else might be listening. We know all about you. We know you used to teach in the high school and then you had some kind of breakdown. You spent the last two years in a mental institution. When you got out you asked if you could come back and teach at a junior high level. The school board hired you, but you're still on probation. I'm betting they keep a pretty close eye on you. If you start telling crazy stories, they'll get rid of you."

Emily turned to the wall, pressing her hands and her cheek against a cold metal locker. She swallowed hard, and discovered there was no moisture left in her mouth. "Get out," she whispered, closing her eyes. "Get away from me."

When she opened her eyes they were gone.

The psychologist was young, Emily thought, not yet thirty; about her own age. She had fine features that were complemented by just the right touch of expensive cosmetics and good fashion sense. Emily knew some men might find the other woman attractive despite the thin, compressed line of her mouth and the infuriating air of superiority she carried with her like the cloying aura of cheap perfume.

The seconds dragged on. The initial rush of relief Emily had experienced when she had finished her story had been short-lived, smothered by the woman's seeming indifference. The psychologist continued to avoid Emily's eyes as she drew concentric circles on a scratch-pad placed on the table between them.

"Well, why don't you *say* something?"

"Quite frankly, Mrs. Terrault, I don't know what to say," the woman said. There was an edge to her voice. She dropped the pencil and looked up. "I just don't know what to make of your story."

"You think I'm lying?"

"Now, I don't say that *you* don't believe—"

"*I* believe, poppycock!" Emily said, half rising from her chair. "I know what you're trying to say!"

"It's not going to serve any purpose for you to get excited, Mrs. Terrault."

Frightened by the strength of her own emotions, Emily sat down again, clasping her hands tightly together. "Do you know what it *cost* me to come to you?" Emily's voice trembled. She could feel herself walking a high wire of words over an abyss of hysteria. She stumbled on. "Don't you suppose I knew the risk I was taking in telling someone that two fifteen-year-old children had threatened to kill me? But it's true. It's *true!*"

"They're much more than just ordinary children, Mrs. Terrault, as I'm sure you're aware, from having them in your class. They both have I.Q.'s in the genius range, and they have already experienced severe trauma in their lives. Their father was hacked to death with an ax, and the killer was never found. The mother then proceeded to withdraw into herself to the point where she could no longer care for the children. Heath and Kathy were placed in a home for children upstate near their own home. Last year they were transferred down here to St. Catherine's. All in all, I'd say they have made a remarkable adjustment to circumstances that would crush lesser children . . . and some adults."

Emily winced under the lash of the last words. "They're monsters," she said very softly. "Monsters. They told me they killed Margie Whitehead."

"Really, Mrs. Terrault. At least twenty other children saw Margie fall under the wheels of that bus, not to mention the two adult bus monitors."

"I know, but even to *say* such a thing a child would have to be terribly, terribly sick. That's why I came to you, that's why I'm telling you all this. I feel they should be helped."

The psychologist sighed. "I must be frank with you, Mrs. Terrault. Heath and Kathy Eaton came in to see me last week."

Emily unconsciously put her hand over her mouth. Suddenly it was hard to breathe.

"They were very upset," the woman continued, "which is quite unusual for them. They said that for some reason they didn't understand, you didn't seem to like them. Kathy said you frightened her, and both children claimed that you picked on them. They asked me if I could help *them* change so that they could please *you*, Mrs. Terrault. In light of that conversation, I'm sure you can see the difficulty of my position."

"When did they come to see you?" Emily's voice sounded apart from herself, an alien echo inside her head.

"Last Tuesday."

"That was the day after I handed back the papers."

Their eyes met and held.

"Mrs. Terrault," the psychologist said, her smile too sweet, too bright, "may I ask you the name of your doctor?"

"Go to hell," Emily said softly. "You go straight to hell."

"Do I have to tell you about it, Mrs. Terrault?"

"No, Mary Ann, you don't. But I would like you to."

"My mother said I shouldn't talk about it. I still get nightmares sometimes."

Emily felt tears spring to her eyes. She understood nightmares, the cold sweat of the mind. She reached out and stroked the girl's thin shoulders. "Mary Ann, I know how it must hurt you to talk about it. Believe me, I wouldn't ask if it weren't very important to me."

"Well, we were all standing in our place outside B wing waiting for our bus. Margie was standing right next to the curb. Bus Eleven had picked up some students and was going around the driveway. Margie fell in front of it just as it was passing us. Her . . . her body made a real funny sound when the wheels went . . . when the wheels—"

"You don't have to tell me that part," Emily said quickly. "Were there many students there when it happened?"

"Billy Johnson was absent that day."

"Yes, but how many other students were waiting for the bus?"

"I don't know exactly, Mrs. Terrault. Fifteen, I guess. Maybe more."

"And Mr. Johnson and Mrs. Biggs were there?"

"They were farther down the sidewalk talking to each other like they always do. Frank Mason said he saw them kissing one time."

"Mary Ann, can you remember who was standing closest to Margie?"

"It's awfully hard, Mrs. Terrault."

"I know, Mary Ann. Please try."

"Well, I was on one side of her. There was Frank Mason, Steve, Kathy and Zeke. I think Sammy was close to her too."

"Kathy Eaton?"

"Yes, Mrs. Terrault, your finger is bleeding."

Emily quickly took her hand from her mouth and wrapped the raw knuckle in the folds of her skirt. "Did . . . Margie have any trouble with anyone? You know what I mean. Did she ever fight with anybody?"

"Do I have to tell the truth, Mrs. Terrault?"

"Please, Mary Ann."

"Nobody liked Margie. She was always making fun of people, and she thought she was better than everybody else just because she was good in Gym." The girl paused. "I'm sorry to say those things about Margie, but you asked me to tell the truth."

"I know, I know, Mary Ann." Emily took the girl in her arms, as much to hide her own tears as to comfort the child. "Was there one particular person she picked on more than anybody else?"

"Margie picked on everybody."

"Did she pick on . . . Kathy Eaton?"

"Margie was always trying to pick a fight with Kathy, always bumping into her in Gym and calling her names. But Kathy never fought back. She'd just walk away. Kathy acts real grown-up. I like her a real lot."

Emily gently pushed the girl away. Mary Ann's head was bowed, her eyes cast down. Emily put her fingers under the girl's chin and pressed very softly until the girl's eyes met her own. "I just want to ask you one more thing, Mary Ann. Please try to think very hard before you answer. Did anything . . . unusual happen that day? I mean, do you remember anything strange that might have happened just before . . . the accident?"

The girl stared thoughtfully at Emily for a few moments, then smiled, as at a happy memory. "Heath was being funny."

"How was Heath being funny, Mary Ann?"

"He came running out of the school door—"

"Was this just before Bus Eleven started up?"

"I guess so. Anyway, Heath came running out of the school, and he was pretending he was an opera star, you know, singing funny and clowning around. Heath didn't usually do things like that, so everybody was staring at him. Everybody was laughing at him except Mr. Johnson and Mrs. Biggs. I think they were mad. Then everybody stopped laughing when the bus ran over Margie."

The dismissal bell rang. Emily made a pretense of searching for a paper, opened her desk drawer and turned on the tape recorder. She left the drawer partially open, then glanced up at the two children who had remained behind.

"You wanted to see us, Mrs. Terrault?"

"Yes," Emily said, then hesitated. She had intended putting on an act, but now discovered that the fear she felt was not at all feigned. She suddenly pushed back her chair and stood. "I have decided to do nothing about Kathy's grades. Now, do you still intend to kill me?"

Heath and Kathy Eaton glanced at each other. They seemed confused.

"We don't know what you mean, Mrs. Terrault," Heath said quietly.

The girl reached out and touched Emily's arm. "Do you feel all right, Mrs. Terrault?"

"Maybe you didn't hear me, Kathy," Emily said, backing away. "I am not going to help you by raising your grades, no matter how much you threaten me. As I told you the other day, in my class you will get exactly what you earn."

"I don't know what you mean by 'threatening you,' Mrs. Terrault. As for my grades, I know how fair you are and I know I'm getting exactly what I deserve. I'm just going to have to work harder from now on. I know that. Isn't that right, Heath?"

"That's right, Kathy."

"Kathy," Emily whispered, "just the other day you and your brother threatened to kill me. You know you did."

Emily watched in amazement as tears began to roll down Kathy Eaton's cheeks. Heath stepped in front of his sister.

"Why are you trying to frighten us?" the boy said. "You made my sister cry."

Emily glanced helplessly back and forth between the faces of the two children. They were so *good* at what they were doing. Even Heath's tone had changed to that of a frightened boy; it was not at all the voice she had heard several days before, or the voice she would hear many hours later.

The insistent ringing tore through the early morning silence. Trembling, Emily picked up the receiver and held it to her ear.

"Mrs. Terrault? This is Heath."

"I know who it is."

"I just wanted you to know that we're not stupid. We'll never talk to you in school again, and this is the last time I'll phone. That's just in case you have a tape recorder and know how to use it."

"Heath! Listen to me, Heath! You're sick! Kathy's sick! Both of you need *help!* Let me help you!"

"Look, *Emily,* we're not the ones who just got out of a nut house, so you'd better just shut up and listen. The only help we want from you is for you to change Kathy's Social Studies grades like we asked you to. You haven't so far because you don't believe we'll do what we say we will. That's a mistake."

"Where are you, Heath?"

"I'm in a phone booth across the street from my cottage. By the time you hang up and call St. Catherine's I'll be back through the window I came out of, in bed. So don't bother. In the meantime you'd better check out your car."

"My car?"

"It's shot. The tires and upholstery are slashed, and all the wiring ripped out. There's also ten pounds of sugar in your gas tank and carburetor. My opinion is that it'll be cheaper to buy a new car than to try and have that one fixed. No charge for the advice."

"Why, Heath? *Why?*"

"Because you're so *stupid,* Mrs. Terrault! *Emily!*" The boy's voice was shrill now, almost hysterical. "*All* of you, you have such little *minds!* And you think that you have the right to *control* people like Kathy and me!"

"Heath, you're mad!"

"Tomorrow, Mrs. Terrault." The voice was calm again.

"Heath—!"

"No! No more talk! Tomorrow! That's the last day. After that we'll do the same to you as I did to your car. Then we'll go cry on that moron psychologist's shoulder about how shocked we are by your death, and how we loved you even if you did always mark Kathy unfairly. Think about it, Mrs. Terrault, and sleep well."

"Over a *grade?*"

"It's not just a grade, Em," Sykes said, leaning back in his leather chair that always squeaked, and propping his feet up on the desk. "After all, you must admit that their logic is impeccable. In four years, this quarter grade could make a difference of, say, a tenth of a point, possibly enough to alter their class ranking. After all, they want to go to Harvard, and they're too smart to underestimate their competition."

"But to *kill!*"

"From what you've described to me, the Eaton children both have sociopathic personalities. To compound the difficulties, they're both extremely intelligent. You see, they've mapped out their whole lives, their goals, like a chess problem, and they're the only major pieces on the board. Everyone—everything—else is a pawn. A sociopath does not feel as you and I feel. It is quite conceivable that, given enough provocation, those children would kill you with no more thought than you might give to kicking a stone out of your path."

Emily shook her head. "I still don't understand. They're only *children.*"

"There is a definite pattern to physical and psychological growth, Em. The pattern of physical growth we can see, while we can only feel the effects of psychological growth. An infant is a raging bundle of *need,* pure id, the center of the universe. Gradually, the pattern grows as the ego—the 'I'—develops, and the ego is perceived in terms of others. In other words, a child knows that he exists as a human being because he sees *other* human beings. But this does not make him civilized. The child will not be truly civilized until he can empathize, to a degree, with other people's pain and wants. Contrary to the public image, a small child is a veritable savage who would gladly kill another in a moment of rage if that other child somehow stood in the way of something the first child wanted very badly. Of course, he doesn't have the strength, and his goals—and his rage—are very short-lived. This allows time for the child to develop a superego; a conscience, if you will, which will modify his behavior toward other people. In a sociopathic personality, the pattern has been broken. How, we can only guess. In this case, the 'how and why' isn't important. If what you say is true, you're probably in a great deal of danger. You may have become a special challenge to them."

Emily closed her eyes, then slowly spoke the words, as if exorcising the demons which had plagued her the past week. "Do you think I've imagined all this?"

"I don't know, Em," Sykes said easily. "What are your thoughts on the subject?"

Emily reached into her pocketbook, took out a neatly folded piece of paper and handed it to the psychiatrist. Sykes opened it, studied it, then glanced up quickly. "This is—?"

"Mrs. Elizabeth Eaton. Heath and Kathy's mother."

"You've seen her?"

"Yesterday. I took a day off from work, rented a car and drove upstate to see her. I got her address from records at the home. I told them I was calling on school business. She's a strange woman, broken, living alone. She was very happy to have someone to talk to. We talked all day."

"What did you talk about?"

"Her children." Emily paused, trying to think of some easy way to phrase what she had to say next. There was none. "Mrs. Eaton thinks that Heath and Kathy killed her husband; their father."

Sykes rose, walked to a window and drew back a curtain. "Did she say so?"

"Not in so many words," Emily said, rushing now, once again feeling panic whispering in her ear. "But I knew that was what she was telling me, in her own way. What woman in her right mind would accuse two children—*young* children—of hacking their father to death?"

"Yes."

The word was spoken softly, but it came at her like a cannon shot. Emily whimpered and put her hand to her mouth, but she would not be denied. She *knew* what she had heard. "There's my car! It's still sitting in the parking lot."

"Along with three others wrecked in the same way, if I remember your story correctly. If Heath did do it, he went to the trouble of making it look like a random act."

Emily slumped in her chair, exhausted, beaten. "What do I do, Doctor?"

"Change the mark, of course."

Emily looked up. Sykes had turned from the window and was gazing steadily at her.

"I didn't say I didn't believe you, Em. It really doesn't make any difference, at least not at this point. Maybe we'll find out more about that in therapy. For the time being, we must assume that one of two things is true: either you are imagining this business with the Eatons, or you are not. If you are imagining it, then no harm will come in any case from changing Kathy Eaton's grade. If you're *not* imagining it . . ." Sykes left the sentence unfinished.

"What then?" Emily whispered.

"Then I suggest that you take a leave of absence for the rest of the year until Heath and Kathy Eaton are transferred to the high school."

Emily was astonished to find herself shaking her head. "I can't. They killed a little girl. Maybe they've killed more. Maybe they'll kill again."

"If so, there's nothing you can do about it, Em. They not only won't believe you, they'll destroy you."

"You're talking about other people."

"Yes, Em. I would have thought that two years of therapy would have taught you that evil doesn't wear a sign around its neck. Just because *you* see evil doesn't mean that others will; sometimes they can't, sometimes they choose not to. In this case I'd say it's a lot of both."

"I can't just leave them free to kill again."

"I'm sorry, Em, but I can't think of any other option. Can you?"

The snow was gone, chased by spring's laughter. Outside the window, down on the athletic field, a lone runner bobbed along the border of trees, nimbly skirting the puddles. Emily turned from the open window. The twins were waiting beside her desk.

"Thank you for coming in after school to see me," Emily said. "Heath, I know you have track practice. I won't keep you long." She smiled. "First, I'd like to compliment both of you on your work the past two quarters. You're by far the best of my students."

It was true. Since Emily had changed Kathy's disastrous first-quarter grades, both children had been model students, earning straight A's. Since then, aside from the stiff formality which was a part of the uneasy truce of silence they maintained, it was as if the incidents earlier in the year had never happened. Emily decided to probe.

"Kathy, you never did tell me why you were so upset at the beginning of the year."

"That's right, Mrs. Terrault, I didn't." The girl was making an effort to sound unruffled, but there was an edge to her voice. There had been no warning that she would be forced to play the role of belligerent, and she was having trouble shifting emotional gears.

"Was it Margie Whitehead, Kathy? Was it because you might have felt just a little bit of guilt at killing another human being?"

The girl started to whimper, but her eyes remained dry.

Heath was more convincing. "Why are you trying to scare us, Mrs. Terrault? You're starting to say funny things again."

"It doesn't really matter, you know," Emily said matter-of-factly. She went to her desk and sat down behind it, folding her hands in front of her.

"Mrs. Terrault," Heath said, "I have to go to track practice, and Kathy has to be home early. May we go, please?"

"Did I ever tell you why I was confined to a mental institution?" Emily said softly. The two children stared back at her, and she smiled again. The Hunter and the Hunted, with the roles continually shifting. But the children did not move. Emily had known they wouldn't, for a new factor had been added to an equation they had thought solved, and they would need time to evaluate it to their complete satisfaction.

"I could not tolerate evil," Emily continued quietly. "More precisely, I could not tolerate the idea that there was so little I could do about the evil I saw. I was really quite pathetic. When I read of a starving child, I could not eat my meals. If I heard a news report of families without heat in their homes, I couldn't face my own blankets. I won't dwell on my past, because I'm not proud of it. I was a very sick woman. Eventually it got to the point where I couldn't function at all. When I wasn't crying, I was breaking things in a blind rage. I lost my husband because of my sickness, and eventually I was hospitalized, as you know. Finally I learned—accepted would be a better term—that the best most people like myself can do is to function *themselves* as good men and women."

"Why are you telling us all this, Mrs. Terrault?"

"I'd like to show you two something." Emily said, opening her purse. She took out a packet of photographs and spread them across the desk. "These are some pictures of the institution where I stayed. Look at them."

The children remained where they were. Kathy had begun to cast anxious glances at her brother, who continued to stare at Emily. A smile tugged at the edges of his lips but never quite materialized.

"You should look at them," Emily said. "You'll see that it's really quite a nice place. Then you'll understand why I won't mind going back there. You see, Heath and Kathy, I'm going to have to kill you."

"Boy, *Emily,*" Heath said, "you really have flipped out."

"Yes, Heath, I'm sure that's what everyone will think. I'm counting on it." Emily opened her drawer, took out the pistol and pointed it at them. She needed both thumbs to pull back the hammer, but the hand holding the gun was steady. "You have no idea how much trouble I had getting this thing," she said casually. "But then practicing was fun." She raised the gun. "I hope it won't hurt. I truly do."

Heath seemed frozen, his mouth half open. His hands trembled. The tears in Kathy's eyes were real.

"They'll kill you if you do this, Mrs. Terrault. You know they will." Heath's voice cracked and he too began to cry. "No woman in her right mind . . ."

"Precisely, Heath. No woman in her right mind would kill two children. But I'm not in my right mind, am I? Certainly that 'moron psychologist' friend of yours doesn't think so. No, only you and I will know how sane an act this really is, killing the two of you. It's simply something that must be done, precisely because there is no alternative. I would gladly die, if need be, but even that isn't necessary, not with my background. I'll be committed. I have a good psychiatrist, and with a little luck I might even be sent back to the same place. Of course, I won't have as much freedom, and it may take me longer to be 'cured' this time, but at least I'll have the satisfaction of knowing that for once in my life I was able to *do* something about a particular evil."

Heath opened his mouth to yell.

"Don't bother," Emily said easily. "Everyone's gone to the middle school for a faculty meeting, and the janitor's half deaf."

"Mrs. Terrault?" The girl's voice was barely audible. Emily swung the gun around until it was pointed at the small, white forehead. "Please, Mrs. Terrault, I don't want to die."

"Neither did Margie Whitehead, Kathy. Neither will God knows how many other victims, people the two of you will kill or maim unless I kill you first. You see, Kathy, your tears mean nothing to me . . . because I have seen your true face. Besides, even if I decided not to kill you, you'd find a way to kill me."

"No, Mrs. Terrault." Heath had come forward and placed both hands on her desk. Emily swung the gun around and he backed away. "We wouldn't, Mrs. Terrault. I promise we wouldn't. We'd confess, and they could send us to a hospital."

Emily laughed. "Who would believe you, Heath?"

"We'll *make* them believe us! I'll tell them about your car! I'll tell them about how we planned it so that Margie's death would look like an accident! I'll—"

"Be quiet, Heath," the girl said suddenly. "She doesn't believe you. She knows better." Emily let the girl come closer. "I know you're not going to believe me, either, Mrs. Terrault, but . . . I'm . . . I think I'm sorry we killed Margie. And I'm sorry we . . . killed . . . our father."

"Did you kill your father, Kathy?"

"Yes," the girl said after a long pause, "but he wasn't our real father. I know he wasn't—and he hated us. When we killed him it was like . . . playing a game."

Emily pointed the gun squarely between the girl's eyes. Kathy's face was completely drained of blood, something carved from marble. Heath sat down hard and retched.

Emily laid down the gun, which was unloaded, reached into her drawer and turned off the tape recorder. She was filled suddenly with a dissonant harmony of laughter and tears. But hysteria was an old friend, and she knew it would pass.

She rose and walked to the window. Outside, a light rain was falling, washing down the afternoon. "I don't know how successful your therapy is going to be," she said, "but I hope this harrowing experience will get you off to a good start. Terror isn't a nice feeling, but it's better than nothing."

She heard the doors close softly, then the easy click of a large man's footsteps. Emily smiled. Suddenly the room was filled with a warm, comforting presence. The terrible tension had almost made her forget that she wasn't alone, and had not been.

"I think Dr. Sykes will want to talk to you now," she said softly.

Dead Week

L. P. CARPENTER

This is L. P. Carpenter's first published story, and in it he demonstrates an understanding of how things at a university can go awry during those pre-exam periods when nothing appears to be happening. Carpenter's own academic experience, during the years 1965 to 1972, was at the University of California at Berkeley, where "Dead Week" takes place. Since then he has held a civil service job that, in his words, "will remain unspecified—since tax auditors seem to have taken the place of warlocks in modern demonology." We think you'll agree that "Dead Week" is a promising debut for a talented new writer.

FROM 6:00 P.M. until 11:00 P.M., Cassy slept the sleep of the hunted. She awoke still dressed, stiff and cold on her cot, and lay for a long time in a semicomatose state watching the ghosts of car lights creep across the ceiling.

Sleeping odd hours was a method she used to cope with her roommates' erratic study habits, and their taste for bluegrass music played loud and long. Now the house below her was finally quiet. The long night lay ahead for a last-ditch effort to prepare for finals next week.

Cassy couldn't understand why no one else ever needed to study. Between her full load of classes, the cafeteria job to supplement her meager scholarship, and the lab requirements for the advanced biology program, she had no time left. The endless talking, socializing, and kicking back that the others engaged in were luxuries she couldn't afford. By accepting a steep increase in rent she had managed to get a room to herself—not a room really, just a cramped vestibule atop the back stairway, probably rented out in violation of fire regulations. But she needed it to study in peace.

Her first task, the one she had been dreading, was to clean off her desk. It was an unexplored drift of papers reflecting the disorder of her own mind—books, lecture notes, handouts, reading lists, and who-knew-what-else dumped there in moments of exhaustion during the semester. Now she would need to review all her course requirements in order to cram efficiently. She dragged herself up, switched on the naked bulb overhead, plugged in her coffee pot, and went to work.

The job went faster than she expected. Most of the papers could be arranged by course number and date or thrown away. The notes were legible, if sparse, and she had really only fallen behind in her reading a few weeks before—so maybe things weren't so bad.

Then she found something. Near the bottom of the mess was a

pink, printed card with the hours and days of a week blocked out like a calendar, bearing the motto "Courtesy of the Berkeley Student Bookstore." The card itself wasn't strange—the times of Cassy's classes, labs, and work shifts were sketched into it with the care of someone mapping out a glorious new life, long before it turned into a murderous routine.

The strange thing was that on Tuesday and Thursday afternoons at 3:00 P.M.—right in the middle of her cherished library study time—were two pencilled blocks labelled "Demo 168."

It looked like her writing, but it puzzled her. She certainly wasn't taking any courses in demonology. Maybe it was demolitions—she laughed, thinking that would make a good poli sci course. On an impulse she picked up her dog-eared schedule and directory and thumbed through the alphabetical listings. There it was, in tiny computer print, underscored in red pencil. "Demography Dept.—Demo 168—133 Dwinelle Hall—TTh 3."

Intrigued and a little disturbed, she plunged into the thick yellow course catalog. "Demography 168. 3 units. The Limits of Population. An exploration of the theoretical and practical limits to population growth, with special emphasis on the roles of birth and death controls in restoring equilibrium. Professors Thayer and Munck."

Slowly, with the elusive quality of a dream, it came back to her. She had indeed considered taking the course in February, nearly five months before. She'd even attended one or two lectures. The subject had sounded interesting—and relevant, she had thought, to the populations of microbes she would be working with in bio. She'd heard that it was a smart precaution to sign up for extra classes in case your first preferences were too crowded.

But the professor had indicated that the course would focus on human populations, using a social-science approach. That was the main reason Cassy had dropped it.

At least she seemed to recall dropping it. She began hunting through the desk drawers. There it was—the green carbon copy of the enrollment card, signed by her faculty advisor. As she read it her heart plunged and her fingertips felt numb. It listed five courses; the fifth one was Demo 168.

But that was crazy! How could she be taking a course without even knowing it? She was sure she hadn't bought any of the texts—at some point she must have just stopped attending and forgotten all about it.

Frantically she searched through the last of the clutter on the desktop. A single sheet, mimeographed in pale purple, came to light. It read, "Demography 168—Course Requirements. The grade will be based sixty percent on the final exam and forty percent on the term paper, to be handed in at the last class meeting. Lecture attendance is recommended. Required reading: *Man against the Ceiling* by Storvich and Smith, Sutton House, 1973; *The Dynamics of Death Control* by E. C. Festung, 1978 ed.; *Sower and Reaper* by G. Hofstaedler, Vendome, 1979. Additional readings to be assigned periodically."

Cassy felt a great, sinking despair. The chance of catching up so late in the semester was nil. She would have to request some kind of administrative relief. Whether it would affect her scholarship, she didn't know.

There was certainly nothing to be done so late at night—and no one she could talk to. She tried to study for other classes, but thoughts of the phantom class kept twisting through her brain. As the night dragged on she accomplished nothing more. Sleep was unattainable.

The most upsetting thing was the realization of her own mental lapse—somehow, under all the demands and stress, her mind had slipped gears. Was it the first time? Would it be the last?

The Berkeley campus seemed deserted the following day as Cassy walked to the Admin Building. Dead Week, students called it—a week of anguished repentance for thoughtless months of procrastination. The sky was steely gray with the fog that can make San Francisco Bay summers colder than its winters. Swishing sprinklers transected the lawns.

Cassy's route passed Barrows Hall, the eight-story math building. She involuntarily glanced at the demolished shrub where a grad student had dived from the roof a few days before. He had been the second suicide to choose the boxlike building this term, the fourth this school year. They were keeping the roof doors locked now.

Sproul Hall loomed impassive on the left, seemingly built of sugar cubes. The plaza wasn't deserted—its bizarre bazaar never ceased. Two die-hard disc throwers, a vagrant guitar player, a revivalist preacher ranting to nobody, and an odd assortment of street people were all doing their things. Cassy hurried through. Somehow the sight of the anonymous social transactions taking place here only intensified her loneliness.

Cassy had friendships, of course—smooth working relationships with the people in her major, her job, and her house. But she felt there was some kind of sustenance she wasn't getting. She knew that she didn't fit the conventional beauty standard; the schoolkid puns about "Cassy's chassis" had stopped being funny after her chassis became a little too stout for most boys' liking. And though she had definitely and finally determined that she was not "pig-faced," it was depressing to have to remind herself of it each time she looked into a mirror.

Not that she wanted a delirious romance. Her schedule didn't allow for it. Summer loomed ahead, with two accelerated class sessions, more hours at the cafeteria, and a visit or possibly two with her mom. She would have liked to do more dating and partying, but lately the guys who approached her always seemed a little slimy. "Let's talk about you," they said; "Tell me about yourself"—willing to give only as much as they absolutely had to. Their attention shifted too easily. The latest one, Howie, had been that way. He had left a message for her a few weeks ago, but she had forgotten to return his call.

Inside Sproul Hall there were long lines at the administration window in spite of Dead Week—students fighting their bureaucratic battles to the bitter end. No one in her line said anything to her; Cassy vainly opened up her biochem text and stared at the chapter on protein synthesis.

When her turn came she tried to explain her situation. The clerk, a bored girl who looked younger than Cassy herself, pointed to an orange bulletin under the glass countertop. "I'm sorry, the last day to add or drop classes was March third."

"But I never really took this class. I mean, I didn't mean to!" She felt herself getting in deeper. "I don't need it . . . I only took it by mistake."

"I'm sorry. The only way to drop now would be to withdraw from the University." The girl peered over Cassy's shoulder to summon the next one in line.

"But that's impossible . . . my other classes. My scholarship! I want to talk to someone else, please."

"You could ask the instructor for a grade of Incomplete."

"Please let me talk to someone else."

"Very well. You'll have to make an appointment to see the dean. His office is on the second floor, in front of you as you leave the stairwell. Next."

After waiting in the dean's anteroom and making an appointment for the following day, Cassy didn't have time to go home before her work shift. Instead she went to the Graduate Social Sciences Library in Stevens Hall. There, at the back of a yellow-lit aisle in the soundless stacks, she was able to find one of the books on the Demo 168 reading list, the Festung text. It was a hardcover maroon volume two inches thick, and it looked as if no one had ever opened it. The glossy pages were densely printed, with graphs of sociological data.

The chapter titles made it sound pretty heavy: "Nature's Inexorable Balance," "Death Controls Versus Human Ingenuity," "The Pathology of Crowding," "The Role of the Unconscious," and so on. The graphs dealt mainly with crime rates and deaths from various causes as functions of population density, in an endless series of uptailing curves. The prose was impenetrable—written in Berkeleyese, a pretentious academic style that tries earnestly to make itself immune to all criticism and ends up qualifying itself into meaningless obscurity.

Typical social sciences material, Cassy thought. There was no hope of making sense of it without the lectures and the teacher's help, if she did end up having to do the coursework.

That was one reason Cassy had majored in biology. It had no shortage of cumbersome facts and figures to grapple with, but there was also the laboratory work—real, concrete procedures that could show the truth or untruth of the theories in solid, life-or-death terms. She was good in the lab, and it was largely on the strength of this aptitude that she'd been accepted into the advanced bio program.

Of course, it had put unexpected demands on her time and cut into her other activities—but she didn't mind. It made her feel good to be valued as a researcher. Much of it was routine work and errand-girl stuff—growing and feeding cultures, caring for test animals, and delivering specimens—still, she was learning a great deal about immunology research. Some of it was quite advanced; she suspected that the lab programs were tied to defense—though her instructors would never admit that, with the current sentiment on campus.

Returning home in a haze of fatigue, Cassy cut across the grassless front lawn and climbed the porch steps of her house. It was a worn, gaudily painted Victorian perched on a roaring one-way street. The front door stood open and an acrid smell drifted out. She headed down the hall, past the communal kitchen, and heard voices raised.

"There she goes now." It was an angry-sounding female, Vickie or Connie, speaking from one of the rooms. An intense murmur interrupted her, and then the voice shrilled, "Well, somebody's got to tell the creep!"

Cassy turned as Dave's tee-shirted figure, built square for soccer, appeared in the kitchen doorway. His face was set grimly.

"Cassy, come here." He jerked his head in the direction of the kitchen.

Cassy complied. Dave stepped back to reveal the room. The acrid smell was heavier here, and the ceiling was smoke-stained. The blackened, ill-scrubbed stove with scorched and blistered cabinets above it resembled an altar.

"We had the fire department here this morning, Cassy," Dave said. "After you left. Did you forget to turn off the burner?"

Cassy felt numb, confused. "Well, maybe . . . I'm not sure . . ."

"Sure she did." Vickie, dressed in tight jeans and Dave's sweatshirt, came through the door that joined their room to the kitchen. "It was her crap piled up on the stove that caught fire. If Bruce hadn't smelt it, we would've all burned to death in our sleep." She thumped across the floor in bare feet and confronted Cassy. "What's with you anyway?"

"I'm sorry . . ." Cassy had only a vague recollection of her hurried breakfast of coffee, toast, and donuts. "I've been so busy lately . . ."

"Busy—jeez!" Vickie threw up her hands violently. "We could be dead right now, and you're busy!" She rolled her eyes ceilingward. "How do we know you won't do it again tomorrow? You sneak around here, and never talk to anybody . . ."

Dave put a hand on her shoulder, gingerly. "Vickie, I think she gets the idea."

"Butt out, Dave." Vickie twisted out from under his hand and went on, "You stay up all night. You know, we can hear you moving around up there. When you walk back and forth, it makes the whole house creak."

Cassy reddened. "Well, that's better than some of the things I've heard coming from your room!" She turned and started down the hall.

Vickie ran out of the kitchen after her. "Bullshit! You almost burned us alive! You leave your coffee grounds all over—and the weird stuff you eat takes up most of the space in the fridge!"

Dave was physically restraining her. "That's enough, Vick."

"I don't care," she screamed. As Casey started up the back stairs, Vickie was yelling, "Why don't you just move out!"

Next day Cassy sat in the office of Dean Moody while he thumbed through her master file. Over his shoulder, visible through the venetian blind, the soaring ivory tower of the Campanile chimed out eleven o'clock. He looked up and pinched his clean-shaven lips into a smile.

"Just an oversight, you say? Well, whatever the cause, I think we can make an exception in view of your excellent academic record. It can be written up as a late drop for health reasons. All that will be required are the signatures of the instructor and your faculty advisor." He took a card from his desk drawer, filled it in partially, and handed it to her. "You can turn it in at the window downstairs."

Cassy had no difficulty getting the signature of her advisor, Professor Langenschiedt. He was so busy between the affairs of the Medical Physics Department and the Academic Senate that he scarcely listened to her explanation before expressing every confidence in her good judgment, signing the form, and hurrying her out.

The approval of the course instructor was another matter. Cassy had some uneasiness about approaching him to tell him she'd lost interest in his class. Every academician takes his job seriously; she didn't really suppose that he'd consider her case important enough to warrant withholding his signature, but she anticipated an unpleasant encounter.

She had reconstructed a fairly clear mental picture of Professor Thayer from the beginning of the term: tall, tweedy, with squared-off tortoiseshell glasses and gray hair sculptured around his brow. His lectures had been dry and dispassionate, giving no hint of his general disposition.

She looked up his office number and went in search of it. Her quest took her through the cavernous lobby of Dwinelle Hall and into its dim, labyrinthine recesses. In building the hall and adding Dwinelle Annex, the designers had violated some basic law of architectural geometry, or else one of human perception. Angular corridors and half-flights of stairs created baffling and often frightening missteps for those who ventured inside. The sickly brown light reflecting off the floor added to the eerie effect. But after many detours and hesitations, Cassy found the indicated door, number 1521, and knocked. "Come in!"

As she opened the door a flood of daylight came through, so that she could see only the outline of the man behind the desk. The tall window looked out on a tree-filled quadrangle, and the north wall opposite was bright with sun.

Professor Thayer closed the book before him and motioned Cassy to a chair. "Hello, Miss . . . uh, I'm pleased to see you. Aren't you in one of my classes?"

"Well, yes, I was . . . I mean I am. That's sort of what I needed to talk to you about. I stopped going after the second lecture."

"Why, that's funny—I thought I'd seen you more than that. I recognize your bangs."

Cassy blushed. Although she had been busy all day formulating excuses, they evaporated now. Cassy told him simply and truthfully what had happened. There was something so reassuring in his manner that she went into more detail than she had done with anyone, and she finished with a lump in her throat. She took the drop card out of her book bag and placed in on his desk.

Professor Thayer nodded at it, but didn't seem in any hurry to sign.

"Tell me," he asked, "how many units are you taking?"

"Fifteen. Besides your class, I mean."

"That's quite a load. You also work part-time?"

"Yes, sir. At the Meals Facility. And my lab requirement is six hours a week, but I usually spend more time than that." Cassy didn't mean to sound abject, but somehow she didn't feel like holding anything back.

"You must be under great stress. I can see how it might cause, uh, a slip of the kind you describe." He smiled. "Of course I'll be glad to sign your card." But instead of reaching for it, the professor folded his arms, leaned back in his chair, and began to profess.

"It's a shame, in a way, that you couldn't have taken my class. It would have given you some insight into a problem that's affecting you—and affecting us all, whether we know it or not.

"The course deals with overpopulation. It's been controversial in the Demography Department, since it probably should be called a sociology or population-ecology course instead; some of my colleagues don't approve of my taking what amounts to a moral stance, by saying just how much population is too much. But since the class deals specifically with human society, and most of the data are here, I've kept it in the department.

"We explore the correlation of increased population density with all the classes of effects—from high rents to disrupted living conditions, stress, violent crime, suicide, *et cetera.* One of the key factors at work is *anomie*—the insecure, faceless 'lonely crowd' feeling discussed by Durkheim and Riesman. It's hard to define an emotion like that scientifically, but it's easy to see its results; they fill the front pages of our newspapers—with gruesome statistics." Professor Thayer prodded a fat green softcover volume of census figures at the side of his desk, so that it flopped shut of its own weight.

"Of course, when you're discussing overpopulation, there's no better example of it than the student body of a large school like Berkeley. In this case, the population pressure is artificial—resulting from the crush of students to a favored institution—but it's intense enough to develop all the classic effects: high rents, crowded living conditions, the overload of facilities, and above all, stress. An interesting microcosm." Professor Thayer gazed speculatively at Cassy for a moment, then resumed.

"The intriguing approach is to view all these social problems not just as ill effects, but as attempts by a dynamic system to balance itself. Death controls, in E. C. Festung's phrase.

"When a population exceeds natural limits, it definitely will be reduced—if not by birth control, then by death controls such as famine and disease. The human species is uniquely fortunate in having the power to choose—though we don't seem to be using that power.

"Festung identified a wide range of behaviors peculiar to man as death controls: war, terrorism, violent crime, transportation accidents, cult suicides, nuclear 'events' "—the professor drew imaginary brackets around the word with two pairs of fingers—"all the unique disasters we take for granted today. He maintains that they all stem from an instinct, inborn in mankind far beneath the level of rational thought, to reduce a population that, unconsciously, we perceive as too large. Like caged birds in the five-and-dime pecking each other to death. In effect, crowding is seen to induce irrational and aggressive behavior. A fascinating theory." This time his pause was punctuated by the sound of sparrows chirping outside in the quad.

"Unfortunately, it all tends to sound very morbid. Many students can't work with it—too depressing. They'd rather just shrug it off, at least until it becomes too big to ignore. Like so many contemporary issues, it's a hard one to face—I've seen some fine minds become paralyzed by a sort of ecological despair." He massaged his chin a moment. "In a way, your little bout of forgetfulness parallels the attitude of all Western society toward the population issue, ever since the time of Malthus. The initial warnings were just too grim, so we thrust it away to the back of our minds. Unfortunately that doesn't alleviate the problem."

The professor lapsed into silence and stared out the window for a while, hands folded. Then he bestirred himself and looked at his watch. "Oh my, I see I've run on for quite a while. You ended up taking my course anyway—the special condensed version. Hope I didn't bore you. Or depress you. Here, I'll sign this."

In a few moments Cassy was being ushered out the door. She

didn't regret having spent so long with Professor Thayer. He was cute, though long-winded—and a lot of what he said sounded awfully unscientific.

Leaving Dwinelle she headed for the lab. After that, home, to do some serious cramming!

So Dead Week ended, if not quite happily, then at least hurriedly. Although the menace of the phantom class was laid to rest, Cassy knew that the distraction and delay had hurt her study effort—perhaps seriously. So she halved her sleep time and doubled her coffee intake to catch up, and in a while agony faded to mere numbness. Perhaps it didn't matter anyway—she had always found that final grades bore no recognizable relationship to her effort or understanding.

To complicate matters, there was a flurry of last-minute activity at the lab. An ill-timed biochemical breakthrough had Cassy making special trips around the campus to deliver files and samples when she should have been doing a dozen other things. In the department she sensed excitement and an unspoken pressure to keep the matter quiet—if not permanently, then at least until summer break, when the majority of students would have gone home and the chance of protest lessened.

On Wednesday the lunch crowd in the Meals Facility was only slightly smaller than usual. A few of the diners moved with the sanctified air of having finished their final exams; others carried stacks of books on their trays and looked haggard. Cassy stood behind the counter doling out portions of stew, chicken, and enchiladas.

A familiar face appeared in the customer line. "Hello, Professor Thayer," she said brightly.

"Why, hello, Cassy! Oh, that's right—you told me you worked here, didn't you?" The professor put on a playfully pensive look. "Hmmm. I wonder what's good today."

"Everyone's having the Caesar salad," said Cassy, smiling. "It ought to be good—I helped make it." She reached for a clean bowl and began to dish up an especially generous helping.

At that moment she noticed the Erlenmayer flask right there before her—from the lab. It was nearly empty of bacterial toxins, type K. It really didn't look much different from the salad-dressing cruet—but that was over on the table by her purse, and it was still full. Again that lightheaded feeling, of gears slipping somewhere.

Cassy and the professor heard a tray crash and looked out across the expanse of tables. Something was happening. A man near the window lurched, fell across a table, and rolled to the floor. There were violent movements elsewhere in the room, and out on the terrace.

Then the screaming began.

Van der Valk and the High School Riot

NICOLAS FREELING

Nicolas Freeling caused quite a stir in crime-fiction circles several years ago when he killed off his popular Dutch detective, Van der Valk, in a novel called Auprès de ma Blonde *(1972). His reason: he felt he had done all he could with the character and wanted to branch out into other areas of crime fiction. This he has done with straight suspense novels and a new series character, Henri Castang. The Van der Valk novels and stories remain popular with readers, however. "Van der Valk and the High School Riot" is one of the earliest (it was first published in 1970) and best of the dozen short stories featuring this sensitively drawn Amsterdam police inspector.*

ANOTHER DEMONSTRATION outside a high school! Banal at first sight. These things broke out like strawberry rash, thought Chief Inspector Van der Valk indulgently from the other end of the street. Bright June morning and the children were letting off steam. And one couldn't blame them! He sympathized secretly; one could find few attitudes more antiquated and rigid than those of the chalky civil servants in the Education Department. These children had to sit passively being stuffed, rows of tiny computers being programmed, and they felt, however obscurely, that whatever education was it wasn't this.

Now they were dancing and screaming like dervishes; wake the teachers up, perhaps. But as Van der Valk got nearer he changed his mind. Throwing stones—that had to be stopped. The little dears were tiresomely incapable of distinguishing idealism and vandalism.

At that moment a police car slowed, turned in off the street, and tried to force a way through 300 or more excited adolescents to the massive, closed front door. A mistake; an active, unintimidated group jumped on the hood, smeared posters all over the windshield, and let the air out of the tires. Unable to get out, the forces of law and order sat fuming and impotent; ordinarily Van der Valk would have laughed heartily. They would simply radio for reinforcements—another instance of too little and too late. Or wagonloads of riot police with the inevitable headlines about police brutality; the dilemma was familiar by now to nearly every police force in the world.

This time, however, Van der Valk decided that the thing to do was to quell the riot without adding to its importance; but he was keenly aware that it was easier said then done. A chorus of slogans broke out, addressed to the pious memory of Che Guevara, and large stones crashed against the façade with an accompanying tinkle of broken glass; no time to imitate brave Horatius on the bridge.

He whisked back along the street and found three hesitant policemen. Four more appeared, probably as a result of calls from the police car which the children were now busily overturning. Ordinary municipal policemen with soft hats and hard sticks against a jubilant and now nasty-minded mob. Van der Valk had to intimidate the rioters; he had no choice.

He mustered his little army on the other side of the street. "Give me your pistol," he said to the nearest. "This thing loaded?" He cocked it, pointed it behind his back at the canal, and fired three shots at two-second intervals. There was a sudden silence.

Decidedly it was an improvement on blowing whistles. The crowd turned to face him, but waveringly. All at once it had thinned subtly; it was less compact. No more than a dozen weak sisters had faded off discreetly round the corner, but the mob was now quiet, staring at him, momentarily open-mouthed. The three policemen in the overturned car scrambled out as best they could and gained the steps by the door.

Van der Valk spoke sarcastically. "You shout louder—but I talk better."

Mistake—a hostile murmur grew and spread. He gave the pistol back, pointed his arm forward in the air like Marshal Murat, and bellowed: "Charge!" Clippety-clop, he thought, heading for the steps. The group before him divided and he bounced up the steps quite pleased with himself. Now they're bumped, keep them bumped. Don't stop to chat and don't give them time to think.

"To your homes, and quick. Any hesitation and I charge you. There are girls among you. Anyone who gets hurt—their lookout."

The fringes bolted, but a solid group of fifty-odd around the dilapidated police car stood firm. A redheaded boy jumped on the radiator.

"They daren't shoot," he yelled. "Throw the pigs in the canal."

"I'll have you," snapped Van der Valk. "Forward!"

The boy jumped down lithely but was hindered by his slower companions. Van der Valk caught a suede jacket, twisted an arm, and brought his captive to a standstill. The rest had run. Inside twenty seconds nothing remained of the battlefield but a few stones and one or two jackets. The forces of law and order were puffing but triumphant. There were five captives, including a girl who twisted, howled, and tried to scratch.

"Let her go," said Van der Valk swiftly. "These three to the bureau. You others stay here and let there be no more nonsense—get that damned car on its feet."

The belated reinforcements had now appeared and two dozen policemen were standing around and looking foolish. The boy twisted suddenly in an effort to break away; the grip must have hurt him because in a fierce movement he turned and spat at the Chief Inspector; this quieted Van der Valk abruptly.

"Bureau," he said again, reaching for a handkerchief. "I'm coming too. We have to have a little talk," he added to the scornful head on a level with his own.

On the bare wooden floor of the police station the boy did not struggle when he was released, but stood looking contemptuously at a ring of ruffled, sweaty policemen.

"You are liable to the following charges," intoned the Chief Inspector formally. "Disturbance of the peace in a public place, refusal to obey an official order to disperse, damage to government property, and incitement to riot and violence. How old are you?"

"Find out."

"Papers . . . Hm, seventeen. You're a juvenile—and my pigeon." He turned to the local commissaire, who was looking at the three boys with an unpaternal gaze. "Your district, Chief. Up to you to prefer charges."

"Carrying any prohibited weapons? Any of you with bicycle chains or such are in real trouble . . . No? Well, Chief Inspector, they're juveniles. You were present, so I'll leave this decision to you."

"Take their particulars and let the other two go with a severe warning, but this boy I want to see more of. With your permission I'll have him taken across to my office."

"Sit down," said Van der Valk mildly.

"No."

"As you wish." He was standing himself, and could for the first time observe the boy at leisure. Tall athletic lad, as tall and almost as wide as Van der Valk himself. Only the depth was lacking—the depth of a man of 40, heavier in the neck and shoulders, thicker in the ribs and thighs.

"We're quite well matched. You're a boxer, I'm a puncher. I've two boys your age. Which gives you youth, and me experience. We can talk. Have a cigarette."

Surprising him, the boy accepted one. He no longer looked hostile, or even sullen. On the contrary he had a sunny, placid look, with more adult assurance than childish self-assertion.

"What have to we got to talk about?" the boy asked innocently.

"Why, I'm in authority over a group. So are you. We have a lot in common, including intelligence and a wish for justice. I've no desire to shout at you. If you refuse to talk, that's your privilege. We could gain understanding from one another. And then, *la paix est fort bonne de soi,* as Jean de La Fontaine remarks somewhere."

The boy thought this over.

"He says something else," he murmured calmly. "According to whether you are in power or in misery, the judgment of the court will whiten you—or blacken you." Van der Valk was brought up short.

"Ah. That's—if I'm not mistaken—the fable about the animals ill of the plague. What year of school are you in?"

"Last—before the university. If there still is any university."

"Social injustice is your theme?"

"What else could it be? Are we on equal terms? I'm in your power; you can bully me or be fatherly, as it suits you. Threaten me with charges and make a delinquent of me. But I'm not afraid of you."

"I very much hope not. You're free to go whenever you wish. I quote you La Fontaine and you quote him back. That's a dialogue, a useful start. I had hoped to show you that you were mistaken to spit at me. I was doing my job—to stop a riot. But you can go now."

"By isolating and arresting the ringleader you break up the followers. Is that it?"

"Just so."

"Sheep," said the boy contemptuously. "None of them has any guts. I'd have had you in the canal—you and the other pigs."

Van der Valk burst out laughing. "What's your name?"

The boy took out his identity-card folder and threw it on the desk, from which it slid to the floor.

"I asked you your name politely. It was to call you by it, not to control your identity. That I could have had done. What can either of us lose by a little courtesy?"

"Robert."

"The animals in the fable—they were ill of the plague and they assembled to discuss what could be done. They decided to confess their sins in public. There's a pretty bitter irony in that story."

"Just so, to quote you."

"The Lion, the Tiger, and the Bear—correct me if I'm wrong—were excused, I think. What crimes could they possibly have committed? None of the other animals, after reflection, could really find anything with which to reproach themselves. Finally a Donkey confessed that he had once eaten some grass which did not belong to him. That's it, they all shouted at once, that's the reason why we all have the plague."

"And so they massacred him."

"Yes. Sounds just like society, eh? But doesn't it strike you that the donkey was rather stupid?"

"The donkey was honest."

"Is that enough, in our society? Aren't you being the donkey? You're a student, still a schoolboy. The world is not what you think it should be."

"I know that you other animals will never admit you're in the wrong. But enough donkeys can kick a lion."

"Will it help? What's your ideal?"

"What we all ask—not to be treated as mental deficients, to be admonished and lectured with a wagging finger by some fat pension pusher if we have the audacity to think for ourselves."

"And for that what will you do? Break a few more windows?"

The boy glared. "We'll build barricades, here too, if you force us to. And stay on them too. And stand up to you. You'll push us off eventually—massacre the donkeys. But that will be remembered—eventually."

Van der Valk sat on the radiator and smoked, saying nothing.

"Sooner or later you know we'll win," said the boy. "That's what you're all afraid of. Violence—but what other resource do you leave us?"

"Well," said Van der Valk at last. "The answer is complex. You won't win, not by behaving like honest but stupid donkeys. I'm a pension pusher, as you rightly say. Don't despise me for that—I may have to face heavier weapons than you used, in a cause I have little respect for; but I'm a civil servant under oath, which I can only break for grave moral need, such as you do not show me. You have ideals and perhaps more courage than I have. I wish you, personally, good fortune and success. But will you take a word of advice? Don't let idealism turn into fanaticism. I am not, myself, ready to yield to violence."

"Will you have any choice?"

"Try passive resistance. You don't lose public sympathy and you don't risk getting beaten up. I broke you up this morning. I was lucky—nobody got hurt. I admit, students haven't the temperament for passive resistance. But if you'd been, for example, barricaded inside your school, your protest would have had more weight and I'd have had more difficulty."

"Not enough of us," said the boy sadly. "Too many are scared—there are too many gutless conformists, afraid of being punished."

"That's always the trouble," agreed Van der Valk cheerfully. "But I suggest that you avoid a direct clash with the police."

"Scared?" the boy said, smiling. He had an attractive smile. His hair was dark red, wiry, handsome. I'm worse than a Dutchman, thought Van der Valk; I'm a bourgeois booby.

"Yes," he said. "The students at Lyon used a truck to charge a police cordon. They killed a commissaire named René Lacroix. He had three children. He didn't run away—he had his job to do. It might have been me."

"And it might have been me. It could be me right now—if that's what it takes. Am I free to go?"

"Completely."

"You will do nothing to me at all?"

"No—donkey. I apologize for twisting your arm. If I bumped you, that's my job. You might perhaps consider apologizing for spitting."

"I'm sorry—I lost my temper."

"What does your father do?"

"He threatens me with prison."

"I daresay he does—it's the most obstructive side of my work. I meant what does he do for a living."

"He's a municipal councilor—Conservative Party."

"Oh, oh. Not a tiger—a bear."

As the boy prepared to leave, slinging his jacket round his shoulders, Van der Valk noticed a subtle change. He was putting on armor against the world. Here he had found a quiet man, who had made cynical jokes, who had been tactful, who had not humiliated him—but outside was a world of animals. He reassumed the air of sneering irony, of impervious ferocity, of not being a donkey. He was the tough one who stiffened an army of sheep, who would not compromise, who would not surrender. Van der Valk felt sadness.

"Robert. You're one individual. I'm another. We have to keep some things clear of our herd instincts."

"Perhaps. But if we meet again, I hit. I'm younger, I hit faster."

"Yes. But it would take a lot of hitting to wear me down. Whereas if I hit you, you'd stay hit."

"I'll remember that."

The boy was gone. Van der Valk could hear steps going two at a time down the stairs, regardless of who might be coming up. He shrugged; he had other jobs to do regarding young men and women who had the misfortune to be pronounced delinquent—"out of their parents' control," was the official phrase—by the children's tribunal of the city of Amsterdam.

He just hoped he would not open a paper one of these days and see a headline: *Schoolboy Killed—Tragic Consequence of Deplorable Riots.* It was always the best who thrust themselves to the front, always the honest donkey that got eaten.

Robert

STANLEY ELLIN

Stanley Ellin's short stories frequently focus on horrors that occur in everyday settings, and ''Robert'' is no exception. To the reader, the sixth-grade classroom seems an innocent place, the children easily handled charges—until Ellin begins describing the strange events that intrude on an otherwise uneventful thirty-eight-year career in teaching. Ellin's own career as a writer began in 1948 with the publication of the classic story ''The Specialty of the House,'' and he went on to write numerous stories, including the Edgar-winning ''The Blessington Method.'' His novels have received less critical attention than his stories, but are nonetheless classics in their own right; among them are The Key to Nicholas Street *(1952),* The Eighth Circle *(1958),* Mirror, Mirror on the Wall *(1972), and* The Dark Fantastic *(1983).*

THE WINDOWS of the Sixth Grade classroom were wide open to the June afternoon, and through them came all the sounds of the departing school: the thunder of bus motors warming up, the hiss of gravel under running feet, the voices raised in cynical fervor.

> "So we sing all hail to thee,
> District Schoo-wull Number Three . . ."

Miss Gildea flinched a little at the last high, shrill note, and pressed her fingers to her aching forehead. She was tired, more tired than she could ever recall being in her thirty-eight years of teaching, and, as she told herself, she had reason to be. It had not been a good term, not good at all, what with the size of the class, and the Principal's insistence on new methods, and then her mother's shocking death coming right in the middle of everything.

Perhaps she had been too close to her mother, Miss Gildea thought; perhaps she had been wrong, never taking into account that some day the old lady would have to pass on and leave her alone in the world. Well, thinking about it all the time didn't make it any easier. She should try to forget.

And, of course, to add to her troubles, there had been during the past few weeks this maddening business of Robert. He had been a perfectly nice boy, and then, out of a clear sky, had become impossible. Not bothersome or noisy really, but sunk into an endless daydream from which Miss Gildea had to sharply jar him a dozen times a day.

She turned her attention to Robert, who sat alone in the room at the desk immediately before her, a thin boy with neatly combed, colorless hair bracketed between large ears; mild blue eyes in a pale face fixed solemnly on hers.

"Robert."

"Yes, Miss Gildea."

"Do you know why I told you to remain after school, Robert?"

He frowned thoughtfully at this, as if it were some lesson he was being called on for, but had failed to memorize properly.

"I suppose for being bad," he said, at last.

Miss Gildea sighed.

"No, Robert, that's not it at all. I know a bad boy when I see one, Robert, and you aren't one like that. But I do know there's something troubling you, something on your mind, and I think I can help you."

"There's nothing bothering me, Miss Gildea. Honest, there isn't."

Miss Gildea found the silver pencil thrust into her hair and tapped it in a nervous rhythm on her desk.

"Oh, come, Robert. During the last month every time I looked at you your mind was a million miles away. Now, what is it? Just making plans for vacation, or, perhaps, some trouble with the boys?"

"I'm not having trouble with anybody, Miss Gildea."

"You don't seem to understand, Robert, that I'm not trying to punish you for anything. Your homework is good. You've managed to keep up with the class, but I do think your inattentiveness should be explained. What, for example, were you thinking this afternoon when I spoke to you directly for five minutes, and you didn't hear a word I said?"

"Nothing, Miss Gildea."

She brought the pencil down sharply on the desk. "There must have been *something*, Robert. Now, I must insist that you think back, and try to explain yourself."

Looking at his impassive face she knew that somehow she herself had been put on the defensive, that if any means of graceful retreat were offered now she would gladly take it. Thirty-eight years, she thought grimly, and I'm still trying to play mother hen to ducklings. Not that there wasn't a bright side to the picture. Thirty-eight years passed meant only two more to go before retirement, the half-salary pension, the chance to putter around the house, tend to the garden properly. The pension wouldn't buy you furs and diamonds, sure enough, but it could buy the right to enjoy your own home for the rest of your days instead of a dismal room in the County Home for Old Ladies. Miss Gildea had visited the County Home once, on an instructional visit, and preferred not to think about it.

"Well, Robert," she said wearily, "have you remembered what you were thinking?"

"Yes, Miss Gildea."

"What was it?"

"I'd rather not tell, Miss Gildea."

"I insist!"

"Well," Robert said gently, "I was thinking I wished you were dead, Miss Gildea. I was thinking I wished I could kill you."

Her first reaction was simply blank incomprehension. She had been standing not ten feet away when that car had skidded up on the sidewalk and crushed her mother's life from her, and Miss Gildea had neither screamed nor fainted. She had stood there dumbly, because of the very unreality of the thing. Just the way she stood in court where they explained that the man got a year in jail, but didn't have a dime to pay for the tragedy he had brought about. And now the orderly ranks of desks before her, the expanse of blackboard around her, and Robert's face in the midst of it all were no more real. She found herself rising from her chair, walking toward Robert, who shrank back, his eyes wide and panicky, his elbow half lifted as if to ward off a blow.

"Do you understand what you've just said?" Miss Gildea demanded hoarsely.

"No, Miss Gildea! Honest, I didn't mean anything."

She shook her head unbelievingly. "Whatever made you say it? Whatever in the world could make a boy say a thing like that, such a wicked, terrible thing!"

"You wanted to know! You kept asking me!"

The sight of that protective elbow raised against her cut as deep as the incredible words had.

"Put that arm down!" Miss Gildea said shrilly, and then struggled to get her voice under control. "In all my years I've never struck a child, and I don't intend to start now!"

Robert dropped his arm and clasped his hands together on his desk, and Miss Gildea, looking at the pinched white knuckles, realized with surprise that her own hands were shaking uncontrollably. "But if you think this little matter ends here, young-feller-me-lad," she said, "you've got another thought coming. You get your things together, and we're marching right up to Mr. Harkness. He'll be very much interested in all this."

Mr. Harkness was the Principal. He had arrived only the term before, and but for his taste in eyeglasses (the large, black-rimmed kind which, Miss Gildea privately thought, looked actorish) and his predilection for the phrase "modern pedagogical methods" was, in her opinion, a rather engaging young man.

He looked at Robert's frightened face and then at Miss Gildea's pursed lips. "Well," he said pleasantly, "what seems to be the trouble here?"

"That," said Miss Gildea, "is something I think Robert should tell you about."

She placed a hand on Robert's shoulder, but he pulled away and backed slowly toward Mr. Harkness, his breath coming in loud, shuddering sobs, his eyes riveted on Miss Gildea as if she were the only thing in the room beside himself. Mr. Harkness put an arm around Robert and frowned at Miss Gildea.

"Now, what's behind all this, Miss Gildea? The boy seems frightened to death."

Miss Gildea found herself sick of it all, anxious to get out of the room, away from Robert. "That's enough, Robert," she commanded. "Just tell Mr. Harkness exactly what happened."

"I said the boy was frightened to death, Miss Gildea," Mr. Harkness said brusquely. "We'll talk about it as soon as he understands we're his friends. Won't we, Robert?"

Robert shook his head vehemently. "I didn't do anything bad! Miss Gildea said I didn't do anything bad!"

"Well, then!" said Mr. Harkness triumphantly. "There's nothing to be afraid of, is there?"

Robert shook his head again. "She said I had to stay in after school."

Mr. Harkness glanced sharply at Miss Gildea. "I suppose he missed the morning bus, is that it? And after I said in a directive that the staff was to make allowances—"

"Robert doesn't use a bus," Miss Gildea protested. "Perhaps I'd better explain all this, Mr. Harkness. You see—"

"I think Robert's doing very well," Mr. Harkness said, and tightened his arm around Robert, who nodded shakily.

"She kept me in," he said, "and then when we were alone she came up close to me and she said, 'I know what you're thinking. You're thinking you'd like to see me dead! You're thinking you'd like to kill me, aren't you?"

Robert's voice had dropped to an eerie whisper that bound Miss Gildea like a spell. It was broken only when she saw the expression on Mr. Harkness' face.

"Why, that's a lie!" she cried. "That's the most dreadful lie I ever heard any boy dare—"

Mr. Harkness cut in abruptly. "Miss Gildea! I *insist* you let the boy finish what he has to say."

Miss Gildea's voice fluttered. "It seems to me, Mr. Harkness, that he has been allowed to say quite enough already!"

"Has he?" Mr. Harkness asked.

"Robert has been inattentive lately, especially so this afternoon. After class I asked him what he had been thinking about, and he dared to say he was thinking how he wished I were dead! How he wanted to kill me!"

"Robert said that?"

"In almost those exact words. And I can tell you, Mr. Harkness, that I was shocked, terribly shocked, especially since Robert always seemed like such a nice boy."

"His record—?"

"His record is quite good. It's just—"

"And his social conduct?" asked Mr. Harkness in the same level voice.

"As far as I know, he gets along with the other children well enough."

"But for some reason," persisted Mr. Harkness, "you found him annoying you."

Robert raised his voice. "I didn't! Miss Gildea said I didn't do anything bad. And I always liked her. I like her better than *any* teacher!"

Miss Gildea fumbled blindly in her hair for the silver pencil, and failed to find it. She looked around the floor distractedly.

"Yes?" said Mr. Harkness.

"My pencil," said Miss Gildea on the verge of tears. "It's gone."

"Surely, Miss Gildea," said Mr. Harkness in a tone of mild exasperation, "this is not quite the moment—"

"It was very valuable," Miss Gildea tried to explain hopelessly. "It was my mother's." In the face of Mr. Harkness' stony surveillance she knew she must look a complete mess. Hems crooked, nose red, hair all disheveled. "I'm all upset, Mr. Harkness. It's been a long term and now all this right at the end of it. I don't know what to say."

Mr. Harkness' face fell into sympathetic lines.

"That quite all right, Miss Gildea. I know how you feel. Now, if you want to leave, I think Robert and I should have a long, friendly talk."

"If you don't mind—"

"No, no," Mr. Harkness said heartily. "As a matter of fact, I think that would be the best thing all around."

After he had seen her out he closed the door abruptly behind her, and Miss Gildea walked heavily up the stairway and down the corridor to the Sixth Grade room. The silver pencil was there on the floor at Robert's desk, and she picked it up and carefully polished it with her handkerchief. Then she sat down at her desk with the handkerchief to her nose and wept soundlessly for ten minutes.

That night, when the bitter taste of humiliation had grown faint enough to permit it, Miss Gildea reviewed the episode with all the honesty at her command. Honesty with oneself had always been a major point in her credo, had, in fact, been passed on through succeeding classes during the required lesson on The Duties of an American Citizen, when Miss Gildea, to sum up the lesson, would recite: "This above all, To thine ownself be true . . ." while thumping her fist on her desk as an accompaniment to each syllable.

Hamlet, of course, was not in the syllabus of the Sixth Grade, whose reactions over the years never deviated from a mixed bewilderment and indifference. But Miss Gildea, after some prodding of the better minds into a discussion of the lines, would rest content with the knowledge that she had sown good seed on what, she prayed, was fertile ground.

Reviewing the case of Robert now, with her emotions under control, she came to the unhappy conclusion that it was she who had committed the injustice. The child had been ordered to stay after school, something that to him could mean only a punishment. He had been ordered to disclose some shadowy, childlike thoughts that had drifted through his mind hours before, and, unable to do so, either had to make up something out of the whole cloth, or blurt out the immediate thought in his immature mind.

It was hardly unusual, reflected Miss Gildea sadly, for a child badgered by a teacher to think what Robert had; she could well remember her own feelings toward a certain pompadoured harridan who still haunted her dreams. And the only conclusion to be drawn, unpleasant though it was, was that Robert, and not she, had truly put into practice those beautiful words from Shakespeare.

It was this, as well as the sight of his pale accusing face before her while she led the class through the morning session next day, which prompted her to put Robert in charge of refilling the water pitcher during recess. The duties of the water pitcher monitor were to leave the playground a little before the rest of the class and clean and refill the pitcher on her desk, but since the task was regarded as an honor by the class, her gesture, Miss Gildea felt with some self-approval, carried exactly the right note of conciliation.

She was erasing the blackboard at the front of the room near the end of the recess when she heard Robert approaching her desk, but much as she wanted to she could not summon up courage enough to turn and face him. As if, she thought, he were the teacher, and I were afraid of him. And she could feel her cheeks grow warm at the thought.

He re-entered the room on the sound of the bell that marked the end of recess, and this time Miss Gildea plopped the eraser firmly into its place beneath the blackboard and turned to look at him. "Thank you very much, Robert," she said as he set the pitcher down and neatly capped it with her drinking glass.

"You're welcome, Miss Gildea," Robert said politely. He drew a handkerchief from his pocket, wiped his hands with it, then smiled gently at Miss Gildea. "I bet you think I put poison or something into that water," he said gravely, "but I wouldn't do anything like that, Miss Gildea. Honest, I wouldn't."

Miss Gildea gasped, then reached out a hand toward Robert's shoulder. She withdrew it hastily when he shrank away with the familiar panicky look in his eyes.

"Why did you say that, Robert?" Miss Gildea demanded in a terrible voice. "That was plain impudence, wasn't it? You thought you were being smart, didn't you?"

At that moment the rest of the class surged noisily into the room, but Miss Gildea froze them into silence with a commanding wave of the hand. Out of the corner of her eye she noted the cluster of shocked and righteous faces allied with her in condemnation, and she felt a quick little sense of triumph in her position.

"I was talking to you, Robert," she said. "What do you have to say for yourself?"

Robert took another step backward and almost tumbled over a schoolbag left carelessly in the aisle. He caught himself, then stood there helplessly, his eyes never leaving Miss Gildea's.

"Well, Robert?"

He shook his head wildly. "I didn't do it!" he cried. "I didn't put anything in your water, Miss Gildea! I told you I didn't!"

Without looking Miss Gildea knew that the cluster of accusing faces had swung toward her now, felt her triumph turn to a sick bewilderment inside her. It was as if Robert, with his teary eyes and pale, frightened face and too-large ears, had turned into a strange jellylike creature that could not be pinned down and put in its place. As if he were retreating further and further down some dark, twisting path, and leading her on with him. And, she thought desperately, she had to pull herself free before she did something dreadful, something unforgivable.

She couldn't take the boy to Mr. Harkness again. Not only did the memory of that scene in his office the day before make her shudder, but a repeated visit would be an admission that after thirty-eight years of teaching she was not up to the mark as a disciplinarian.

But for her sake, if for nothing else, Robert had to be put in his place. With a gesture, Miss Gildea ordered the rest of the class to their seats and turned to Robert, who remained standing.

"Robert," said Miss Gildea, "I want an apology for what has just happened."

"I'm sorry, Miss Gildea," Robert said, and it looked as if his eyes would be brimming with tears in another moment.

Miss Gildea hardened her heart to this. "*I apologize, Miss Gildea, and it will not happen again,*" she prompted.

Miraculously, Robert contained his tears. "I apologize, Miss Gildea, and it will not happen again," he muttered and dropped limply into his seat.

"Well!" said Miss Gildea, drawing a deep breath as she looked around at the hushed class. "Perhaps that will be a lesson to us all."

The classroom work did not go well after that, but, as Miss

Gildea told herself, there were only a few days left to the end of the term, and after that, praise be, there was the garden, the comfortable front porch of the old house to share with neighbors in the summer evenings, and then next term a new set of faces in the classroom, with Robert's not among them.

Later, closing the windows of the room after the class had left, Miss Gildea was brought up short by the sight of a large group gathered on the sidewalk near the parked busses. It was Robert, she saw, surrounded by most of the Sixth Grade, and obviously the center of interest. He was nodding emphatically when she put her face to the window, and she drew back quickly at the sight, moved by some queer sense of guilt.

Only a child, she assured herself, *he's only a child,* but that thought did not in any way dissolve the anger against him that stuck like a lump in her throat.

That was on Thursday. By Tuesday of the next week, the final week of the term, Miss Gildea was acutely conscious of the oppressive atmosphere lying over the classroom. Ordinarily, the awareness of impending vacation acted on the class like a violent agent dropped into some inert liquid. There would be ferment and seething beneath the surface, manifested by uncontrollable giggling and whispering, and this would grow more and more turbulent until all restraint and discipline was swept away in the general upheaval of excitement and good spirits.

That, Miss Gildea thought, was the way it always had been, but it was strangely different now. The Sixth Grade, down to the most irrepressible spirits in it, acted as if it had been turned to a set of robots before her startled eyes. Hands tightly clasped on desks, eyes turned toward her with an almost frightening intensity, the class responded to her mildest requests as if they were shouted commands. And when she walked down the aisles between them, one and all seemed to have adopted Robert's manner of shrinking away fearfully at her approach.

Miss Gildea did not like to think of what all this might mean, but valiantly forced herself to do so. Can it mean, she asked herself, that all think as Robert does, are choosing this way of showing it? And, if they knew how cruel it was, would they do it?

Other teachers, Miss Gildea knew, sometimes took problems such as this to the Teacher's Room where they could be studied and answered by those who saw them in an objective light. It might be that the curious state of the Sixth Grade was being duplicated in other classes. Perhaps she herself was imagining the whole thing, or, frightening thought, looking back, as people will when they grow old, on the sort of past that never really did exist. Why, in that case—and Miss Gildea had to laugh at herself with a faint merriment—she would just find herself reminiscing about her thirty-eight years of teaching to some bored young woman who didn't have the fraction of experience she did.

But underneath the current of these thoughts, Miss Gildea knew there was one honest reason for not going to the Teacher's Room this last week of the term. She had received no gifts, not one. And the spoils from each grade heaped high in a series of pyramids against the wall, the boxes of fractured cookies, the clumsily wrapped jars of preserves, the scarves, the stockings, the handkerchiefs, infinite, endless boxes of handkerchiefs, all were there to mark the triumph of each teacher. And Miss Gildea, who in all her years at District School Number Three had been blushingly proud of the way her pyramid was highest at the end of each term, had not yet received a single gift from the Sixth Grade class.

After the class was dismissed that afternoon, however, the spell was broken. Only a few of her pupils still loitered in the hallway near the door, Miss Gildea noted, but Robert remained in his seat. Then, as she gathered her belongings Robert approached her with a box outheld in his hand. It was, from its shape, a box of candy, and, as Miss Gildea could tell from the wrapping, expensive candy. Automatically, she reached a hand out, then stopped herself short. He'll never make up to me for what he's done, she told herself furiously; I'll never let him.

"Yes, Robert?" she said coolly.

"It's a present for you, Miss Gildea," Robert said, and then as Miss Gildea watched in fascination he began to strip the wrappings from it. He laid the paper neatly on the desk and lifted the cover of the box to display the chocolates within. "My mother said that's the biggest box they had," he said wistfully. "Don't you even want them, Miss Gildea?"

Miss Gildea weakened despite herself. "Did you think I would, after what's happened, Robert?" she asked.

Robert reflected a moment. "Well," he said at last, "if you want me to, I'll eat one right in front of you, Miss Gildea."

Miss Gildea recoiled as if at a faraway warning. *Don't let him say any more,* something inside her cried; *he's only playing a trick, another horrible trick,* and then she was saying, "Why would I want you to do that, Robert?"

"So you'll see they're not poison or anything, Miss Gildea," Robert said. "Then you'll believe it, won't you, Miss Gildea?"

She had been prepared. Even before he said the words, she had felt her body drawing itself tighter and tighter against what she knew was coming. But the sound of the words themselves only served to release her like a spring coiled too tightly.

"You little monster!" sobbed Miss Gildea and struck wildly at the proffered box, which flew almost to the far wall, while chocolates cascaded stickily around the room. "How dare you!" she cried. "How dare you!" and her small bony fists beat at Robert's cowering shoulders and back as he tried to retreat.

He half turned in the aisle, slipped on a piece of chocolate, and went down to his knees, but before he could recover himself Miss Gildea was on him again, her lips drawn back, her fists pummeling him as if they were a pair of tireless mallets. Robert had started to scream at the top of his lungs from the first blow, but it was no more than a remote buzzing in Miss Gildea's ears.

"Miss Gildea!"

That was Mr. Harkness' voice, she knew, and those must be Mr. Harkness' hands which pulled her away so roughly that she had to keep herself from falling by clutching at her desk. She stood there weakly, feeling the wild fluttering of her heart, feeling the sick churning of shame and anguish in her while she tried to bring the room into focus again. There was the knot of small excited faces peering through the open doorway, they must have called Mr. Harkness, and Mr. Harkness himself listening to Robert who talked and wept alternately, and there was a mess everywhere. Of course, thought Miss Gildea dazedly, those must be chocolate stains. Chocolate stains all over my lovely clean room.

Then Robert was gone, the faces at the door were gone, and the door itself was closed behind them. Only Mr. Harkness remained, and Miss Gildea watched him as he removed his glasses, cleaned them carefully, and then held them up at arm's length and studied them before settling them once more on his nose.

"Well, Miss Gildea," said Mr. Harkness as if he were speaking to the glasses rather than to her, "this is a serious business."

Miss Gildea nodded.

"I am sick," Mr. Harkness said quietly, "really sick at the thought that somewhere in this school, where I tried to introduce decent pedagogical standards, corporal punishment is still being practiced."

"That's not fair at all, Mr. Harkness," Miss Gildea said shakily. "I hit the boy, that's true, and I know I was wrong to do it, but that is the first time in all my life I raised a finger against any child. And if you knew my feelings—"

"Ah," said Mr. Harkness, "that's exactly what I would like to know, Miss Gildea." He nodded to her chair, and she sat down weakly. "Now, just go ahead and explain everything as you saw it."

It was a difficult task, made even more difficult by the fact that Mr. Harkness chose to stand facing the window. Forced to address his back this way, Miss Gildea found that she had the sensation of speaking in a vacuum, but she mustered the facts as well as she could, presented them with strong emotion, and then sank back in the chair quite exhausted.

Mr. Harkness remained silent for a long while, then slowly

turned to face Miss Gildea. "I am not a practicing psychiatrist," he said at last, "although as an educator I have, of course, taken a considerable interest in that field. But I do not think it needs a practitioner to tell what a clearcut and obvious case I am facing here. Nor," he added sympathetically, "what a tragic one."

"It might simply be," suggested Miss Gildea, "that Robert—"

"I am not speaking about Robert," said Mr. Harkness soberly, quietly.

It took an instant for this to penetrate, and then Miss Gildea felt the blood run cold in her.

"Do you think I'm lying about all this?" she cried incredulously. "Can you possibly—"

"I am sure," Mr. Harkness replied soothingly, "that you were describing things exactly as you saw them, Miss Gildea. But—have you ever heard the phrase 'persecution complex'? Do you think you could recognize the symptoms of that condition if they were presented objectively? I can, Miss Gildea. I assure you, I can."

Miss Gildea struggled to speak, but the words seemed to choke her. "No," she managed to say, "you couldn't! Because some mischievous boy chooses to make trouble—"

"Miss Gildea, no child of eleven, however mischievous, could draw the experiences Robert has described to me out of his imagination. He has discussed these experiences with me at length; now I have heard your side of the case. And the conclusions to be drawn, I must say, are practically forced on me."

The room started to slip out of focus again, and Miss Gildea frantically tried to hold it steady.

"But that just means you're taking his word against mine!" she said fiercely.

"Unfortunately, Miss Gildea, not his word alone. Last weekend, a delegation of parents met the School Board and made it quite plain that they were worried because of what their children told them of your recent actions. A dozen children in your class described graphically at that meeting how you had accused them of trying to poison your drinking water, and how you had threatened them because of this. And Robert, it may interest you to know, was not even one of them.

"The School Board voted your dismissal then and there, Miss Gildea, but in view of your long years of service it was left for me to override that decision if I wished to on my sole responsibility. After this episode, however, I cannot see that I have any choice. I must do what is best."

"Dismissal?" said Miss Gildea vaguely. "But they can't. I only have two more years to go. They can't do that, Mr. Harkness; all they're trying to do is trick me out of my pension!"

"Believe me," said Mr. Harkness gently, "they're not trying to do anything of the sort, Miss Gildea. Nobody in the world is trying to hurt you. I give you my solemn word that the only thing which has entered into consideration of this case from first to last has been the welfare of the children."

The room swam in sunlight, but under it Miss Gildea's face was gray and lifeless. She reached forward to fill her glass with water, stopped short, and seemed to gather herself together with a sudden brittle determination. "I'll just have to speak to the Board myself," she said in a high breathless voice. "That's the only thing to do, go there and explain the whole thing to them!"

"That would not help," said Mr. Harkness pityingly. "Believe me, Miss Gildea, it would not."

Miss Gildea left her chair and came to him, her eyes wide and frightened. She laid a trembling hand on his arm and spoke eagerly, quickly, trying to make him understand. "You see," she said, "that means I won't get my pension. I must have two more years for that, don't you see? There's the payment on the house, the garden—no, the garden is part of the house, really—but without the pension—"

She was pulling furiously at his arm with every phrase as if she could drag him bodily into a comprehension of her words, but he stood unyielding and only shook his head pityingly. "You must control yourself, Miss Gildea," he pleaded. "You're not yourself, and it's impossible—"

"No!" she cried in a strange voice. "No!"

When she pulled away he knew almost simultaneously what she intended to do, but the thought froze him to the spot, and when he moved it was too late. He burst into the corridor through the door she had flung open, and almost threw himself down the stairway to the main hall. The door to the street was just swinging shut and he ran toward it, one hand holding the rim of his glasses, a sharp little pain digging into his side, but before he could reach the door he heard the screech of brakes, the single agonized scream, and the horrified shout of a hundred shrill voices.

He put his hand on the door, but could not find the strength to open it. A few minutes later, a cleaning woman had to sidle around him to get outside and see what all the excitement was about.

Miss Reardon, the substitute, took the Sixth Grade the next day, and, everything considered, handled it very well. The single ripple in the even current of the session came at its very start when Miss Reardon explained her presence by referring to the "sad accident that happened to dear Miss Gildea." The mild hubbub which followed this contained several voices, notably in the back of the room, which protested plaintively, "It was *not* an accident, Miss Reardon; she ran right in front of that bus," but Miss Reardon quickly brought order to the room with a few sharp raps of her ruler, and after that, classwork was carried on in a pleasant and orderly fashion.

Robert walked home slowly that afternoon, swinging his schoolbag placidly at his side, savoring the June warmth soaking into him, the fresh green smell in the air, the memory of Miss Reardon's understanding face so often turned toward his in eager and friendly interest. His home was identical with all the others on the block, square white boxes with small lawns before them, and its only distinction was that all its blinds were drawn down. After he had closed the front door very quietly behind him, he set his schoolbag down in the hallway, and went into the stuffy half-darkness of the living room.

Robert's father sat in the big armchair in his bathrobe, the way he always did, and Robert's mother was bent over him holding a glass of water.

"No!" Robert's father said. "You just want to get rid of me, but I won't let you! I know what you put into it, and I won't drink it! I'll die before I drink it!"

"Please," Robert's mother said, "please take it. I swear it's only water. I'll drink some myself if you don't believe me." But when she drank a little and then held the glass to his lips, Robert's father only tossed his head from side to side.

Robert stood there watching the scene with fascination, his lips moving in silent mimicry of the familiar words. Then he cleared his throat.

"I'm home, mama," Robert said softly. "Can I have some milk and cookies, please?"

The Turncoat Journal of Marc Milton Stearns

BARRY N. MALZBERG

Barry N. Malzberg is no ordinary writer, and therefore "The Turncoat Journal of Marc Milton Stearns" is no ordinary crime story, academic or otherwise. Its effects and implications are at once subtle and powerful; and its literary blending of crime and scholarship makes it an appropriate final entry for this anthology. In his somewhat controversial career (writers with idiosyncratic approaches to fiction are always controversial) Malzberg has published an impressive number of works in a variety of fields: close to three hundred short stories, articles, and essays, and an aggregate of one hundred novels, collections, nonfiction works, and anthologies. After a self-imposed three-year hiatus from fiction writing, he has once again begun to produce novels and short stories—good news, indeed.

August 2: The appalling series of murders of senior English faculty continues; departmental rivalries are to be expected in academe but this is pushing matters too far. Marilyn M. Weems, associate professor and former Fulbright holder, was found sprawled across an open, illuminated manuscript of "The Pardoner's Tale" in her carrel at the Upham Library. "Aprill is the cruellest month," she had written me jestingly on the occasion of my sixtieth birthday but four months ago; however, she had not contended with August. She is the fourth of us to be murdered since the first of this year and I feel a distinct unpleasantness, one might even say a chill, in the atmosphere.

August 3: "Stearns," the police lieutenant says to me in my offices, after having completed what he calls a "summary investigation," "have you considered the possibility, as we have, that these murders might be the work of some graduate assistant or nontenured faculty member who is desperately trying to create vacancies in the department?"

I tell him that this is inconclusive, a wholly bizarre theory, but of course one never can tell in this era of desperation . . . scholars in Marlowe or Chaucer forced to eke out miserable livings as adjunct faculty, only to be fired after a few semesters; doctors of philosophy in the most esoteric areas performing manual labor or seeking retraining through computer centers. "Anything is possible," I concede.

"What is your own specialty?" the lieutenant asks.

"The Jacobean revenge drama," I say, "elements of restoration comedy."

"Revenge drama," the lieutenant says, looking thoughtful; "are there any adjuncts, any untenured faculty with a similar specialty?"

I stare at him. "What a repellent implication," I say.

"I was just exploring the issue," the lieutenant says. "Four of you people are dead; this is obviously not random work."

"I dismiss the implication," I say.

Nonetheless, after the exit of the official, I give the issue some thought. Marilyn Weems (whom I must admit I detested; a resolute feminist of the new breed who seemed to have neither kindness nor compassion) was a Chaucer specialist and so are two of the junior nontenured faculty, Harry Hobson and George Williams, who joined us in September, shortly before the murders began on Halloween Eve. Furthermore, both of them are qualified to teach in the areas of the modern American novel, Shakespeare, and Byronic poetry—which were the areas of expertise of the other victims. Perhaps the lieutenant has a point. These are desperate times in academia, although I would not credit anyone with the *sitzfleisch* to acquire a doctoral degree with the raw circumstances of murder. Still, one does not know.

I ponder the issue at some length and wonder if I should indulge an old interest of mine—participate in some free-lance investigation. After all, the lieutenant himself has planted heavy intimation. On the other hand, it might be a dangerous pastime for an overweight, preoccupied, sixty-year-old full professor of English. Still, it is worth some thought. These murders cannot go on. They are foul and disgusting and the fact that all of the victims have been found on the campus, with distasteful photographs in the newspapers, can only have a deleterious effect upon our reputation. One finds it difficult to think of facing the MLA, scant months from now, with such a scandal.

I believe that I will investigate this issue; however, I will do so with the greatest caution.

August 4: The trimester system with its abolition of the old academic year, its happy churning of students throughout the entire course of the year with requisite breaks only for national holidays or to meet contract provisions, means that circumstances at Upham Library are most amenable to investigation (to say nothing of murder), the full faculty being present now even in what once was called the dead of summer. Accordingly, I was able to proceed directly with my investigation, the results of which I will now disclose.

Both Harry Hobson and George Williams were interviewed by me in my offices early this afternoon and interesting revelations came forth. "That's a ridiculous allegation, Dr. Stearns," Hobson said. "I am happily married to a wife with an inheritance and resigned to being an academic tramp for the next ten years; I love my work under any conditions."

Williams was hardly less forthcoming. "How can you even think that?" he said when I raised the issue shortly after he had walked into my offices. "There must be something terribly wrong with you. Is this some kind of an unsplendid joke?" I am trying to catch the flavor, so to speak, of their rhetoric, although it is difficult. "This is the most bizarre conversation I have had in many years," Williams said, "and now I am going to terminate it."

Perhaps this can be interpreted as suspicious activity, although Hobson, too, ended our interview most abruptly. Both of them, rather seedy young men in their early thirties with elaborate mustaches, men of a type I have come to increasingly dislike as they flood into the colleges (it is possible at this age that I am beginning to lose my grip, that the sere, the yellow leaf predominates, but I do not think so; I find my judgments sound), both of them engaged in fervid denials of a sort which, in classical detective novels (of which I have read more than a few, hence my interest in amateur investigation) would reveal potential culpability. My root conviction is that one of these young men, or perhaps both of them in collaboration, planned and executed these murders with terrific verve and panache, expecting that after the sensation had faded and a suitable number of specialists had been shuffled off to the final stage of tenure, they could reputably compete for permanent positions; however, I must admit that I do not have the hard evidence at this time to turn them in, so to speak, and so I must dedicate my efforts toward finding that stray and tightening link that will enable the police to close the case. This is quite interesting, surely the most interesting series of events in which I have been involved in years.

My suspicion centers on Hobson. There is a strained and tormented aspect of his visage; also his bachelor's, master's, *and* doctorate are from the same state university of Illinois. One cannot trust a man who would spend nine years in the same place and also, as Harry Truman once said, we already have too many land-grant universities.

August 5: The lieutenant was most impolite; he was, as a matter of fact, thoroughly alienating.

"That was a facetious suggestion," he said to me in his offices after I insisted upon seeing him, "it was merely a means of making conversation." He looked away from me distractedly; screams from some interrogee undoubtedly being tortured for information drifted up like smoke from the basement. "We have some very interesting, some very credible leads, and we expect a break in this investigation shortly."

"I think that this should be taken very seriously," I said. "Both of these men, particularly Hobson, are acting strangely and the motivation is ample. I remind you that *you* initiated this plan of action."

The lieutenant looked back at me and sighed. "It was *not* a plan of action," he said. "I don't know what got into your head; I don't know, sometimes, how you professors think. I made a silly suggestion, more or less to relieve the tension of a very tragic, ominous situation, and you seem to have taken it literally. It's not necessary for you to go on with this; surely this is a police matter. Look, Dr. Stearns; I don't mean to patronize you but you're a sixty-year-old, sedentary specialist in your Jacoby revenge, a casual reader perhaps of English mystery novels and—"

"Jacobean," I said fiercely, "*Jacobean* revenge and I am also, in the event of the chairman's sabbatical, the acting chairman of this department of English and it is my responsibility to deal with the matters affecting my faculty; you can understand that these events have had a *most* disconcerting effect upon scheduling, to say nothing of the tragic, emotional implications, and the sooner we can reach some kind of resolution, find the culprit—''

But the light behind his eyes, so to speak, had flickered away; there was no posture or attention in his aspect and I could tell that any further exposition would lead only to patronage; perhaps he regarded me as a babbling fool.

''Be that as it may,'' I said, standing with dignity, ''I would pursue this matter which arose from your own inspiration, beginning with Hobson, who I consider to be a most dangerous man. Even if these murders cannot be ascribed to him you will find, I think, certain damning unpleasantnesses in his background.''

The circumstances of my exit need no further description (and Jacobean revenge plots make little reference to transitional material) but I can assure myself in these highly confidential pages that it was not undignified, although it *was* assaulted by tremors of doubt: what if I were acting irrationally? But that, of course, is not and cannot be the case: if Hobson and/or Williams are not guilty of these bizarre murders, I will eat an illuminated manuscript. At the MLA convention reception desk. In full academic costume.

August 6: In her most famous and perhaps her best novel, *The Murder of Roger Ackroyd*, Dame Agatha Christie uses a first-person narrator involved (as an assistant to the detective) in the investigation of a murder. This narrator, a humble country doctor, *turns out to be the murderer himself*, Christie having artfully concealed the act of murder and those thoughts relating to it in the consciousness of the narrator. It is a most sensational and bizarre device, although one regarded as unfair by a significant minority: and the debate goes on.

In making reference to that novel here, I intend to warn the reader (these diaries, like all my papers, are prepared with the idea of eventual public disclosure) that a similar device may appear to be in the offing here. *This is absolutely not the case.* I am not responsible for the death of poor Marilyn Weems, or anyone else. I find the thought of murder horrifying, and yet I sustain precisely that accusation now. Let me explain.

The lieutenant arranged for my arrest shortly after his visit to my apartment this morning. "Hobson was able to point out the identity of his killer before he died," the lieutenant said; "the gunshot apparently destroyed his brain but not his will. '*Department*,' he said to the first officer on the scene, '*department*.' Then he died. Furthermore," and here the lieutenant shockingly brandished a pair of my own monogrammed collar pins, "these were found at the scene of the crime. I think that you are most satisfactorily tied into these unfortunate events, Professor Stearns, and I would caution you from this point onward that anything you say might be used against you in a court of law and counsel should be summoned—"

I believe that at this point I am somewhat awkwardly attempting to paraphrase the so-called Miranda warning, but it should not be necessary to continue in that vein as I am already occupying rather unpleasant quarters at what is called a holding facility, and at the advice of my attorney, Winston R. Smathers of Boca Raton and later St. John's Law School, am making no statements whatsoever, preferring to leave these horrendous matters in his incapable but willing hands.

Except to report the substance of an interesting conversation with George Williams which occurred *before* the instance of the arrest but *after* Hobson had been unpleasantly shot in his carrel.

"He tried to kill me, Stearns," Williams said earnestly, reason in his eyes, color in his academic face, "*he* was the assailant all the time. I knew that when he came blundering in here with that gun shouting about how tenure was the bane of the new academic class and then pointed the gun at me; I reached for it, his foot slipped on the copy of Henry James's *The Ambassadors*, which fortunately had been dropped on the floor while I pursued later texts of the master, he went off-balance, I grabbed the gun and shot *him*. But now everybody's going to think that *I'm* the murderer because of the circumstances.''

The logic of this allegation was stunning; meanwhile blood pooled crazily from Hobson's head. His face, in rictus, had the earnestness of one approaching doctor's orals. ''You must think I did it, too,'' he said. ''You don't believe a word of this.''

''Oh,'' I said delicately, ''oh, that isn't necessarily so.''

''He wanted to kill me,'' Williams said, ''and maybe he was doing me a favor; I have a wife who's about to leave me, two small children, no tenure, enormous debts, no prospects; I don't even have a doctorate.''

''The lack of a doctorate is certainly a problem,'' I conceded. ''You can't last at even a community college without one these days.''

''I ran out of money,'' Williams said unhappily, ''but it doesn't matter anymore. Here,'' he said, ''here's all the evidence you need,'' and he handed me the gun. ''I don't care any more. It's out of my hands. Tell them what you want. Do what you must.''

I felt the gun slide into my hand with the cool insistence and dry certainty with which a lover might greet a half-familiar breast, and looking then at the drenched face of Williams, considering Hobson's condition, I felt a kind of compassion, a peace that passeth all understanding drifting into the receptacle of self, and I said, ''If that is the case and your distress so great, then as the assistant chairman of this department I feel it is incumbent upon me to protect you.'' I considered the gun carefully. A cockroach, liberated from a facsimile quarto to better possibilities, scuttled with delight up Hobson's arm. ''I will take the rap,'' I said magnificently.

Williams stared at me.

''Isn't that what they say in detective novels? I've read a few. *Murder of Roger Ackroyd* and so on. I will take the responsibility for the crime. After all, why shouldn't I? I'm sixty years old, blocked at this academic level, blocked at this miserable little third-rate university, my powers decline, enrollment shrinks, students sit with spittle on their lips and read with their fingers when I try to educate them. No one is interested in historical antecedents either; it's all science fiction or rock lyrics that they want—"

"But we're defending Western civilization," Williams said hopelessly. "That's what I believed. That's what they said to me when they asked me to take the graduate assistantship in my senior year."

"Western civilization," I said. "Exactly. It isn't much but it is all we have. Maybe you're right."

"The mind is the cutting edge of the soul," Williams said in a rather rambling fashion, "the library is the repository of civilization."

"Precisely," I said, humoring him. "And now we must leave this library at once."

We prepared to leave the library at once. I removed the collar pins, leaving them beside Williams, knowing that in the long run everything has a purpose after all. Hobson continued to remain dead. The cockroach waved tentative feelers. I seized Williams by the shoulder and dragged him from the room. I made certain at the end not to double-lock the door.

August 6, later: Winston R. Smathers, late of St. John's, has reviewed these notations and said that they must be released at once, even though they are not evidentiary. "For God's sake, do you know what the prosecution will do with these? They'll blow us into the water. Still, we have to try."

"You don't understand," I said, "these are for your eyes only. I do not want them released."

This remark appeared to undo, for him, the consequences of an eastern education. "Don't want them released?" he said. "But why?"

"I have my reasons," I said. I took the papers from his trembling fingers. The guard—there is always a guard—stared incuriously. Smathers said more. Then he said less. Then he went away.

His reaction, his exit, disturbs me, but in no way which can be convincingly shared with him. Soon enough I know they will be coming down the hall to transfer me; in fact I think that I can hear them now.

"It's time," they will say, "it's time, Stearns, hurry up please, it's time," and to that what can one say? Can I say, "It isn't time, gents?" Can I say, "It isn't time because one generation will not die or go away while the others must wait, so I have made a noble sacrifice?" Could I say this? Could I say, "The Jacobeans knew, so did Medea, that not only the young must kill for the young." Should I say that? But what would the attendants make of all this? What could they make of it? What—I will bring up this point if necessary in open court at the end—given such dreadful evidence of my implication, would I make, then, of myself?